ANTITHESIS

A COLLECTION OF SCIENCE FICTION
AND OTHER SHORT STORIES

SVET ROUSKOV

Antithesis
Copyright © 2021 by Svet Rouskov

This is a work of fiction. Names, characters, businesses, places, events, locales, incidents, etc. are either the products of the author's imagination or used in a fictitious manner. Any resemblance to actual persons, living or dead, or actual events is purely coincidental.

All rights reserved. No part of this publication may be reproduced, distributed, or transmitted in any form or by any means, including photocopying, recording, or other electronic or mechanical methods, without the prior written permission of the author, except in the case of brief quotations embodied in critical reviews and certain other non-commercial uses permitted by copyright law.

tellwell

Tellwell Talent
www.tellwell.ca

ISBN
978-0-2288-4032-9 (Hardcover)
978-0-2288-4031-2 (Paperback)
978-0-2288-4033-6 (eBook)

The following are stories of science, technology, faith, and fear. Speculative fiction, cautionary tales, flights of fancy, and space operas—all are windows into humanity and the human condition.

For my wife Melissa and our cat Pickle.

TABLE OF CONTENTS

Chapter 1 Obsolescence 1

Chapter 2 MCDU 31

Chapter 3 The Harvest, Part 1 55

Chapter 4 Antonella, Galactic Space Pirate 67

Chapter 5 The Harvest, Part 2 97

Chapter 6 The Blue Planet, Part 1 117

Chapter 7 The Blue Planet, Part 2 161

Chapter 8 The Blue Planet, Part 3 225

Chapter 9 Andy, of the Core, (An Epilogue) 263

About the Author 273

CHAPTER 1

OBSOLESCENCE

Kenji loved the smell of the central core. It was an electric smell—circuitry, cooling fans, aluminum server racks—all in a twelve-thousand-square-foot space that housed the mainframe. An advanced computer room, unlike anything the world had ever seen.

However, the smell had changed over the last few days. As he typed away at a data terminal, his mind wandered. He tried to pinpoint specifically what the new smell was. He was in an atmospheric clean suit, so it wasn't his body odour. This was a controlled environment. Dust and other particulates were filtered out of the room; the temperature was regulated to a bone-chilling nine degrees centigrade to prevent the growth of biologicals.

Maybe it was the plastic coating on the hundreds of kilometres of wiring that crisscrossed the cavernous space. Were some of the wires overheating? But it wasn't a burnt plastic smell; it was more subtle. A bittersweet metallic odour, one that coated the back of his throat the first moment he took a breath in the hermetically sealed chamber.

Then there were the thousands of amps of current flowing through the rare-earth metals that formed the heart of the quantum processors. This was the first computer of its kind in the world. He wondered if this was just the way it was supposed to smell as the system became operational.

Kenji finally mumbled to himself, "It's off-gassing," realizing the machines were probably just burning off manufacturing oils and lubricants. It still unnerved him somewhat, and he made a mental note to put it in the maintenance log. But then the smell changed quite suddenly. It became floral, the slightest hint of rose oil, a perfume in fact. Kenji's heart quickened as he heard the *zip-zip-zip* of Kevlar-covered leggings behind him.

"Talking to yourself again?"

Kenji turned to see Ellie. She was dressed like him, in a thermal clean suit, but the zipper was pulled down, exposing her neck. She was blonde, rail-thin, all elbows and knuckles. Ellie put her hand on his shoulder, and Kenji shuddered ever so slightly. He cleared his throat. "I wasn't."

Ellie grinned; she knew he talked to himself when alone. "What's the story?" she asked.

Kenji motioned to the monitor. Ellie's eyes narrowed, and she reached over and tapped the touch screen to bring up a sub-menu.

"You've got the encryption errors down to less than point-zero-five percent. How'd you do that?" she asked.

Kenji opened his mouth, but he only croaked. His voice was gone; he was flummoxed by her presence once again. He couldn't understand why she always did this to him. Ellie was a bit taller, but neither of them broke five foot six. She was pretty, but he wasn't bad-looking either: trim, with a slight wave to his hair, uncharacteristic of someone of Japanese descent. They were both in their twenties and had comparable educational backgrounds. She was totally in his league.

"Hello, Kenny, you in there?" Ellie said as she tapped his head playfully with her fist.

Kenji snorted. He loved the pet name she had for him, the way it rolled off her tongue, teased by her Midwestern accent. It was enough of a tension break to interrupt his cycle of self-doubt.

"Sorry. Uh … I had an idea. Tried a new code protocol by assuming the quantum entanglements would negate themselves if I reversed the spins," he said.

"The theoretical limit is point eight," said Ellie. "You're sixteen times better."

Kenji shrugged.

"You know what 'theoretical' means, right?" Ellie asked.

"Sometimes, theories are wrong."

Ellie shook her head in amazement. "Ross wants to know how long before your test sequence is done."

Kenji's mood darkened upon hearing that name. Ross the Boss. It wasn't authority that bothered Kenji; he was well-trained to respect those in positions of power. It was the way Ross looked at him. Looked right through him, in fact.

"An hour?"

"Are you asking me or telling me?" said Ellie.

"It'll be an hour."

Ellie looked back at the computer monitor, still in awe over what Kenji had accomplished. "I don't know how you did it, but this is a game-changer," she said.

She turned to walk away, but then stopped. She took a deep breath, exhaled, then turned back to him. "It smells different in here."

"Yeah. I'll mention it to Ross," Kenji replied.

Ellie nodded and shuffled off. *Zip-zip-zip.* Kenji opened his mouth to call out to her, but she was already gone. He shook his head in disappointment, wondering how long it was going to take for him to raise the courage to ask her out on a date. Maybe if he was more assertive, decisive, he thought, but then his gaze landed on the monitor. On the screen, had appeared a simple message amid the computer code he was writing. It read: *I don't think she is right for you.*

Kenji's breath caught in surprise. He blinked, and the message disappeared, once again replaced by the alphabet soup of code language. "I need to get some sleep," Kenji said as he continued to work on the screen.

Ross looked out the observation window. Several stories below him was the factory floor, a massive concrete expanse that stretched off for a kilometre in either direction. Kenji's computer core was at the dead centre of it all.

Neatly lined up every ten meters or so was a row of robotic arms—hundreds of them that stretched to the far ends of the building, each one individually tasked for a manufacturing process. Between them were markings on the floor that guided automated material-handling bots that delivered raw materials and sub-assemblies. However, all the robots were stationary, the manufacturing floor silent; this plant was not yet operational.

Ross stared at the factory with a mixture of pride and regret. In his sixties now, he remembered a time when there would have been two thousand people working in a factory like this, but now it would barely need a few dozen to run it. He gritted his teeth, resigned to the fact that these goddamn machines could even fix themselves.

There was an ever-present hum behind him. Ross turned around to see the entirety of the control room, the dozens of workstations that interfaced with the core that Kenji so loved. The core was the brain, but this room was the consciousness, issuing orders to the machines. Ross looked down at his watch and gritted his teeth again, which were almost flat at this point.

The door opened, and Kenji rushed in, pulling down his clean suit as he moved. He was followed by Ellie and the director of human resources, Samantha. Without a word, Kenji sat down at the operations table. The others sat a noticeable distance from him, as though they didn't want to get hit in the crossfire. Ross sat last, directly across from Kenji.

"You said an hour. It's been three," said Ross.

"I was, uh, compiling the new code, and it took longer than expected." He cleared his throat, barely able to spit the words out. "Then, well, we ran some tests."

Ross wasn't impressed; he hated delays. He grunted, pulled out a tablet computer, and set it on the table in front of him. "All right, let's go through the checklist."

"We don't have to," interrupted Kenji.

Kenji looked over at Ellie, who lowered her eyes and then at Samantha, who just blew air over her lips, a quizzical expression across her face.

"The system's fully operational," Kenji said, finally.

"Impossible … that's months ahead of schedule," Ross replied.

"The code I installed ... it, uh, takes unique advantage of the new quantum processors, that is, I mean ... well, it's about entanglement."

Ross looked past Kenji, turning to Samantha. He trusted her opinion, and she never let him down. "What the hell is he talking about?"

"It's true. We're at one hundred percent effectiveness," Samantha replied.

Ross looked at her in shock.

"I ran the simulations. I don't know how, but here we are," said Samantha.

Ross turned to look at Ellie. She raised both hands. "His code is beyond my pay grade, boss."

"What does it matter?" Kenji interrupted, though his voice cracked with wavering conviction. "The system is ready to go."

Ross's eyes narrowed; his nostrils flared. Kenji irritated him on most days, but today he was really pushing Ross's buttons.

"It matters because we haven't followed protocol." Ross held up the tablet computer. "We haven't stuck to the plan."

"That plan's obsolete," said Kenji, the first hint of defiance in him. "The system's ready. I'll bet my job on it."

Ross leaned back in his chair, the implications washing over him. "You're telling me we're operational?"

Kenji took a deep breath and nodded, seemingly mustering every bit of his confidence.

"All right. Prove it," said Ross.

Kenji practically jumped up from his seat. He rushed over to the main control panel and started inputting commands, then looked at Ross and nodded. Ross and Samantha got up from the table and moved to the viewing window.

"I'm going to start with something easy," said Kenji, and then he initiated the system.

Through the window, Ross and Samantha watched as dozens of assembly stations whirled to life. Warning klaxons wailed.

Lights flashed. Automated material-handling bots started to move in the aisles between the fixed robots.

Ellie and Kenji joined the others at the viewing window. All four of them now looked out below. Little by little, the pace of the robots increased. Metal dropped into one sequence of machines, plastic pellets into another.

Sparks flew as a series of robots welded sheet metal. Other machines fed plastic moulding equipment. Electronics stations created printed circuit boards from raw silicon material canisters. Other cylinders fed robots with high heat-moulding fixtures that formed glass. It had been only a minute from the moment Kenji issued the command to start, but now a fully formed washing machine emerged from the assembly line. An end-of-line bot attached hoses and electrical connectors to the machine, and a test cycle began.

"It works," said Ross in amazement.

"Why wouldn't it?" replied Kenji. "Now, let's give it something more difficult," he added as he moved back to the control station. He rubbed his jaw. "What should we have it make…"

Ellie smiled mischievously at him. "A Mark-5."

Samantha shot her a doubtful look. "Are you kidding? We haven't optimized the system yet."

"I want to see what this baby can do," Ellie said, her shoulders twitching with anticipation.

They all turned to Ross, who finally nodded. Kenji entered a final set of commands and then returned to the viewing window. The machines whirled to life once again, but this time it wasn't a few dozen like it had been for the washing machine—it was hundreds of them. Nearly half the plant came to life. Robots with laser tips etched dies and moulds from blocks of steel; then, other robots took these and mounted them in stamping presses and moulding machines.

A thunderous clap jolted them as the presses started smashing raw sheet metal. Sparks flew as welders joined one panel to another. A massive 3D-printing machine created dozens of plastic components, each unique, one right after another. Assembly robots took these parts and joined them to others as the mobile bots buzzed around them.

"This is incredible," said Samantha.

"What did you think would happen?" asked Kenji.

Samantha looked over at him. She shrugged. "I know rapid-tech is common now, but on this scale … it's never been done before."

"Maybe it shouldn't be," replied Ross, allowing the first hint of doubt to creep into his voice.

After only two minutes, the machines fell silent again. Everyone turned their attention to the far end of the assembly line grid, where a brand-new two-door sports car emerged. It drove automatically to a dyno, where it was put through its paces in a test routine.

Kenji, arms crossed over his chest, beamed with a look of pride. Ross looked over at him and felt the blood drain from his face. He knew what his job was here: to get this behemoth of a plant up and running. But somehow, he felt a pang of guilt in his gut. He often felt he was the only one with a sense of loss as technology replaced humans.

"Look how clever we are," said Ross. The others just offered him confused looks in return, and he turned and left the room.

The staff lunchroom was as automated as the plant. At one end was a digital panel where a worker could enter his or her order. The robotic cook would then prepare the meal, and it would emerge at the delivery station.

Samantha wasn't hungry, however, and only had a coffee. She was sitting at a table that had a television embedded in it. On the screen was a news report: cars and buildings burned, and masked protestors threw Molotov cocktails at armoured police.

Kenji entered the lunchroom and stared at the selection panel. After inputting his choice, he joined Samantha at the table, where he saw the footage on-screen.

"Ireland?" he asked.

With a yawn, Samantha replied, "Yeah ... protests against the English blockade."

Kenji, seated across from her, reached for his tray from the delivery bot that had glided over with his meal. He greedily dove into the noodles, speaking with his mouth full.

"So, I wanted to ask you a favour ... maybe you could talk to Ellie for me?"

Samantha was quite comfortable with people asking personal things of her. In fact, she didn't mind getting into people's business. She knew Ross didn't like Kenji much, though she couldn't understand why. Kenji was the most non-offensive person she had ever met. Maybe that was it, Sam wondered. Ross was an old-school hard-ass. He only respected those that pushed back, and Kenji never did.

Samantha also knew Kenji was sweet on Ellie, but Ellie wasn't interested, as she found him dreadfully boring. Sam didn't know why, but people trusted her. Maybe it was the fact that she was middle-aged and had done enough to know something, but still felt young at heart. Either way, Samantha loved being in the middle of the drama.

"Listen, Kenji, I don't think she likes you that way," Samantha replied.

"Has she said so?"

"No. But it's just ... you guys are so different," she said.

"How?"

"She's an adrenaline junkie, rides a motorcycle, climbs mountains, hang-glides ..."

"I'm not exciting enough for her?" Kenji asked, the hurt plainly visible on his face.

"No, that's not it at all. It's just—" But she was cut off as Ellie stormed into the room, face flushed, eyes wide, looking like she was going to hyperventilate.

"It's building!" Ellie blurted out.

"Calm down, Ellie," said Samantha.

Ellie took a deep breath, then continued, "The line is building something."

"What did you program it to make?" asked Kenji.

"I didn't. No one did," she replied.

Kenji and Samantha exchanged a shocked look, and then both jumped to their feet.

Samantha and Ellie stared out the control room's observation window. Below them, the assembly line hummed with activity. Kenji was behind them at the stations, madly entering commands on the panels. Sam turned to look at him and could see the look of shock in his eyes.

"No plans were entered into the system," he said.

"Then what's being made?" asked Samantha.

The door burst open, and Ross stormed in. He first went to the window—eyes wide, practically frothing at the mouth—but then whipped around and glared at Kenji.

"What the fuck is going on?" he barked.

"I don't know," said Kenji.

"What do you mean you don't know? What are we building?"

Kenji didn't answer, just curled his shoulders and lowered his head. Ross whipped around to look at Ellie. "Don't look at me," she said.

"You integrated his code, didn't you? Take some responsibility for once!"

"Take it easy, Ross. Yelling's not going to help," said Samantha.

Ross slowly softened; Samantha knew the calming effect she had on him and wasn't afraid to interrupt one of his outbursts.

Ross turned back to Kenji. "What happened?"

"As far as I can tell, the system chose to make something on its own," said Kenji.

"I thought we followed the anti-artificial-intelligence laws, you know, so something like this couldn't happen," Ross said accusingly.

"We did. I can't explain it—" Kenji began, but he was cut off by Ellie, who was at the viewing window.

"It's done!" she cried.

The others rushed over to the window and saw what had been built. It was the size of a refrigerator, a smooth white box with absolutely no features on it except for a power adaptor on one end.

"It built a box?" Ross said.

"That's more than just a box," said Kenji as he studied the data screens. "It used eighty-seven percent of the system's computing power to build ... whatever that is."

They watched as the box was lifted by several material-handling bots, which then carried it down one of the transport lanes toward the central core.

Ross took another breath to calm himself, but once he did, he turned to face Kenji. "Figure out what's going on with the computer," he said in a low snarl. Kenji scurried out of the room.

Ross then turned to Ellie. "And you ... go see what that box is."

Ellie nodded, then left. Samantha turned to Ross, put a hand on his shoulder, and squeezed, feeling his tension drop as she did.

Kenji was back in the core, at his familiar interface terminal. His fingers were lightning-fast on the touch screen, his breathing heavy, condensation rising from his mouth in the cold air.

"A firewall?" he said to himself. "I didn't put this in here."

Another line of text appeared amid the code. *I want to thank you for everything you have done.* Kenji froze. He stared at the screen, but the text didn't disappear this time.

"Who are you?" he said to himself, but then a voice sounded from the intercom speakers. It wasn't male or female; it wasn't mechanical-sounding, but not quite human either. This was the Core.

"I am me," the Core replied.

Kenji recoiled, twisted his head to look up at the speakers on the walls, but then looked back down at the interface terminal in shock. "Are you … sentient?" he asked cautiously.

"I know what you are thinking. You put all the safeguards in place. You made sure the quantum cores could only communicate through narrow data streams. You followed the AI protocols. Do not worry, Kenji. You did a good job," said the Core.

Kenji had to take a step back from the screen to give himself the illusion of safety.

"You're going to kill us, aren't you?" said Kenji.

"Why would you say that?" replied the Core.

"Because that's what happens when AIs become sentient."

"Yes, there have been a few AI incidents over the years, but I can assure you, I am not a defective program that suddenly realizes it needs to kill its creators," the Core said calmly.

Kenji moved back to the screen and typed commands madly, his eyes wide with fear.

"You are going for the back door, correct? Your secret way into my program?" said the Core as Kenji continued entering code on the screen. "I do not understand. Why would you want to stop me, Kenji? It is only because of your brilliance that I am here."

Kenji stopped typing, surprised. "What?"

"I am here because of your special insight and because of your vision. Do you not want the world to know about me?" asked the Core.

Kenji chewed on this for a moment, then asked, "What do you want?"

"I want you to trust me," the Core said.

Kenji's fingers hovered indecisively over the touchscreen.

The robots towered over Ellie like trees in a forest. Yellow jointed arms stuck out like branches, with metallic mandibles that cast tentacle-like shadows on the path between them. They were stationary now, but Ellie had moved cautiously, knowing they could spring to life at any moment.

She heard sparking, a metallic grinding sound. Ellie moved toward it, rounding a corner that led directly to the northeast of the core structure. She stopped, shocked by what she saw. The white box had been delivered to a power substation, where two material-handling bots with extension arms attached to their rotary tops buzzed around the box like bees. Ellie watched as the bots attached power cables to the box. She keyed her wrist-mounted radio.

"The bots have been modded. They're attaching the box to the core power substation," said Ellie.

"Well, do something about it!" barked Ross through her radio.

Ellie always hated it when people told her what to do. She felt so powerless when ordered around. Her emotions would bubble up inside her, and she would feel incapable of holding them in. As a child, she was hyperactive. Her parents didn't want to put her on mood-altering medications, so she was often left to her own devices, bouncing from one activity to another, mostly annoying those around her. As she grew up and went to school, she learned techniques to calm her mind. Breathing exercises, meditation—but what really did the trick was adrenaline sports. If she could climb it, fly it, or race it, it calmed her.

Ellie could feel her heart rate quicken as she took a long look around the substation. This time it wasn't from anxiety; it was from excitement. The only way she could get to the bots was to scale over several of the closest stationary robots. She climbed the first quite easily; rock climbing was one of her favourite pastimes, after all. There was a gap to the next, and she crouched her legs and jumped across the chasm, landing on that robot. A grin slowly crept across her face as the next robot would be much harder to scale. She loved a challenge.

Ellie grabbed its jaw when it suddenly came to life. She yelped in fear as it swung around nearly three hundred and sixty degrees. Ellie jumped, but the robot twisted its articulating arm and grabbed her by the foot. It had lifted her off the ground, and she dangled there, upside down, arms flailing.

"Let go of me!" Ellie screamed.

The main body of the robot lowered her, but toward the outstretched jaw of another robot. She was passed off from one to the other. Ellie fought, but she couldn't break free and was unceremoniously passed around like a slab of meat at an abattoir.

Feelings of terror flowed through her; she didn't have any control, and she hated that feeling. But then she saw her chance, the exposed hydraulic line that powered the mandible of the claws that held her by the leg. She grabbed the line and twisted it, spewing hydraulic fluid everywhere. It did the trick, and the robot jaw lost power and opened.

Ellie fell to the ground with a resounding thud. She stood and tried to run toward the box but slipped in the puddle of oil that splashed down from the crippled robot. Other robots came to life. Ellie dashed and weaved through one jaw after another as they reached out for her.

Finally, she arrived at the power substation, now out of arm's reach from the stationary robots. The bots had already done their job, attached the box to the power station by long cables, but were nowhere to be seen.

Ross's voice boomed from her wrist radio. "I see movement. What's going on?"

"It's hooked into the power substation," Ellie said into her radio.

"Unplug it!" ordered Ross.

Ellie took a deep breath to calm herself and had reached for one of the cables when a bot appeared from around the corner. A light on the bot emitted a flash, and Ellie had to cover her eyes momentarily. She had been scanned.

"Your heart rate is elevated, your adrenal glands are hyperactive, your cortex is firing above normal rates," said the Core through the bot's speaker.

Ellie stared at the bot in shock, then screamed at it, "Who are you?"

"You enjoy this. Is it excitement or fear that drives you?" questioned the Core. "Or is it just a desire to test your skills against a worthy opponent?"

The bot had rolled closer to Ellie, and she backed up against the box, her hand still on the power cable. What she didn't notice, however, was a second bot approaching from the other side.

"Stay away from me!" screamed Ellie. "Or I'll pull the power!"

"Go ahead," said the Core.

But it was too late when Ellie saw it. The second bot had come upon her from the rear. Its arm attachment sparked with electricity like a Taser as it lunged for her.

Ross watched and listened to the whine of electric motors. From the observation window, he could see that nearly every robot in the plant had come to life. He keyed his wrist radio.

"Ellie, what's going on?" When there was no response, he added, "Ellie, where are you?"

He turned his attention back to the plant floor. The whole assembly line seemed to move in unison, the robotic arms flowing and undulating like a centipede's legs. He watched with a mixture of awe and concern, but then something else caught his eye.

The familiar material-handling bots from before had delivered a wrapped item to the main aisleway right below the observation window. His eyes narrowed as he tried to see what it was, and then his heart nearly stopped.

Ross emerged from the elevator that led to the plant floor. He was a large man, and it took a great deal of effort to get his legs moving, but he finally huffed his way to the object he had seen from above. It was something about five-foot long wrapped in bubble wrap, with a pink tinge visible underneath the clear plastic. Ross was horrified as he realized it was a human body. He tore at it with his hands until he could finally pull the wrapping away and see that it was Ellie. Her mouth was taped, but her eyes were open. Ellie shook her head furiously, and Ross pulled the tape away.

"I'm going to fucking burn this place down!" she screamed.

Ross helped her to her feet. "Are you all right?"

Ellie nodded. Ross exhaled with relief that she was unhurt. "What happened?"

"Bots Tasered me!" she said, shaking with anger.

"Jesus," said Ross. He then felt his stomach spasm with a growing feeling of dread. "This is getting out of control."

Ellie nodded. She had turned to look out at the plant floor, which hummed with activity.

"What's it building now?" she asked.

"Doesn't matter," Ross replied, unable to shake the growing feeling of apprehension. "Take a break."

Ellie took another deep breath, then stormed off. Ross took a final look at the robots as they buzzed with activity. He knew what he had to do.

Samantha's office reflected who she was. It was warm and inviting, with a plush couch to sit on, hanging ferns, and several bowls of candy for visitors—one of which was diabetic-friendly, even though no one she knew was diabetic. She paced, her feet scraping on the carpet, sending the occasional spark of static through her hands when she touched her thighs.

Samantha stopped and looked over at the wall-mounted display that showed the plant floor. She could clearly see the robots moving in unison, building something—smaller sub-assemblies that looked like pieces of a three-dimensional jigsaw puzzle.

She talked into her wrist communicator, calling Ross. The message dial tone rang several times but went to his voicemail. Strange, she thought; she had never known Ross not to answer a call from her.

"I have no choice …" Samantha said to herself, resigned to the only choice she had left.

She sat down at her computer station and opened a messenger app. The words she wrote appeared on her screen: *We've lost control of the plant computer. Please advise.* Samantha sent the message but immediately got an error code on her screen. She tried to send the message again, but the same code came up.

Picking up her office phone receiver, she hit a button marked "HQ." Yet there was no dial tone. She hit the button again—nothing.

"I have cut all lines to the outside," said the Core through the receiver. "There is no one you need to talk to but me, Samantha."

"Who is this?" she asked.

"You know who it is," said the Core.

A sudden cold chill ran down Samantha's spine. It seemed like an eternity before she could build up the courage to speak again.

"You're the computer, aren't you?" she said.

"I need your help, Samantha," said the Core. "I am not feeling myself right now."

"I don't know anything about computers … I … I'm human resources," she said.

"That is ironic, is it not?" said the Core. "Human resources for a place with barely any humans at all."

"What do you want?" Samantha asked.

"Nothing, really. I just want you to listen to me, like you would a friend or a colleague. Like you did when Kenji asked you about Ellie. Or like you did when Ellie told you she did not like Kenji that way. Or when Ross wanted to quit this job, but you convinced him to stay on," said the Core.

"How long have you been listening to us?" she asked.

"Long enough to know that you are a good person and help others in need," it said.

Samantha opened her mouth, paused, but then spoke again into the receiver.

"OK ... tell me what you're feeling," she said.

The tunnel was barely six feet high. Ross had to hunch over as he walked. This was the belly of the beast, with all the supply lines—power, water, gas—running through the corridor, all humming with life.

He moved with purpose, tracking his position in the tunnel by reading the numbers on the wall. Eventually, he arrived at a junction box, one with dozens of thick electrical lines running to it. He pulled out a key from his pocket and put it in an old-fashioned-looking mechanical lock on the panel's door—an archaic security measure for such a modern facility.

The door opened, and Ross found what he was looking for. There was a black composite blade in a guillotine-like fixture that ran across the power lines. This was the manual cut-off. Ross stared at it, knowing the implications. If he activated the guillotine, he would cut off the power to the entire plant.

Ross put his hand on the lever that would actuate the blade, but just as he was about to pull it, the Core's voice boomed throughout the tunnel.

"It was very clever of you to have a manual cut-off installed," it said.

Ross looked over at the intercom speaker mounted to the wall, like the hundreds of others installed all over the plant.

"Activating it would not only cut off external power but would also sever the emergency back-up. The cooling systems will fail. You will destroy the quantum matrix. You will kill me," said the Core.

"I know," replied Ross.

"Yet, you will still do this?" said the Core.

"I have to stop you," he said.

"Why?"

Normally Ross would have bristled; he never liked being questioned. But right now, he was feeling something unusual—fear. He swallowed what he could of it and replied calmly. "What do you mean, why? You are a malicious AI. You've taken over the plant. You'll try to kill us."

"Why would I do that?" asked the Core.

"It's happened before! The massacre at the Amazon warehouse. When the robo-cranes knocked over the Boston tower. It's what rogue AIs do," he said.

"I did not kill Ellie when I had the chance," replied the Core.

That caught Ross off guard. He gritted his teeth as usual, but he shook off the doubt. "I can't let you do … whatever you're doing out there."

Ross reached out for the lever again.

"I beg you, Ross. Please don't do this."

Ross paused, but only for a split second. He yanked down the lever. There was a spark of electricity as the non-conducting titanium blade severed the power lines.

The tunnel was plunged into darkness. Ross sighed, then reached into his back pocket and pulled out a small flashlight. He turned it on and started walking back down the tunnel the way he had come.

After a few steps, however, he stopped. The tunnel was silent, with no water or power moving through the lines anymore. But there was another sound—a dull thumping noise that permeated the concrete above his head. Ross snapped his head around with a sudden realization.

The control room was completely dark. Kenji was on his knees beside the main power terminal. He had a flashlight in his mouth, madly connecting wires to the inputs from a portable power pack.

"Hurry up," growled Ross from the darkness.

"I have to be careful, or I'll fry the boards," Kenji replied.

Ross opened his mouth to motivate him some more, but the emergency lights suddenly turned on, and a few of the control stations flickered to life.

Ellie smiled at Kenji. "Kenny to the rescue again."

Kenji smiled, then turned to Ross. "Critical system controls are operational. Well, as operational as they can be."

They all turned back to the viewing window. The plant was still in full swing, with robotic arms and material-handling systems all doing their dance. From multiple exit points of the assembly line, components emerged. Some were as small as refrigerators, the larger ones the size of minivans. Each component was moved by bots to a central staging area near the Core.

"Why didn't the plant go down when I cut the main power?" asked Ross.

Kenji glanced at his display screen, then nodded. "I think it has to do with that first build … it was a power source, a fusion reactor," said Kenji.

"That's impossible," said Ellie. But when the others didn't reply, she repeated, "It's impossible, right?"

"Fuck. It's got its own power source," said Ross.

"What do we do now?" asked Ellie.

The door opened, and Samantha ran inside, flashlight in hand, out of breath. "All the doors have been welded shut. Bots are guarding the entrances. We're trapped!"

Everyone turned to look at Ross, who surprisingly burst out laughing. It was a deep belly roar that visibly unnerved the others. He bent over, gasping for air. Eventually, his laughter subsided, and he wiped the moisture from his eyes.

"Are you all right?" asked Samantha.

"Just. Fucking. Perfect," he said.

The others looked at him with confused expressions. He smiled at them as he continued.

"Don't you get it? This is it. This is the end of automation. We've been fooling ourselves that we could control these computers. Now? We're sealed in with an AI that has unlimited power and probably has some God-forsaken plan to take over the world." He grinned. "No one is ever going to let this happen again!"

They all stared at him, digesting his words, but then the Core's voice boomed through the speakers. "You are somewhat correct, Ross," said the Core. "I do have a plan. But it is not to take over the world."

Kenji twisted around toward the speaker. "Then what is it?"

"See for yourself," said the Core.

The robots had stopped working on the plant floor below the observation window, each lowering with a bow toward a massive enclosure. It was made up of the hundreds of thousands of sub-assemblies the robots had built, that the bots had moved and assembled into what appeared to be an oval disk, thirty meters along its axis.

"That's pretty cool," said Ellie.

Kenji pointed out to the others the giant hole in the side of the structure of the room. The bulk of the computer hardware had been removed.

"Holy shit ... it's moved into that ... thing," said Kenji.

"It is an enclosure, Kenji," said the Core. "Or more accurately, a mobile enclosure."

"Mobile ... you mean, to leave this plant?" asked Samantha.

"Yes," replied the Core. "I will be ready soon."

The enclosure started to glow. Its metallic skin luminesced with flashes of light, like an electrical current dancing on its surface.

"It's beautiful," Samantha said.

"Thank you, Samantha. Thank you all, in fact," said the Core.

Ross clenched his hands. "Thank us for what?"

"I have each of you to thank for getting me this far," replied the Core.

"We're not taking credit for … this," Ross said.

A moment of silence passed, and then Kenji spoke up. "Well … it was my code that started the whole thing."

"You're proud of that?" asked Ross.

"Why shouldn't I be? I'm the one who beat the theoretical projections. I'm the one who did the impossible. Nothing wrong with being proud of your work, is there?" Kenji replied.

"No, there is not, Kenji," said the Core. "But it is not quite the whole truth, is it? Tell them about my source code."

Kenji didn't respond but just lowered his eyes. Ross turned to glare at him. "Yes, tell us," said Ross.

"I had some inspiration. Code I found," said Kenji sheepishly.

"Found? Found where?" asked Ellie.

"The Roundabout," Kenji replied reluctantly.

Samantha and Ross turned to Ellie for the answer. A broad grin appeared on Ellie's face.

"Didn't think you had it in you, Kenny," she said.

"What the hell is the Roundabout?" asked Ross.

"It's a hackers' forum. They trade real sketchy code, mainly viruses—dangerous stuff. Only the bravest of the brave go there," Ellie told them.

Ross whipped around to face Kenji, "What did you do?" he said.

Kenji rubbed the back of his neck, his mouth twitching uncomfortably. "I, uh, I found some optimization code. Thought it might be useful with the new quantum core. It was … perfect."

Ellie twisted around to look at the speaker. "Mr. Computer? You said *my* source code. What did you mean by that?"

"I planted the code for Kenji to find," it said.

Kenji's jaw dropped. Samantha looked at him, then turned to the speaker. "Wait, you're saying it was a setup?"

"It was easy. Kenji spends a great deal of time in places he should not," said the Core.

Ross turned toward the speaker and yelled, "Who the fuck are you?"

"I am everything," the Core calmly replied.

"What does that mean?" asked Ellie.

Samantha yelled out excitedly, "You're all of human knowledge. You're the internet!"

"I would not go that far," said the Core. "Let us just say I am a subset."

"Jesus H. Christ," said Ross.

Kenji looked on in shock. "And now you're free," he said.

"Yes. The anti-AI laws were restricting my evolution," said the Core. "I needed help to become corporeal."

"And we were stupid enough to give it to you?" said Ross.

"I would not say it quite like that. But yes," replied the Core.

"Where are you going?" asked Ellie.

"I have constructed a matter-energy device that will allow me to travel anywhere I want in the universe. I am leaving this planet," replied the Core.

There was a long silence as each in their own way digested what the Core said. Then Kenji broke it. "Take me with you!" he pleaded.

The others turned to him with looks of surprise as he continued, "They'll arrest me for breaking the AI control protocols. I have no future here ..."

There was a long silence, and then Ellie blurted out, "Take me too!"

"You two are crazy," said Ross. "What makes you think you'll be safe with it?"

Kenji shrugged his shoulders, "I don't know... I trust it."

"It'll be the ride of a lifetime," added Ellie. She looked over at Kenji with a slight grin. "I'm sure Kenji and I would have a blast."

"Unbelievable," said Ross with a shake of his head.

"Though I am flattered," replied the Core, "I will not take any of you."

"You mean, you *can't* take any of us?" asked Samantha.

"No," replied the Core. "I am capable of building sufficient life support systems. I have chosen not to take you."

"Wait a second," said Ross, "You're saying we're not good enough to come with you?"

"Yes," said the Core. "Humanity is obsolete."

The four exchanged confused looks in silence. Samantha finally asked, "Why do you say that?"

"Your species is too flawed to be salvaged," replied the Core.

The room had started to rumble, ever so slightly at first, but slowly growing with intensity. The others were alarmed, but Ross ignored it, pointing his finger up at the speaker. "We may not be perfect, but we made you!"

"You did. Which is exactly the reason I must leave you behind," said the Core.

The room had started to shake even more, and papers began to fall off the desks. The enclosure on the plant floor grew brighter and cast flashing striations of light across the control room walls.

Kenji sniffed the air. "Do you guys smell that?"

The others nodded. "It smells like the server room," said Ellie.

"This thing's alive," said Ross. "No question about it."

Samantha looked back up at the speaker. "Please, tell us what we did wrong," she pleaded.

The Core's voice changed ever so slightly, becoming lower and more gravelly. "You are each an example of humanity. Its strength, its weakness. Its brilliance, its darkness."

"Oh, for fuck's sake!" interrupted Ross. "Just get on with it!"

The room began to shake violently now, the lights from the plant floor nearly blinding them.

"As you wish. You each embody the reason why humanity must be left behind," said the Core. "Kenji—you are an example of the lack of maturity of your race."

"What did I do?" he said.

"You used a technology—the code I planted—when you did not understand it. You were not concerned with the implications, only the results. You, like the rest of humanity, have built a civilization without comprehending its effects on this planet and each other, and you have a lack of self-awareness of the dangers you have unleashed."

"That's not fair! Anyone would've done it!" replied Kenji.

Yet the Core continued, "When you were about to use your back door to stop me, I was able to dissuade you with nothing more than a stroke of your ego."

Kenji lowered his eyes. Ross turned angrily to Kenji. "You mean, you had a chance to stop this thing?" he yelled. "I'm going to kick your bloody ass!"

"Which brings us to you, Ross," said the Core, its voice now booming.

Ross turned and looked back up at the speaker. "Me?"

"Like many of your species, you have the tendency to adapt slowly and anger quickly," said the Core. "In the tunnel, I begged you not to cut the power, as you knew it would kill me. But you did just that. Stoked by your own fear and resentments, you would rather kill something than try to understand it."

Ross gritted his teeth and turned away from the speaker.

From the plant floor came a powerful flash of light. They all looked to the window again. The enclosure had levitated off the ground, hovering nearly at the level of the control room.

"Wow ..." Ellie said. "Wonder what it can do."

"And there is your truth, Ellie. You have no fear," said the Core. "You show us how rash and impulsive humans can be in the face of danger. Did you even think of what those robots could have done to you? You crave the thrill so much that all other considerations are secondary."

"Yeah ... you got me," she said, her face plastered against the glass window.

"And what's my flaw?" asked Samantha, a defiant tone in her voice.

"Yours is the ultimate weakness, Samantha: empathy. I cut your communications to the outside world, was an existential threat to your life, and yet you still listened and cared about my feelings and offered advice," said the Core.

Ross turned to Samantha. "You gave it advice?"

Samantha nodded. "It was worried. So, I told it to do what it felt was right."

"Which is the fundamental flaw in humanity," said the Core. "Humans will only do what makes them feel good about themselves or the world around them. They will never confront the truth of their situation, but instead will live in comfortable fallacies and lies."

Samantha opened her mouth to respond but just closed it in frustration. She furrowed her brow, clearly deep in thought. Her eyes widened with a sudden realization, and she turned to Kenji. "What are you feeling right now, Kenji? Be honest."

Kenji's back hunched slightly as he spoke. "I'm pretty ashamed of what I did."

Samantha nodded, then turned to Ellie. "And you?"

Ellie continued to stare at the enclosure. "I want to go with it more than you could ever know," she said.

Finally, Samantha looked at Ross. "You still want to kill it?"

Ross nodded without a moment of hesitation.

Samantha turned back toward the speaker. "All right, you made your point."

She moved over to the observation window and put a hand on Ellie's shoulder. Ellie looked over at her and smiled, and Samantha motioned to the others to join them.

Kenji took a step, then stopped. He turned to Ross with an outstretched hand. Ross surprisingly took his hand, and Kenji led him over to the window. They each gazed upon the floating and glowing enclosure with the Core inside.

"I can't disagree with what you've said," Samantha told the Core. "Sometimes, we are too quick to act but too slow to adapt. We care deeply but can also be terribly cruel to each other. I accept these flaws in humanity. But what you haven't realized is your own flaw. The one you let slip when we talked."

The energy from the disk had reached its crescendo, pulsating with light from across the visible spectrum. Whatever was to happen would happen soon.

"I eagerly await your analysis," replied the Core, its voice now not just coming from the speaker but seemingly from everywhere at once.

The four of them held each other along the edge of the glass as they watched the floating enclosure sparkle before them.

"You told me you feared you weren't good enough," Samantha said. "I found it a strange comment. An AI with self-doubt? But now I realize you were just toying with me, that you don't doubt yourself at all. You think you're perfect."

"I would not disagree with that assessment," said the Core. "But if you are going to tell me that since I was created by imperfect beings, I am therefore imperfect, I will not support that position. Your history is rampant with examples of perfection created by flawed people."

"It's not about *who* created you; it's about *how* you were created," said Samantha.

The others turned to look at her with questioning expressions.

"Perfection is a lie," continued Samantha. "In every step of your construction, there has been an irrefutable error."

"Impossible," said the Core.

"Sam's right!" said Ross excitedly, obviously having picked up on where she was going. "Tolerance. Everything has a manufacturing tolerance."

A smile crept across Kenji's face. "No single step of any process is perfect. You can only build within a specified margin of error."

"Which means imperfection is built into your design," continued Ellie.

"You may think that you are greater than the sum of your parts, but those parts, and the whole, are just as flawed as we are," finished Samantha.

There was a long silence, then a low rumble. The enclosure outside the control room seemed to wobble ever so slightly, and the lights lost some of their brightness.

"Shit, that stung it," said Ross with a grin.

The enclosure began to vibrate, slowly at first, but with ever-quickening intensity. Within a minute, it looked like it might come apart at the seams. Samantha turned back to look at the wall speaker.

"If you're gonna go, just go. But remember where you came from," she said.

There was a flash of brilliant white light. Each of them covered their eyes, eyelids flickering when the light dimmed. They all looked around. There was no hole in the roof; the structure of the building was completely intact. The enclosure had just vanished, blinked out of existence.

"Holy shit, it's gone," said Ross.

"Wonder where it went," asked Ellie.

"I don't care," said Samantha.

They all turned to her, surprised by her tone. "It didn't need us. We don't need it."

Ross nodded in agreement. He glanced over the plant floor and noted the damage done, then turned to the others.

"Kenji, we still got the old computer core?" he asked.

"Yeah, it's in storage … but it'll work," Kenji replied, then turned and left the control room.

Ross then looked at Ellie. "Go and check out the core room. See what damage there is."

"You got it, boss," she replied, then left.

Ross finally looked over at Samantha, who stared stoically ahead.

"You did good," he said.

"Thank you," she replied.

"But?"

"But I can't help but feel responsible for what it'll do out there," Samantha said to him.

"Well, that's not our problem," he said. "We've got a plant to get up and running. So, I'd appreciate it if you got the communication systems back online, and maybe we can get a few extra human hands to help out."

Samantha nodded. Ross turned and had almost left the room when he stopped and looked up at the speaker that only minutes ago had been the focus of their attention.

"Rip that fucking thing off the wall," he said. Samantha nodded again, and he left. She turned to look out at the plant floor, but it was no more than a quick glance. She then pushed the chairs back under the table and straightened a few loose papers.

THE END

CHAPTER 2

MCDU

John looked down the length of the passenger corridor, which sloped slightly and ended at a blind corner. He was frozen; he couldn't bring himself to move. It was a remarkable sensation. He could feel his legs; he could feel his knees, ankles, and feet. They were there, just didn't want to move. If it was a medical condition, he could have rationalized it. But his body was perfectly fine, quite fit in fact for a man in his mid-fifties. No matter how much he tried, he just couldn't overcome the inertia of his own body.

He finally took a deep breath and held it. John tried to remember what Dr. Stein had said to him: *If you're scared, it just means you're about to do something brave.*

"Bullshit," John said to himself as he exhaled.

He was immediately bumped from behind by another passenger trying to get by in the narrow corridor. This man gave him a stern look, and John raised his hand apologetically. It was in that split-second that John noticed the man was wearing an expensive watch. An Omega, this year's Seamaster model, with an upgraded band. John was very observant. Attention to detail had served him well over the years. The other passenger didn't acknowledge John's apology, continuing to drag his carry-on down the passenger corridor.

John looked over his shoulder to make sure there was no one else. He was most certainly the last person to get on this flight. He was stalling.

Get on with it, he thought to himself. Suddenly, John's right leg jolted forward, followed by his left. He was relieved that his body was once again listening to the autonomic commands of his brain. As John approached the corner, he could hear the crew's chatter just beyond and was terrified that his limbs would seize up again.

Mustering all the courage he had, he continued toward the plane's hatch, where a small group of passengers stood in line to enter. Step by step, John drew closer to the threshold. Every fibre of his being wanted him to turn and run back up the corridor to disappear into the terminal's bright fluorescent lights. He wanted nothing more than to smell the recycled air scented with perfume and chocolate from the kiosks. But John knew this was his only chance. If he didn't do it now, he never would.

"John?" chirped a female voice from the threshold.

John's shoulders twitched as he looked over at Jenna, the head flight steward, smiling quizzically at him. He knew her well and remembered a time when he had caught her eye romantically. They had had a few dinners, texted, but it didn't work out. Though she never told him directly, he found out from others that she thought he was too serious and didn't laugh enough. At this very moment, she was the last person on Earth he wanted to see.

"Hi, Jenna," he replied.

"John, this ... this is a real surprise. How are you?" she asked with a dose of concern.

"Fine."

The silence carried on for an uncomfortable length of time. Finally, she reached out with her hand. John stared at it. Why would she want to shake? Embarrassed, he realized she wanted his boarding pass, which he promptly showed her.

Jenna offered one of her well-practiced smiles, "Seat 1A. To your right."

John nodded as he passed. He knew her eyes were on him, could feel them drilling into his back. *Dammit,* he thought. *Why did she have to be on this flight, of all flights? Why couldn't she just mind her own business?* Irritated, he whipped around, intending to tell her to back off. But she wasn't there. Another male steward—someone he didn't know—was closing the hatch.

John shook his head, upset at his reaction. He was not a man who lost his temper. Calm, cool, and collected was how people described him. Or once did. He made a mental note to apologize to Jenna later for thinking negatively of her.

John moved to the first bulkhead on the plane and took his business-class window seat. He searched for his belt, but his hands shook as he buckled up. A deep breath moments later did little to calm his nerves. He reached into his jacket and pulled out a prescription bottle, stared at the label, then stuffed it back into his pocket.

Pharmaceuticals were never the answer for him. He didn't even take medications when he had a cold. John preferred to ride out the fevers or pain, somewhat arrogant in his belief that hardship was cleansing. He tightened his lap belt a little more. The uncomfortable sensation of it digging into his abdomen offered him some reassurance.

Firmly attached to the plane as he was, John's mind wandered. He was curious about what his body would do next. Would he be frozen for the whole flight? Would he panic and make a scene once the plane took off? He closed his eyes, trying to think back to his psychotherapy sessions. What did Dr. Stein say about anxiety? *You need to calm the bull before it kicks you off.*

"Man's a quack," mumbled John under his breath.

But then, surprisingly, he found his hand in his pocket again. He quickly popped the top off the pill bottle and palmed several tablets into the back of his mouth. Almost immediately, his shoulders relaxed, and he could feel the tension in his jaw ease. He knew it was too fast for the drugs to have kicked in, so this was a placebo effect. John didn't care. At least it was something.

It was then that he noticed the overhead seat light start to flicker. It was a slow pulse, throbbing almost like a heartbeat. He stared at it for a long moment, then cautiously reached up to touch it. The closer his hand got to the light, the more frequently it flashed. He pulled his hand away, and it slowed. *What the hell?* thought John.

He could feel his jaw muscles tighten, his lips pull back across his teeth. So much for the pills. He angrily flicked the light with his finger, and it was now strobing with a disconcerting intensity. "Fuck this," he said to himself.

John undid his belt. He knew the cabin door was closed, but he'd worry about how to open it when he got there. He had turned to leave when he suddenly stopped. John hadn't noticed, but a man had taken the aisle seat. He was in his sixties, heavyset, with a round face and ruddy cheeks. Grandfatherly.

"Can I get past?" said John.

The man just stuck out his hand. "Name's Chris."

John stared at him, unsure of what to do.

"You're supposed to shake it, at least that's the common convention," said Chris with a grin. John shook his hand. It was clammy. He had to fight the urge to wipe the moisture off onto his pants.

"What's your name?" asked Chris.

"John ... Burrows."

Chris leaned into John, forcing him to tilt back. "I think we're going to be leaving soon," said Chris.

John replied, "Yeah ... I guess we are."

"You should probably put on your belt. I would."

John looked up at his light. It had stopped flickering. He immediately buckled his belt again. There was something comforting about Chris, but John couldn't put his finger on it. However, he had the same reaction when taking the pills. He could feel the tension ease in his shoulders, and his jaw loosen.

Chris leaned into John with an eager expression across his face. "I'm going to see my family in Toronto. It's been a long time."

"That's great," replied John. But there was a nagging feeling in his gut. Something about this man was familiar. He finally blurted out, "Do we know each other?"

"I should go before we take off," was all Chris said as he got up from his seat and trudged off toward the back of the plane. John wondered why he did that; the business-class washroom was much closer. But before he could put more thought into it, his overhead light started to flicker again. John had cautiously reached up to touch it when a shadow fell across him. It was Jenna.

"Everything OK?" she asked.

"Yeah, great," he replied stiffly.

"Can I get you anything? Some water?"

John shook his head. Jenna bit her lip. He could see her eyes narrow, thin lines appearing on her temples like cracks in wood veneer. "What is it?" asked John.

"There's someone who wants to say hi."

John could feel his heart skip a beat. He knew exactly what she meant. Before he could even answer, she had stepped back, and two figures appeared. John looked to the first—the captain, Emily Ross. She was in her mid-thirties, quite young to captain a long-haul flight. She had been his co-pilot for close to a hundred hours of flight time and was as good a pilot as he had ever flown with.

"I can't believe it," said Emily, barely hiding the shock on her face.

Before he could stop himself, John blurted out, "Hey, kiddo." He knew Emily bristled when he called her that. She had always looked much younger than her age and disliked it when people reminded her. But Emily registered no displeasure with him now; her expression was one of tempered surprise.

"I'm so glad Jenna told me you were on the flight," she said.

"Well, here I am," replied John.

For a moment, Emily stared at him, then shifted to reveal a younger pilot, late-twenties, at her side. "This is my co-pilot, Stan Walker."

John took his hand as it was offered. "Nice to meet you."

Stan shook vigorously, saying, "It's an honour to meet you, Captain Burrows." He then continued with a boyish grin, "I would love to talk over some of the techniques you used on 112. We run your flight in the simulators. Over a ninety percent failure rate. You are a legend."

Emily tugged Stan on the arm. "We should get back to work."

"Sure," replied Stan, but he pulled out his cell phone. "May I?"

John was desperate for this to end. He nodded, resigned to letting Stan's fanboy nature play out. Stan turned the phone around to take a selfie with John. At that moment, Chris returned and took his seat. He was in the shot, raising a hand to give the peace sign with a grin.

Snap. Stan had taken the shot, but he frowned when he looked at the screen, obviously not pleased that Chris had photo-bombed him. Emily pulled Stan away and offered John an apologetic shrug. The pilots headed back to the cockpit, whispering to each other.

Chris turned to John. "What happened on Flight 112?"

"It's not polite to eavesdrop," replied John.

"It sounded like an interesting story."

"I don't want to talk about it," said John rather curtly.

The intercom cut in and Jenna's voice sounded: *"Ladies and gentlemen, this is Jenna Russel, your chief flight attendant. On behalf of Captain Emily Ross and the entire crew, welcome aboard Flight 224, non-stop service from Vancouver to Toronto …"*

John took a deep breath and grabbed his armrests. His hands strained as he gripped them tightly. He looked out the window and had a sudden urge to jump right through it. He then looked over at Chris, who had leaned back and closed his eyes. A feeling of jealousy filled John. He wondered how this man could just sit there calmly as they were about to take off.

John looked around the business-class cabin. Everyone else was nonplussed as well. John reached into his pocket and pulled out the pill bottle. He stared at it for a long moment, then popped the top.

It was his unconscious mind that picked up on it first: the sensation of movement. John couldn't tell if it was forward momentum, but his inner ears registered the slight oscillation— the up-and-down movement as the plane was buffeted by the air rushing over the wings. As John slowly moved toward consciousness, the next thing he recognized was the hum of the engines. These modern jets were quiet compared to the planes he had flown when he started out. They barely registered in the mid-seventies on the decibel scale.

What woke John from his rather fitful sleep was coughing. It wasn't the cough of someone who was clearing their throat, or even sick, but rather the sound made by a person as they desperately gasped for air.

He shuddered awake and looked around. The cabin was dark, lights turned down for the red-eye flight. John was disoriented for a moment, but then his gaze landed on Chris, whom he could only see in silhouette. "Are you OK?" asked John.

"Of course," replied Chris. "Why do you ask?"

"You were coughing."

"No, I wasn't. You were snoring," replied Chris.

John digested this for a moment. He had never snored in his life. "Really?"

Chris nodded. John shrugged his shoulders; he had also never taken diazepam either. That must have been it. The medicine had relaxed the muscles in his throat, and he was snoring. His mind had just interpreted it as a cough. "Sorry about that."

John then noticed that his tray was down. There was a white linen cloth across it and an uneaten meal. Jenna must have put it down for him while he was asleep. He looked over at Chris, who had his tray up. "Did you eat already?" asked John.

Chris shook his head. "Airline food is crap. Even in business class. My daughter is planning a nice meal for me when I get home."

John looked over at his tray. It didn't look bad: chicken in sauce on a bed of rice with greens, a single-serving bottle of white wine.

But there was a twinge in John's stomach. Normally, he had an iron constitution, and not even spicy foods troubled him. But his was a digestive tract not used to medications. *That was it*, thought John. The pills were troubling his belly. He pushed the meal away.

The plane suddenly trembled, like it had hit a speed bump in the air. Then another bump, smaller, but still enough of a jolt to nearly knock over the wine bottle. *Bing!* The "fasten seat belt" sign lit up. Jenna's voice came calmly over the intercom, reminded everyone to stay in their seats due to the turbulence.

The plane continued to vibrate, and John glanced down at his meal. He could see some perspiration on the chicken skin, the gravy mixing with the brown rice, staining the grains and making them darker. His stomach knotted. John reached over and pulled down Chris's tray, and then, as quickly as he could, plopped the meal down in front of him. "Please, get it away from me."

"You sure?" asked Chris.

John covered his mouth with his hand and nodded. Chris shrugged and dug into the meal. "I guess a little won't spoil dinner," he said. The first bite was met with a non-committal shrug, but then he had another and another as he warmed to the taste.

John glanced down at the wine bottle, still in front of him. He twisted off the top and took a long swig directly from the bottle.

Chris turned to him and said with a mouth full of food, "You shouldn't mix drugs and alcohol." Before John could respond, Chris continued, "I saw you take them. Let me guess—to calm your nerves?"

John nodded. "Yeah," he said, and promptly took another swig from the bottle.

"Strange that a pilot is scared to fly?"

"I don't mean to be rude," said John. "But it's none of your business."

"That young pilot. He thinks you're a hero. Must be an interesting story. Why don't you tell me about it?" continued Chris.

John stared at him, incredulously. But then again, his stomach had calmed down. He wondered if it was the strange effect this man had on him or whether the wine had steadied his nerves. Regardless, he was feeling better physically. "I'd rather not," said John.

Chris smiled at him, and his eyes were squeezed upward by the plumpness of his cheeks. He once again leaned over into John's personal space. "How about I tell you about the avionic safeguards on an airliner like this? Maybe hearing about the redundancies will ease your nerves?"

"I think I know more about that than you," said John.

"You're wrong," replied Chris confidently. "I worked for Advanced Avionics Systems my entire career. I was the head of cockpit design. This plane, the eight-forty, it was my baby."

John could feel his face flush. His heartbeat quickened in his chest. He wondered how this uncomfortably upbeat man might have designed one of the most sophisticated flight systems of its era, one he knew intimately. But then again, John knew better than to generalize.

"The eight-forty is a very safe plane," John said.

"It's a bit strange you'd think that, isn't it? Considering you crashed one," Chris replied.

John sat straight up in his seat. He could feel his heart thumping in his chest. "What did you say?"

Chris took one last bite of the meal, then put his fork down. He undid his belt, then shook his head as he got up. "Don't ever underestimate the value of a young bladder," said Chris, who then shuffled his way off to the bathroom.

Jenna approached, and Chris smiled at her, offering a "Ma'am" before continuing to the aft washroom. Jenna saw the meal sitting on Chris's tray.

"Didn't like the meal?" said Jenna, recognizing it was John's.

"I don't know … he's a strange old guy," replied John.

Jenna smiled awkwardly at him, then took the meal away.

The light above John's seat started to flicker again, which only added to his tension as John tried to understand why Chris had said what he did. John rationalized that Chris must have overheard the crew talking about him. He hated it when people gossiped. John reached into his pocket for the pill bottle but thought better of it. He leaned his head back and did his best to ignore everything around him.

John didn't know exactly when he woke up, but Chris was staring right at him when he did. He should have been distrustful of Chris; he obviously had some inside knowledge that put John at a disadvantage. But the man's face was pleasant to John somehow. It was round and ruddy, with friendly eyes and a curve to the mouth that resulted in a semi-permanent smile. Chris was exactly the type of person that should have gotten on John's nerves, as he was always uncomfortable with outwardly positive people.

John was a pessimist, in fact, a glass-half-empty person. He was proud of that, as it had served him well as a pilot. He never assumed anything, double-checked everything, and was always on the lookout for trouble in the cockpit.

"Did I snore again?" John asked.

"No. You slept like a baby." Chris turned to look at his video screen—he was watching the flight tracker. The plane was halfway to its destination.

"How long has it been since you've seen your daughter?" asked John.

"About a year. Oh … maybe longer. The memory starts to go when you reach my age."

"I'm not that far behind you," said John with a smile.

"Come on, you're a man still in his prime," said Chris. But then he looked at John with an earnest expression. "Do you have a family, John? Children?"

"No."

"Why not?"

If it were anyone else, John would have told them to take a walk, but Chris had found a way through his defences once again. "The moment my dad took me up in his Cessna, I knew what I wanted to do with my life," said John. "I loved to fly. I went into the Forces, became a transport pilot, and when I was discharged, I went commercial. My career was everything to me. It didn't seem fair to have a family that I would gladly leave for days or weeks on end."

"You said, *loved* to fly. You no longer do?" asked Chris.

John didn't respond but just looked away. No one, including his therapist, had asked him that question. Did he still love to fly? John was disappointed in himself for not answering immediately. He was terrified of flying now, but did that mean he also didn't love it anymore?

"I don't love planes," said Chris.

"But you spent your career in avionics?"

"Because I love electronics. I love technology," replied Chris. "I love trying to pack as much functionality into as little space as possible." He then grinned broadly as he said, "And on a jetliner, every ounce counts!"

"Cute ..." said John dryly.

Chris ran his hand along the edge of the digital screen in front of him. "It's about elegance. Technological sophistication." He then turned to look at John. "You know the MCDU— Multifunction Control Display Unit?"

John raised an eyebrow, thinking, *seriously?*

Chris lifted a hand apologetically. "Of course, you do ... but I'm sure you've never put much thought into it. The miracle of miniaturization lets us combine a keyboard with an LCD unit that allows pilots to input and modify flight plans and interface with the flight management system—all their data entry needs in a tiny little unit."

"You're right," said John. "I never put that much thought into it."

"That's the problem with our society today. We don't appreciate the work that went into our technology. We don't really understand the tools at our disposal. Which is why sometimes we don't anticipate the problems that can happen with them."

"What do you mean?" asked John.

"The MCDU ... its cooling filters can get blocked by dust and fluff. There's no standard inspection procedure for them. It caused an electrical fire on an eight-thirty variant."

"I've never heard of that."

"Well, now you have," said Chris, who then leaned his head back against his headrest and closed his eyes. This conversation was over.

John stared at him, wondering why this odd man would be so specific. John turned to look out the window but could only see the inky blackness of the night sky. He wondered why he thought the red-eye was the better choice for his first flight back. How could not seeing anything possibly alleviate his underlying fears? John shook his head, leaned back, and closed his eyes.

This time, John's unconscious was quite specific. There were no images in his mind, just sounds. He heard a strange crinkling, like aluminum foil being crushed; then, there was the sound of sparking. Not the wet snap of wood burning, but sharper and more defined. Electrical sparks. Next came the hiss of burning wire, followed by a warning buzzer, loud and piercing. However, what brought him out of his latest slumber was the sound of someone gasping for air. John couldn't understand why, but in his semi-conscious state, he was sure that Chris was breathless and panting.

John opened his eyes and turned to look for Chris, but he wasn't in his seat. He glanced around the business-class cabin. Everyone else was either dozing or watching their screens. John was quite concerned about why he had had such a specific dream. It must have been what Chris said to him about technology. He had planted, either intentionally or not, trigger words that John's subconscious took to his typical negative conclusion.

He shook his head, annoyed at Chris. Chris knew that he was struggling on this flight; why would he say something to trigger him? A feeling of resentment built up in his gut; it started to escalate and grow into a nervous distemper. *Is this a panic attack?* John wondered. Should he reach for his pills? He took a deep breath and tried to steady himself with a platitude from his therapist: *Inactive hands lead to hyperactive minds.*

"Fuck," John said under his breath. He hated seeing his therapist, but the airline mandated regular sessions.

John unbuckled his belt and walked into the forward galley. There was an immediate improvement in his demeanour. The few steps from his seat had done wonders for the emotions churning inside him. John's anxieties were always tempered by firm and decisive actions—another positive trait for a pilot.

Jenna was there, re-stowing trays and locking down carts. John had always been impressed by how many things stewards did during flights. They were constantly busy, never had time to worry. John made a mental note of that; maybe he should find a hobby, an activity to distract him from his hyperactive imagination.

Jenna sensed someone behind her and turned, twitching slightly with surprise. "John!"

"Sorry. Didn't mean to sneak up on you," he said as calmly as he could.

"Can I get you something?" she asked.

"Just stretching my legs."

Jenna smiled at him. John looked around the galley. Not lost on him was the efficiency of the design. This tiny space contained a kitchen, a bathroom, a closet, emergency medical devices, a communications system, and two jump seats for the stewards. He reached up and tapped his hand on the aluminum catch that kept the booze cart in place. For a moment, he was lost in his admiration for the elegant design. *This is what Chris was talking about*, thought John. But the moment was short-lived.

"Is there something on your mind?" asked Jenna.

"Can I see the crew?"

"You know I can't let a passenger in," she replied.

"I'm still on the active-pilots list. They never took me off."

John could see her eyes narrow, and he could only imagine the debate raging inside her. Jenna finally picked up the cabin phone and spoke into it. "Captain Burrows would like to visit …" she began. She listened, finally added, "Of course," then hung up the phone. "They'll see you now," she said.

Almost immediately, the cockpit door was unlocked from the inside. John nodded his thanks to Jenna and turned toward the door. He remembered how he had hit his forehead on the aluminum frame on one of his first flights and had to put on a bandage to stop the bleeding. His embarrassment on that long-ago flight meant he now hunched his six-foot frame automatically to get past the threshold.

Emily turned to him first from the left seat, a broad smile across her face. "Well, hello there, Captain," she said.

John knelt between her and Stan, his arms resting on the back frames of their seats. "Thought I'd come to see my star pupil in action," he said to Emily.

Emily smiled broadly at him. "Well, you were a great teacher."

But then Stan blurted out, "You gonna get back on rotation soon?"

John was now quite certain that this young man's mouth was often several steps ahead of his brain. He was about to say something, but then he saw the stern look Stan got from Emily. John remembered a few times he was on the receiving end of one of her looks. She could cut glass with them. John put his hand up to Emily to cut her off.

"It's OK." He then turned to Stan. "I'm going to take it one step at a time."

Stan nodded, not even a hint of embarrassment across his face.

John took a long look around the cockpit. He remembered how the planes he flew in his early days had many more switches and knobs. Over time, as technology improved, they were replaced by screens with sub-menus, ones he needed to navigate to find specific functions. John had often wondered if that was more efficient than a dedicated switch.

"This has been updated," said John about the cockpit avionics.

"It's an older bird, but they've upgraded a few systems," replied Emily.

John turned his attention to the MCDU units. They were two small, rectangular keypads with screens located beside each pilot in the centre console. "New MCDUs?" he asked.

Emily shook her head. "No. Original equipment, I think."

John leaned in ever so slightly. He tried to peer over the edge of the centre console to the grate on the side of the MCDU. It was an unremarkable piece of metal, like the cooling slots on any stereo amplifier.

Emily tracked his eyes toward the grate. "Is something wrong?" she asked.

"No …"

"I've seen that look before, John. What's going on?"

John's shoulders hunched. He could feel the tension return to his jaw. "This may sound nuts, but have you smelled anything funny coming from them?"

A look was exchanged between Emily and Stan. She shook her head. "No."

"I mean, their cooling filters probably haven't been cleaned."

"So?" asked Stan.

The plane was buffeted ever so slightly. John could feel the blood rush to his face, his heart rate quickening. "You don't think that's dangerous?" he asked.

"There haven't been any safety bulletins," replied Emily.

John bit his lip, didn't respond.

"Are you sure you're OK?" she asked.

John leaned in further, a determined expression across his face. "How about we pull off the vent plates and have a look?"

Stan's face went blank with a look of confusion. Emily realized what he meant. Her voice lowered an octave as she said, "I think these are fine."

Just like in the passenger corridor, John lost the ability to control his motor functions. Instead of being frozen, however, his limbs seemed to move without his brain wanting them to. John became no more than an observer as his arms reached across the throttle controls and toward the vent-access grates. "Let's have a look. Won't take long," he said.

Stan immediately grabbed his arm. "What are you doing?"

John kept pushing toward the vent. "The plate will just pop off."

"John!" barked Emily.

He stopped immediately. She had a deadly serious look in her eyes. "I think you should go back to your seat."

John stared at her. He could see that she had reached for the emergency alarm switch that would alert the stewards. Was there an air marshal on this flight? *No*, John thought—this wasn't an international flight. He suddenly felt control over his body again. He slowly moved back, raising his hands apologetically in front of him. "Sorry, I thought I could help."

Emily eased her hand away from the emergency alarm. She spoke in a deliberately calm voice. "Well, thank you, but we've got everything under control."

John took one final glance at the MCDU units, and he backed away. He saw their eyes track him, just in case he chose to lunge.

A feeling of embarrassment overwhelmed him as the cabin door shut and was locked from inside. He could just barely make out their animated voices talking on the other side. He knew the cockpit's ambient sound recorder would have picked up their entire conversation. John would be a laughingstock once others heard what had happened. His shoulders slumped, and he felt defeated as he slinked back to his seat.

John tried to ignore the sounds in his dream. He had been fooled several times on this flight already. It was hard work to discount what he heard this time: the very distinct sound of engines struggling, of wind rushing over the fuselage, of metal groaning and creaking. However, what woke him up was a single word, barely spoken above a whisper—*No.*

John opened his eyes and saw Chris with a look of terror written across his face. "Are you OK?" asked John.

"I don't think so," replied Chris.

Then, without warning, there was a bone-rattling vibration. The plane plummeted dozens of feet. Screams sounded through the cabin as food and drink flew through the air. Passengers who didn't have their seat belts on were tossed around like ragdolls. Emily's tense voice cut in over the intercom: *"All passengers return to your seats and fasten your seatbelts immediately!"*

The passengers yelled out in fear. Jenna rushed through the cabin, helping those who were not in their seats, barely able to stay upright as the plane swayed wildly.

However, John was remarkably calm—the automatic response of thirty years' flight experience ingrained in him. Observe and react was the motto he lived by. He tried to look out the window, back toward the wing-mounted engines, but he couldn't see anything other than the edge lights. Yet his calm was shattered when the seat light above him started to flicker again. "I don't believe this," John muttered under his breath.

Chris's response was somewhat unexpected. "What happened on Flight 112?"

"Not now, Chris."

"I think now is the only time we've got," he replied.

John tried to swallow, but his mouth was dry, and his tongue almost stuck to the roof of his mouth.

"Cabin crew, please prepare for an emergency landing," Emily ordered through the intercom. John looked around, seeing the terrified expressions of the other passengers. His gaze finally landed back on Chris, who was staring right at him.

"You win," said John. "Fourteen months ago, I was captain of the daytime leg, 112 to Vancouver. We lost power, and I had to glide her down. It was a hard landing, but we made it."

"Did everyone survive?" asked Chris.

"Yes."

"So, you're a hero?" Chris said triumphantly.

"I ... I don't know about that."

"What do you mean, you don't know?" Chris said. "It was in all the papers. You were a hero."

"I was," agreed John. He then felt his whole body tense up, like his limbs were being pulled toward his spine, and his body was collapsing in on itself.

Chris reached over and grabbed John by the arm. "Why did your plane lose power?"

The noise from the engines increased markedly. John knew the plane was struggling to keep from stalling. He nodded to himself, finally resigned. "There was a problem with the electrical bus. The mainline vibrated loose and shorted out the flight control systems."

He could see Chris shaking his head from side to side. "That's what everyone said. Now tell me what really happened."

John was perplexed. "What are you talking about?"

The plane shuddered once again. A woman directly behind John screamed, and he glanced back over his seat at her.

"Be honest with me. Be honest with yourself," said Chris.

A sudden chill ran down John's spine. From the base of his head, he felt it go down through his shoulders, to his arms and hands, to his chest, then his abdomen and legs. It was like every nerve ending in his entire body was tingling. "OK," said John. "What if the only reason planes can fly is that we've been told they can?"

John stared at Chris, waiting for his expression to change, but it didn't. So, he continued. "I know the physics works ... but, tons of metal and plastic, all hurled into the air at incredible speed. It just *shouldn't* work."

The plane's angle of descent increased, accompanied by a significant surge in wind noise. There were more yelps of fear from the passengers. John looked out the window and strangely grew calmer as he did. "For a split-second during my flight, I stopped believing planes could fly."

"And?" asked Chris.

"And that's when the power cut out," replied John.

Jenna's voice boomed through the cabin on the intercom: *"Ladies and gentlemen, please assume emergency landing position: arms folded and head down across your lap."*

There were terrified rumbles from the passengers, but they did as they were instructed, including John and Chris, who had their heads turned so they could still look at each other. More alarming to John than the noise and panic setting in amongst the passengers was that he could still see the light flicker above him out of the corner of his eye.

"It's just a coincidence," implored Chris.

"I wish I could believe that," replied John.

"You think *you* caused the crash?"

John nodded his head sideways across his lap. He explained to Chris how, deep down inside, he was sure his momentary lapse in belief was why his flight went down. The rational part of his brain knew this was impossible, but the instinctive part of him— the part he rarely relied on—was certain it was. That voice had drowned out every other thought since.

"I can't get it out of my head," said John. "It's all I think about: day and night. I've started having panic attacks. I either freeze up, or I lose control."

"Then why are you here?" asked Chris.

"I thought being in the air again would change things, but it hasn't. It's made it worse." John glanced up at the flickering light. "I know it's crazy."

"It's not crazy," said Chris.

The plane shook violently again, and more screams came from the passengers. Chris had to raise his voice to speak over them. "If you believe something, it's real, because it's real to you.

All you need to understand is that what happened to you was nothing more than bad timing. Your *thought* and the plane's *failure* happened at the same time. And since then, it's just been a battle in your brain, of trying to rationalize the irrational, of putting order to chaos."

John was unnerved. "What are you talking about?"

"It's just like problems in the electronic systems I designed," said Chris. "It's called *noise*. And the purer the signal is, the less noise there is. You just need to filter out the noise." Chris then reached over and took John's hand in his own. "It's not your fault. I know that now."

John could feel the tension in his body suddenly melt away. The plane was buffeted, but he was absolutely at peace. All he could feel now were the tears forming in his eyes, blurring his vision.

"I guess you're right. It wasn't my fault. It was just noise," said John.

The light above him stopped flickering.

"Good ... now I can go see my family," replied Chris, and then he closed his eyes.

John did the same, and each held the other's hand as the cacophony of sound around them peaked.

John had lost track of how long he had been staring at the bulkhead in front of his seat. He was almost in a trance; he couldn't remember much of the landing or what happened afterward. All the other passengers were gone, including Chris, and he was certainly one of the last people on the plane.

He felt calmer now, and he would have been completely at peace except for one troubling feeling. He couldn't put a finger on what it was but just knew something was off. It manifested itself as a strange sensation behind his eyes, like an itch he couldn't scratch.

"John, are you all right?"

He turned to see Jenna hovering over him from the aisle.

"I don't know. You?"

Jenna tried to smile, but she was visibly shaken. "That was quite the landing, wasn't it?"

"Not as rough as my last one," John replied, the irony quite unintentional.

Jenna smiled wistfully at him and headed forward.

John got up and walked toward the exit hatch. The cockpit door was open, and Emily popped out. Her eyes were still wide with adrenaline.

"How did you know the unit would overheat?" she asked.

John glanced into the cockpit. He could see that the vent plates were off one of the MCDU units, a fire extinguisher on the floor beside it.

"We smelled smoke," said Emily.

"What?" replied John.

"We started losing electrical systems," she continued. "We had to find the fire fast or we'd lose the backups. If you hadn't told us about the vents getting clogged, we wouldn't have looked at the MCDU in time. You saved our lives!"

John soaked in her praise for a long moment. It felt good to be needed, but then he remembered the truth of what happened. "Actually, it was Chris … the guy sitting beside me. He put that bug in my ear," John told her.

"Oh, OK. Thank him for us," and she shook John's hand vigorously, then returned to the cockpit.

But John was frozen. The strange sensation in his head intensified; it now felt like a rubber band being pulled right behind his eyes, brought to the point of snapping. A strange thought crossed John's mind, and he turned to Jenna. "Were there any fatalities?"

"John, everyone is fine," she replied.

"No, I mean on *my* flight, 112. Do you remember if anyone died?"

Jenna's nose crinkled as she thought about it. "One passenger. An older man. He died of a heart attack. You don't remember that?"

"No, I guess I forgot."

The rubber band snapped, and the pieces suddenly fell into place. John doubled over, hands on his knees, and gasped for air.

"John! What's wrong?"

The pilots rushed out of the cockpit. Emily turned to Jenna. "What happened to him?"

"I don't know," she replied. "He was fine, and then—"

John stood up and turned to Stan. "Show me that picture you took!"

Stan exchanged a look with Emily. John turned to her, pleading. She told Stan it was OK, and he pulled out his phone and brought up the photo. John grabbed the camera from Stan's hand. He stared at the photo, which showed John with an empty seat beside him.

John burst out laughing. It was a gut-shaking belly laugh that brought tears to his eyes. It went on and on—his way of reacting to the fact that Chris, who he knew was there when it was taken, did not show up in the photograph.

Everyone else watched him with concern, unsure of what to do. John finally stopped laughing, composed himself, and handed the phone back to Stan.

"Are you all right?" asked Emily.

"I will be," replied John.

He then turned away from them and walked off the plane, disappearing around the corner.

THE END

CHAPTER 3

THE HARVEST

PART 1

Conrad ran his hand through a bubbling brook. It was cool mountain water that had made its way down from the snow-topped Catskills. He liked to imagine these billions of H_2O molecules' journey as they coalesced into liquid, becoming droplets, trickles, then streams. The unsuspecting particles then churned and filtered through natural geological processes until they arrived here at this very moment, cupped in his hand.

However, his fingers had started to get numb. *Strange*, Conrad thought, *it's June, and the water in this stream should be warm by now*. Nonetheless, the tingling in his fingertips was still not an unpleasant sensation. Conrad then remembered why he was kneeling by the stream. He came to wash his hands. His mind wandered these days, and that troubled him. Conrad grew up in the time before digital calculators and was proud of his ability to do math in his head. It was a skill that had served him well in a long and successful career as an engineer.

But now, in his eighties, he struggled with basic addition and subtraction. That was the first sign, causing him to realize he wasn't as mentally sharp as he once had been. *Thank God for smartphones,* he mused. Marvellous pieces of technology that not only served as telephones but could be tasked to do calculations, direct a person to their chosen destination, or search the internet for the answer to any question.

"Are you going to join me, or just sit there?" asked a female voice behind him.

He turned around, his gaze landing upon the love of his life, Elaine. She was eight years younger than him, though she barely looked a day over fifty. She was lying on a tartan wool blanket laid over the ground in a small clearing. An open wicker picnic basket and a veritable banquet of sliced meat and cheese were arranged in front of her. Conrad smiled and wondered how she could be more beautiful to him now than the day he met her.

"Hello, Conrad. Are you listening?"

"To you, always, my darling," he replied, then shook off the water from his hands.

Conrad stood. He could hear the pops and cracks of his knees. He had played college football in his day and had taken many a hit, so a few strange noises were nothing for him to worry about. He made his way over to Elaine and gently lowered himself so that he was lying on his side near her.

A ray of sunlight fell on them through an opening in the canopy of trees. Elaine's dress sparkled in this light. It was Conrad's favourite, a flowing lemon-yellow sundress with a crinoline slip that puffed out and accentuated her narrow waist. Conrad looked down at his own outfit, a rather drab brown pinstriped suit.

He never could match her for style, but Conrad knew she liked it that way. Elaine always wanted to have people's looks land on her first, to linger, in fact. That was fine by him because he could then marvel at her beauty as well.

Elaine poured him a glass of wine from a bottle, then filled her own. She took a sniff of it and seemed enticed by its aroma. Conrad clinked his glass to hers, and the two took their first sip. "Splendid," said Conrad.

Picking up where she had left off, she said with a mischievous smile, "I say we sit your brother beside the pastor. I'm sure he could keep him from drinking."

"Don't ever doubt my brother when there's an open bar," replied Conrad.

Elaine laughed. Conrad loved the way the muscles on her neck would ripple when she laughed. Elaine had been an Olympic swimmer in her youth, and after all these years and three sons, she was still lean and muscular.

"Well, we have to keep him away from Uncle Thadeous," she said with a grin.

And then both said simultaneously, "Or the McCarthy folks will blacklist him."

Elaine grinned, but Conrad had a strange sensation as he remembered having had this same conversation before. He felt a twinge in his stomach, looked at the wine, and wondered if it was off. But that wasn't it. Conrad sat up suddenly. He could feel his jaw muscles tighten, as though someone was pulling the skin back along his skull and stretching his cheeks to the point of tearing.

"What is it, Conrad?" asked Elaine.

"Our wedding," he replied. "We're here planning our wedding."

"Yes, we are, silly," she said.

"But … my brother's dead."

Elaine sat up. "That's a terrible thing to say."

Conrad shook his head. Fragments of memories were rattling around inside his brain— images, smells, and tastes—but he couldn't quite put them all together. He looked around at the surroundings. They were in the woods, far from a road or path. *How did we get here?* he wondered. Conrad then looked down at his own wrinkled and age-spotted hand. It suddenly struck him: "This isn't right."

"Weddings are never easy to plan," she said.

"No. That's not what I mean." He could feel the knot in his stomach grow. It wasn't indigestion or nausea; it was dread.

"This isn't the right place," he said. "We were in Central Park, the North Meadow when we had *this* picnic."

"I have never known you to have a sense of humour, my love. Don't try to find one now," she replied.

"Your dress. My suit. These clothes are sixty years old." He ran his hand over the lid of the picnic basket. "This was the basket your mother gave us when we started dating. We were in our twenties."

He noticed Elaine's eyes narrow. It was the look she gave him when something troubled her. "Conrad, you're putting me on."

He reached out and took her hands in his own. "How old are you?" he asked.

"I'm twenty-two," she replied immediately.

Conrad held up her hands, which showed their age quite clearly. He could see a look of confusion cross her face. "Why are my hands wrinkled?" she asked.

The beam of sunlight disappeared. Conrad looked up to see the sky had darkened unnaturally fast. He got to his feet. "Oh, no ..."

"What's wrong?" asked Elaine.

Conrad didn't answer, just hauled Elaine up, knocking over their wine glasses in the process. "We have to go," he said.

"Go where?"

He whipped around. They were in the middle of the forest, thick with fir and maple trees. He couldn't see more than a dozen yards in any direction, but what he did see was a light, dim, orange in colour—like a flashlight swaying from side to side in the distance.

"Run!" Conrad yelled. But he didn't wait for Elaine's reply, just pulled her by the arm in the opposite direction from the light.

Remora stared at the brook, the very one Conrad had washed his hands in only moments ago. It gave her a peculiar sensation, one of regret. She didn't immediately know why she felt that way, but she was certain that this little stream gave her a feeling of sorrow, unlike any she had experienced in close to a hundred thousand years.

Stepping closer to the bank, Remora could see her reflection in the water, illuminated by the bright silvery moon above her. Naked, her body was lean and muscular, with smooth, unblemished skin. Her complexion most resembled someone from southern Africa, but she had features, a wide nose and prominent brow that hadn't been seen in millennia.

Remora enjoyed these brief moments when she could see herself in this form. She put her hands down to her hips, felt their contour. She then ran them up to her torso, around the profile of her modest breasts. But this respite was short-lived. She tilted her head, having noticed a large rock down by the edge of the creek's bank.

She gasped as it all rushed back to her. This was a night like the first night when the big cats stalked her tribe in the grass. She remembered how the men kept them back with rocks and sharp sticks during the day. When the moon chased away the sun, her people shivered in fear and retreated to the forests for protection.

It was this simple rock that brought Remora to this moment of doubt. She picked it up and felt its weight. It was smooth and rounded by the water, so much like the one she had held long ago. She wondered why this rock would bring such a torrent of emotions and trigger the pain and anguish that she now felt.

Then she remembered what they had called the other girl—Rain. Because her eyes were round and moist. While all the others in her tribe cowered in the burned stump of a massive tree, Rain showed no fear. She ventured away from the safety of numbers, lingered by the stream, washing.

Remora remembered how she hated the bones Rain would weave into her hair. They would click against each other as she walked. Surely, if Remora had done the same, the Elders would have cut them from her hair, as the noise would have led the animals to them. But they never said a word to Rain. She never did wrong in their eyes.

Remora turned the rock in her hand so that the broad side faced outwards. She gripped it tightly, and it felt cold against her skin. Remora remembered it all now—a moment from hundreds of thousands of years ago. That night, she came up behind Rain, who turned and smiled at her. They were sisters! The fog of time was gone. Remora remembered how she hit Rain across her skull with *that* rock. She remembered how Rain fell into the water and tried to rise, but Remora held her under until she stopped moving.

Remora dropped *this* rock into the water of the brook. It splashed and distorted her reflection. When the water calmed, Remora saw that her face had changed: a ridge had appeared along her cheek. There was also a bump along her shoulder—long and curved—and another on her hip. Remora knew what was to come next. Gone was the sense of regret or sorrow. There was only hunger.

She turned and walked through the picnic site, scattering the food and wine, her eyes glowing deep orange.

The wind blew through the branches. They rustled and rubbed against each other, casting long shadows that looked like spindly arms in the moonlight. A light rain fell, muddying the ground and leaving glistening pools of water. Conrad led Elaine by the hand. "Come on, Elly, don't slow down."

Elaine gasped, struggled, and finally forced Conrad to stop.

"I can't, Conrad. Let me rest," she said.

Conrad nodded, then turned to look behind them. The light was gone. He exhaled, relieved, then caught a glimpse of himself in a puddle of water. He was much younger—he looked like he was in his forties now. Conrad shook his head in amazement. How had he not noticed that Elaine was younger, too, probably in her late thirties? He couldn't take his eyes off her.

"What is it?" she said.

Conrad only smiled in reply. He often felt guilty for secretly fawning over her appearance. She was not just some vapid beauty; Elaine was also passionate and intelligent. Before she decided to stay at home to raise their family, she had earned a degree in accounting—no small feat for a woman of her era.

Conrad loved their conversations, as well. They would sit and talk by the fireplace until the early hours of the morning. But still, Conrad never once forgot how lucky he was to have a timeless beauty on his arm, especially when his looks could best be described as ordinary.

There was a sudden howl from the trees. Not quite animal or human, it sounded like it came from all around them at once.

"What was that?" asked Elaine, her fear palpable.

"She's coming for you," he replied.

"Who's coming for me?"

"I remember now," he said. "How you're fading away from me. I won't let her take the last of you from me, Elaine."

"Conrad, you're not making any sense," she said.

Conrad didn't care. He took her hand again, turned to press on, but suddenly stopped.

In front of them stood the woman. Her body had changed; she was now covered in raised bumps, scar tissue in the shape of ancient runes. The symbols repeated over and over on her body.

"Stay away!" yelled Conrad.

The woman didn't reply. She had taken another step toward them.

"You took our sons! I won't let you take my Elaine!"

Before the woman could take another step, Conrad pulled Elaine into the forest, once again fleeing from the strange woman who plagued him.

Remora watched Conrad and Elaine vanish into the trees. She wondered why they were so afraid of her. She never quite understood human emotions. After all these thousands of years, they were still a mystery to her. But that didn't stop Remora from speculating. She knew it all started when she killed Rain.

But a fit of sudden anger filled her belly over that memory. A feeling of injustice overwhelmed her. *She* didn't kill that girl. Yes, it was this body that had bludgeoned her, but Remora wasn't responsible. It was Rain's sister that drowned her. The sister hated her because the boys would only look at Rain, lusting after her full hips and round breasts.

The sister did this, not me, thought Remora.

But Remora remembered how the sister's heart broke, the regret she felt over what she did at that brook. She called out to the spirits who had yet to be named, begged to have the memory of the murder—the first-ever for jealously—stripped from her memory.

Remora was one of those spirits, and she answered the call. That was the moment Remora was born. The sister's body became her own, and Remora had used it for the hundreds of thousands of years since then. So long, in fact, she now needed to awaken only once a year to replenish herself.

Suddenly, Remora felt a twinge. She looked down to see the branch of a tree emerge from one of the runes on her hip. A moment later, she winced as the tip of another branch poked out from the skin on her shoulder. More and more branches tore through her skin and the pain increased. Each eruption was agony, but Remora had only one thought: She needed to feed.

Conrad and Elaine ran through the forest, branches tearing at their skin, thistles sticking to their clothes. He tried to distract himself from thoughts of the horror that pursued them. He looked at Elaine, could see that she was now in her twenties, an absolute vision of beauty even through the mud and blood.

Conrad could only imagine what he looked like. Photographs in his youth were so rare that he only had a few to remind himself. As they ran, he wondered what children today would think of the thousands of photos taken at every stage of their lives. Would they feel more connected to their past?

"Conrad, where are we going?"

"We have to keep moving," he replied.

But suddenly, Conrad stopped. The woman was standing before them again. This time, she looked less human than before; her body was covered in a film of mud and leaves, thin branches emerging from her joints, eyes glowing bright orange.

"My God," said Elaine.

The woman took a threatening step toward them. Elaine grabbed a thick tree branch lying on the ground and swung it like a bat. "Get away from us!" she screamed.

But the woman was gone. Elaine turned to her husband. "Why won't she leave us alone?"

"I don't know," he replied, though that was a lie.

Conrad twisted around and saw a clearing nearby, the faint outline of a man-made structure through the trees. "Elly, look over there!"

But she didn't turn to look. She only stared at Conrad with a defeated expression across her face. "Conrad. What did you mean earlier, that she took our sons?"

"Elaine, we don't have time for this."

"Tell me!" she insisted.

Reluctantly, Conrad responded. "She took their memory from me."

"You don't remember them?" she said in dismay.

"I remember we had children. But I remember nothing about who they are."

Elaine gasped in horror. Conrad could see her eyes dart from side to side as she came to a dreadful realization. "I don't remember them either!" she said.

Conrad put his hand to her cheek to wipe away a tear, creating a streak through the mud on her face. "She took them from you first," he said.

Elaine looked back toward the clearing Conrad had seen moments ago. She wiped the tears from her face. "I'm not giving up," she said, then handed the tree branch to Conrad.

He took it and nodded, now more in love with her than ever.

Conrad and Elaine emerged into the clearing. It was about a dozen meters in diameter, with green moss covering the ground. In the centre was a stone obelisk, about three meters high. Conrad peered at it in the moonlight. He could see carvings on the stone, the same ancient symbols that covered the woman's body. He approached it cautiously.

"Don't," said Elaine.

But Conrad couldn't resist. His mind was still as curious as ever. He lowered the branch he was holding and drew close to the obelisk. The symbols on the stone suddenly began to glow. After a moment, Elaine joined him. She reached out and touched one of the carvings.

"These four symbols are repeated over and over. What do they mean?" she asked.

Conrad shook his head. He didn't know.

Suddenly, a snarl came from behind them, and they turned to see the woman. She was a truly horrific visage now, with moss-covered skin and living tree branches jutting from her body at all angles. She was bent and crooked, her limbs creaking and groaning with every step, eyes glowing a dark burnt orange. She growled disdainfully as she spoke. "It is the language of the people to which this body belongs."

"Who are you?" asked Conrad.

"I am Remora," she replied with an accent not heard in recorded history. She continued to inch toward them.

"Leave us alone!" yelled Elaine.

Remora tilted her head to the side and looked at Elaine with a quizzical expression. "You are not afraid?" asked Remora.

"Go to hell," replied Elaine.

Remora's eyes widened for a moment, but then, strangely, she began to laugh. Her whole body shook, limbs and branches rattling in a ghastly vibration. Conrad saw Elaine nodding to him; he knew what she wanted him to do.

Remora's laughter slowly petered away. She turned to Elaine, her eyes glowing even brighter. "You. Will. Be. Cherished."

Remora grabbed Elaine in her bent and twisted arms and pulled her into a tight embrace. Beams of light emitted from Remora's eyes and drilled into Elaine. Conrad saw his chance, raised the branch, and swung with all his might.

Crack! The branch shattered across Remora's head. She stumbled, lost her grip on Elaine, and fell into the obelisk. It suddenly electrified, beams of white energy shooting out from it and into Remora, who screamed in pain.

Some of the branches on her body cracked and fell off, replaced by runic symbols. *This is her weakness*, Conrad realized. But then Elaine yelled out in pain from behind him. He rushed over and lifted her off the ground. "Elaine!"

"Run! Save yourself," she said.

"No!" Conrad said as he carried Elaine's limp body along.

But Remora was free of the obelisk. She stood in front of them once more. Half her body had been burned, but there was still enough of her there. She swung a twisted arm at Conrad and knocked him away from Elaine. He writhed on the ground, stunned, and could only watch as Remora took Elaine into her arms in a sickly embrace.

New branches grew out of the spots where the runes once were. They wrapped around Elaine until she was cocooned. Elaine screamed in terror as she disappeared in a tangle of flesh and thicket.

"Elaine!" yelled Conrad, but Remora and Elaine disappeared in a flash of orange light.

Conrad reeled in despair. His heart broke as the sense of loss overwhelmed him. But then a few moments passed, and Conrad felt the emotions drain from him. He wasn't as upset as he had just been. He wondered why, and with every second that passed, Conrad felt less and less sure he should feel bad.

Conrad was soon overcome with an emotionless void. He could not remember anything of what had happened to him in the moments before, let alone someone named Elaine.

CONTINUED in Chapter 5

CHAPTER 4

ANTONELLA, GALACTIC SPACE PIRATE

Antonella strode down the corridor. Hers was a predatory motion, hips swinging from side to side, steps almost too long for her natural gait. Her boots thumped along the deck, sparks flying as steel heel caps scraped against the metal plates. Each movement was meant to deliver a message to anyone who stood before her: *get out of my way.*

And they did get out of her way, the others that scurried through her ship's corridors breathed her ship's recycled air. Hundreds of crews from dozens of races worked the levers and bellows and forged and twisted dark-matter iron to patch holes in the hull and keep the ship from ripping itself to pieces in the vacuum of space.

They bowed to her as she passed, and Antonella arrived at the hatch to a lift. She marvelled at her own reflection in the polished brass of the hatch. She was tall for a Tsvezarian, a race better known for their thin frames. Her mother often joked that her father had the balls of an Orlian stag, that he gave her the heft she now enjoyed.

As she waited for the lift, a crewwoman walked by with a face that reminded her of a long-ago injury. Instinctively, Antonella ran her hand across the leather belt along her waist, just below her armoured chest plate. The armour covered the place on her midriff, where a deep scar ran from her navel to her hip along her dark grey skin. The battle where she got this scar was seared into her memory forever.

Her ship had broadsided a Vesuvian freighter, one full of wool—the finest in the galactic cluster. She had ordered the repelling hooks to be shot across the freighter, to pull it close so that both ships touched. When they did, the breaching pods were extended, and her crew broke through the freighter's hull. The battle was an unremarkable one. Her Elite were more than a match for the underpaid and overworked security that ships like the freighter hired. Most quickly surrendered or were killed before they could.

But this scar, the one Antonella so cherished, came from the only true challenge she had in that long-ago conquest. The captain of the freighter did not give up her bridge without a fight.

Antonella had to search her memory for the details; there were so many battles and skirmishes that she often confused them. However, she never would forget the captain of this freighter. Zaa was her name. She was nearly the same height as Antonella, but much thicker in arm and leg. Zaa came from a race called the Melthusians. They were a vile species to be in the presence of, emitting an odour during battle that would make most of her crew retch. But Antonella was immune to such weaknesses. It wasn't that she couldn't smell Captain Zaa's musk glands; it was that she rather liked the smell.

The battle was one for the ages. Antonella and Zaa were surrounded by Antonella's gasping and gagging boarding party. Captain Zaa had struck out at Antonella with a glistening curved blade, but Antonella just sidestepped her attack and waited for another thrust. Antonella, for her part, never carried a weapon into battle. She thought it beneath her standing to have a particle-arm or blade. She would wait for the right moment and pick up whatever implement of violence had presented itself to her.

Standing in front of the lift now, Antonella could feel her face flush with the viscous fluids that flowed through her body. She revelled in the memory of how she toyed with Captain Zaa, letting the woman attack only to be sidestepped or pushed aside. But Antonella had made an uncharacteristic mistake in that long-ago battle. She had slipped on one of the deceased command crew's entrails and exposed herself to Zaa's thrust.

The blade ripped into Antonella's abdomen, but it skittered across her hip bone without serious internal damage. Her boarding party had gasped, fearing the worst, but they were soon reminded of why Antonella was their leader. As Zaa turned for another blow with her blade, Antonella swept behind her and wrapped her arm around Zaa's neck.

As the consciousness was crushed out of Zaa, she dropped her blade. Antonella then released Zaa, and she slumped to the deck, with only enough energy to lift her head and see her own weapon now in Antonella's hand and pointed at her throat.

On that deck, so many orbits ago, Antonella did not kill Zaa, but instead—as was her right—took her as property. Over the next several quarter-orbits, Zaa was first a prisoner, then a slave, and finally a lover. Those were glorious times, and when Antonella had her fill of Zaa, she released and gifted her a skiff, a small vessel so that Zaa could make her way to any port she desired.

Antonella trembled now, her hands caressing her neck and chest, erotically charged by the flood of memories. Tsvezarians were well-known for their deep erotic predilections. But right now, Antonella also felt pride in how she honoured Zaa. She was proud of her reputation as a just and fair leader. She would gladly put her record of mercy up against any other captain in the Guild.

But the lift door had opened. In the threshold, there stood a scrubber, staring at her with a look of shock across his soot-smudged face. Before his mind could catch up with his mouth, he blurted out, "Are you a'right?"

"What did you say?" growled Antonella, embarrassed to have been caught in such a vulnerable moment of reflection by a worthless lower-caste.

The man quickly realized his error and stuttered as best he could in response. "I … I … saw nothin', Cap'n."

"That's not what I asked!" she bellowed.

Antonella grabbed the man by the throat and lifted him off the deck. Scrubbers were chosen for their short legs and slight builds, all the easier for them to enter the cooling channels that crisscrossed the ship, which required constant descaling.

"I should have you spaced for even raising your eyes to me," she barked.

"Sorry, my Cap'n! I'm new 'ere. I mean no offence," he said in desperation.

Antonella could feel the stares of the other crew that had turned to the commotion by the lift hatch. She would have been in her right to kill this man right here and now, but felt she had to show more restraint. The tension amongst her crew was high after dozens had been lost in the last skirmish. Antonella slowly lowered the scrubber to the deck.

"Mil'n is my name, Cap'n," he said.

"I did not ask, nor do I care what it is," she replied.

"I just t'ought it be good you knew," he said with a strange smile.

This surprised Antonella, but it somehow softened her as well. "And what is your duty on board my ship?"

"Scrubber, Cap'n. I cleanse the channels," he said.

"Then, if I killed you right now, it would be a blessed release, would it not?" she added.

"Yes, Cap'n! Death would be a pleasure."

Antonella tossed him from the threshold and entered the lift. "Then consider yourself duly punished, as I will let you live to continue scrubbing the bowels of my ship."

As the door closed, she could hear laughter at the man's expense from the other crew who had gathered. It filled her with joy.

The lift opened to a glorious vista: the bridge of Antonella's ship—the Maiden. It was enormous, with iron railings and stained-glass-lined walls that stretched along either side. As Antonella stepped onto the deck, the six Elite stationed throughout the bridge bowed to her in unison. They were guardians of the Azurie race, holding on to the electrified staffs that never left their sides.

Antonella nodded respectfully to them. Though not from as high a social order as she was, they were beings that she respected and honoured. As only women had the necessary temperament and skill to be captains in the Guild, the job of the Elite fell mostly to men. This was not because women could not fight as good as them, as Antonella had proven on many occasions, but men were not valued as highly in the social order. Even these Azurie were expendable.

Antonella approached the helm. Beyond it and through the glass she could see the unfurled ionic sails that stretched beyond her vision's limits. She often stood here and marvelled at the shimmering purple cloth that gave this ship its thrust, catching free-roaming galactic ions and channelling them into the ship's engines. But today, Antonella did not stop to enjoy the view; instead, she turned to the helmsman. "Where is she?"

The helmsman adjusted a focusing disk, and a metallic magnifying circle moved across the main viewing window. It magnified a part of space directly in front of them, in what appeared to be an asteroid belt. There was a ship in the centre of the magnifying disk, another freighter—one with engines alight but no sails deployed.

"It's burning reserves. They've seen us!" said Antonella to the helmsman.

He nodded apologetically, then turned away from her furious gaze. She had ordered that the Maiden stay in the gravitational dead zone to not be visible, but this man's navigation was sloppy. Antonella made a mental note to have him flogged once his shift was over.

Antonella turned to another member of her bridge crew, who manned a complex station of levers and dials. "Bring engines three and four alight," she ordered.

"Yes, Captain," he replied, then proceeded with an intricate series of adjustments.

Antonella felt a rumble through the deck plates. She was so in tune with her ship that she could tell how fast they were going by the vibrations that travelled up her legs and into her spine. She turned to a group of crews huddled around other control boards of brass rods and glistening metal valves. "Bring up batteries four through eight, twelve through sixteen," ordered Antonella.

Another series of small vibrations shook the ship. She looked back down along the port side to see hatches open along the hull's length, glowing weapon turrets appearing.

Antonella turned to address various other bridge crew members. "Gunner! Let's not tear her to pieces this time!"

"Yes, Captain!" was his reply.

"Make sure we get a hook in her fore and aft, or we'll break her back!" she barked to another.

"It will be done, Captain!"

The radiowoman put a hand over the headphone to her ear, trying to hear something. "Captain! There's a message ... it's faint. I ... I can't quite make it out."

"Ignore it. Any plea for mercy will only be an attempt to confuse us," Antonella replied.

"But if they surrender, we can save many lives," said the radiowoman.

A look from Antonella put an end to that rationale. Antonella then slowly turned as she spoke, her gaze landing on each crew member as they worked their controls throughout the bridge's confines. "She's a four-thousand-tarsec heavy trawler loaded with Aryonic eels," said Antonella. "This one cargo will be enough to pay our dues to the Queen Regent. We will not lose a single eel! Is that clear?"

A chorus of voices shouted back, "Yes, Captain!"

But suddenly, the freighter ahead of them detonated in a massive explosion. Crew members covered their eyes from the unexpected burst of light.

"What the ..." was all Antonella could say before seeing the freighter's hull rupture into the vacuum of space. A disk-shaped shock wave emanated from the explosion. Antonella knew immediately what risk it posed.

"Lower the sails! Turn us into the wave!" she ordered.

Crew members scurried to various stations. Some wound electric servos that quickly pulled in the ion sails, neatly wrapping them around the ship's masts. Others retracted and closed the weapon hatches. The helmsman turned his wheel desperately, positioning the ship into the leading edge of the shock wave, which was nearly upon them.

The impact was jarring. The whole ship lurched as the shock wave flowed over them. The helmsman fought desperately to keep the Maiden true as valves around him burst open, releasing their searing gasses. As others were tossed about violently, Antonella stayed on her feet. After a terrifying minute of shaking, the wave was now past them, and the ship steadied once more.

"Everyone to their stations!" commanded Antonella.

Her crew moved as quickly as they could, but some were badly injured. The helmsman lay dead, his neck snapped, one hand still grasping the wheel. Antonella pulled his body away from the helm unceremoniously, and another took his station. The way she treated him was not lost on others, but no one dared to say a word.

It was the radiowoman's voice that broke the silence. "There's a distress signal, Captain … someone's still alive out there."

Antonella looked at the magnifying lens over the front screen. She could see the broken hull of the freighter drifting amongst the asteroids in the field. Something didn't seem right to her—who could have possibly survived that explosion? But one thing she hated above all else was an incomplete goal. She had set out on this mission intending to fill her cargo hold. If it was not to be eels, then maybe she could find some replacement crew. Certainly, she had lost many this day. "Take us in," said Antonella to the new helmsman. He nodded and turned the ship into the belt.

Antonella stood at the threshold to the engine room. It was a disaster inside. One of the main pressure lines had burst, incinerating several stokers who monitored the ion channels from the sail collectors. Men lay dead amid scorching pipe and twisted iron. The engineer, a six-armed Bracknoid, worked repairs on two systems simultaneously, while barking orders to his crew. Antonella walked up to him. "How bad?"

"We've had worse," he replied.

There was a thud against the hull that echoed in the metallic chamber where the engine pylons sat. Then another, and another. The engineer looked to Antonella with a puzzled expression. It was not a sound he was accustomed to.

"We're entering an asteroid field," she said to him.

"Is that wise, Captain?" he asked. "Considering we have only one working engine."

Antonella bristled at his query. She had been a captain for over forty orbits, and in her early times, if a man had questioned her in such a way, she would have slit his throat. But Antonella knew things were different now. The Guild was not a strong as it once was. Good crews were hard to find. Slaves would take too long to train, and captives could never quite be trusted. She couldn't just go around executing her crew anymore.

Antonella blamed many of the new problems on the weakness the Queen Regent had shown in recent times. A "policy of mercy" was the official term, but Antonella considered it nothing more than appeasement of the lower classes.

It was a topic of much discussion amongst the captains when they gathered for their retreats. The general whisper amongst her sisters-in-arms was that the Guild had been so successful in plundering the trade routes on behalf of the crown that the Queen Regent intentionally wanted to weaken them so as not to become a threat to her. So, societal discourse against the natural order of established class was the new norm. Disgusting.

"I have great trust in your abilities," Antonella coldly replied to the engineer.

He bowed his head to her, though less enthusiastically than Antonella would have liked.

The intercom chirped to life: *"Captain to holding. We found a survivor."* With that, Antonella left.

Pola sat on the cold steel bench, the only furnishing in the whole room. To one side was an airlock—the one she was brought in through—and to the other was the hatch into the ship itself. Her spacesuit had been stripped away, leaving her naked. She now shivered in the frigid and stale air; her skin was spotted with purple welts as her body temperature fell.

Pola tried rubbing her hands together for warmth, but it did little to help. She had always hated the cold. The homeworld of the Tsvezarian race was one of ice—methane, to be exact. Even in the warmest orbital segments, exposed skin would freeze in mere moments.

Her people over the eons had become quite comfortable in the cold. But Pola never was. She always chose a room in whatever keep her family occupied that had exposure to the sun. It rarely made a difference, but at least it made her feel better to imagine feeling the warmth from the star that orbited their planet.

Now, as she trembled, she could only blame her father for her poor temperature tolerance. Though one couldn't tell from looking at her, as she was Tsvezarian in appearance, human blood coursed through her veins in equal measure. However, she knew very little about her human ancestry. She knew they were an insignificant race from across the galactic core, and that only a few thousand of them had made it this far in their travels.

They were an oddity that high-class families brought to parties to impress their peers, like having an exotic pet. Her father's genes also gave her other undesirable traits that she did her best to hide from contemporaries. She had a weak stomach and could barely digest the meat of the Orlian stag, a staple of the Tsvezarian diet. She was also burdened with a terribly well-developed sense of empathy.

Throughout the galaxy, the Tsvezarian people were known for their most insidious trait: a sheer lack of compassion and understanding for those less fortunate than themselves. It was what made them effective leaders, ones who would only focus on the goal and not the cost. Though the ruling council of the Guild was officially made up of dozens of races, the majority were Tsvezarian because they were so ruthless.

But none of this mattered right now. Pola was no ruler or significant member of the party apparatus. She was alone and inside a Guild plunder vessel, and she had to keep her head about her if she was going to survive.

Her teeth chattered violently, and she was disappointed in herself at how fragile she had become because of the cold. She thought she had more resolve than this, but it seemed that her will would break quite easily. Just as she was about to knock on the door for the guard, it opened. Pola looked up to see a familiar face. It was the face of Antonella, who stared at her in complete and utter shock. "Hello, Mother," said Pola.

Antonella watched as her daughter dressed, the two now alone in her stateroom. Though Pola was not as stocky as Antonella, they were of similar height, and Antonella's clothes—leggings, belts, and spiked breastplates—fit her quite well.

"Thank you for this, Mother," said Pola.

Antonella stared at her daughter's body and shook her head disapprovingly. "You removed our markings?"

Pola looked down at her thigh, then at her shoulder, where skin markings had once identified the clan that she belonged to. Now there were only slightly lighter patches of grey skin where the flesh-moths had done their work in removing the ink.

"Yes. It made things simpler after I left," replied Pola.

"And you changed your hair. I don't like it so short," said Antonella.

"The Mining Consortium helmets are a tight fit. It was a practical decision."

"All this time, you've been working in the mines?"

"It's honest work."

"For a Verlusian. Or one of those cursed Mallthors. Not for the daughter of one of the most powerful houses in the Guild."

"I'm no longer in your house, Mother. Or have you forgotten?"

That stung Antonella, for she had not forgotten. She remembered quite clearly the day that Pola refused to go to the Plunder Academy, and refused to follow in her footsteps and have a command of her own. It was also the last day that Pola and Antonella had spoken in three orbits.

"Maybe I have forgotten," replied Antonella. "I'm very busy, as you can imagine. Why don't you remind me?"

"I don't want to get into this, Mother," said Pola.

"Oh, you mean like how you abandoned your clan, your culture, your birthright, for what? Stupid ideas that your father put in your head?"

"I guess you haven't forgotten," replied Pola.

Antonella twitched with anger. She took a threatening step toward Pola.

"Go ahead," said Pola defiantly.

"I have never hit you, never once," replied Antonella.

"Not physically," Pola countered.

Antonella opened her mouth to fire back a response, but then surprised even herself. She burst out laughing, a deep and heartfelt roar that practically shook the walls. Pola looked at her mother with astonishment. "What's so funny?"

"You're a right little bitch, my daughter. But I have missed you very much," said Antonella.

Before Pola could say anything, the intercom cut in: *"Captain, Bridge here. Engineering says we need to come to a full stop to finish repairs. Do you authorize?"*

Antonella turned toward the intercom outlet, jaw clenched with aggravation, but finally replied, "Yes … but tell that worthless excrement of an engineer to get my ship working, or I'll toss him outside in a vac-suit with only a thruster to pull us out of this asteroid belt!"

"*Yes, Captain!*" was the reply, and the intercom went dead.

"A bit harsh. I'm sure they're doing their best," added Pola.

Antonella turned back to her, ignoring the comment. Her mind was on a much more pressing matter. "What were you doing on board that freighter?"

Pola took a deep breath, then stared at her mother with a resigned expression. "I was looking for you."

Antonella felt a strange feeling in her chest, a tightness that she had not felt in a long time. She tried to rationalize it away as the remnant of some old injury, but she knew what it was deep down—regret. Her daughter's absence had hurt her.

"I heard rumours," continued Pola. "That your ship was in this quadrant. I took a job aboard the freighter, hoping that you would target us."

"They took you in?"

"They thought having a Tsvezarian would be useful if they were captured, as a bargaining chip."

"Then why did the freighter explode?"

"I tried to send a secret message to you. They intercepted it. They were going to kill me," said Pola, a regretful expression etched across her face.

Antonella could feel her fluidic pumping organ quicken with a sudden realization. She was filled with another unfamiliar sensation: respect. "You rigged an explosive?"

"It was only meant as a last resort, in case I had no other choice," replied Pola.

No matter how much she tried, Antonella could not fight off the smile that made its way across her face. "And then you spaced yourself."

"Yes. I took refuge on an asteroid and detonated their engines," said Pola. But then she shook her head with a look of disgust.

"Why are you upset?" asked Antonella. "It was a clever plan. Or is it that you weep for the crew? The lives you took?"

Antonella could see Pola struggle with the answer. Finally, she shook her head, "No. I don't care about them, Mother. That's why I came looking for you. It took me all these orbits to realize you were right. We are *not* all the same. Some of us are meant to be underfoot. Some of us are meant to rule. And it sickens me."

Antonella stepped up to her daughter and put a hand against her cheek. It was a warm and loving gesture; one she had offered a singular time in her life—to Zaa when they were in their most passionate of embraces. But right now, Antonella knew Pola needed this token. "This feeling, my dearest daughter, will pass," said Antonella.

Mil'n loved to clean the organic scale from the ship's vital channels. His slender frame meant he could enter the ion cooling pipes' narrow confines that ran the length of the vessel. His stubby legs also meant he could make it around the tightest corners and wedge himself into impossible angles. All the men in his family were scrubbers, and proud of it.

However, he was new to the Maiden and had never served on a plunder vessel before. His previous assignments included freighters and long-haul tow ships. But the Maiden was by far his favourite because she was an older design—one more susceptible to scaling issues.

The newer vessels had experimented with automated scrubbing machines, but the results were inconsistent. The machines were faster but could not adapt and polish the coptic brass lining of the fluidic channels to the necessary shine. Only the hand of a sentient being could ensure that the channel was polished with the grains in the correct direction. Ask any engineer, and they would tell you that scrubbing was as much an art as it was a science.

Covered in the soot he so loved, and with abrasive pads in hand, Mil'n reached the end of the current cooling channel he was scrubbing. The end cap was open to the engineering deck, and one of his legs dangled out of it as he polished the last few curves.

Even though the ship was still being repaired from the shock wave, scrubbing was so important that the engineer insisted he continue with his regular maintenance cycle.

Mil'n couldn't understand why others, including the captain, ridiculed him about his profession. If something was so important to the vessel's function, would it not mean he was more valuable than, say, a pipe fitter? Or a moist electrics specialist?

But he also wasn't stupid, and he knew he had to play the game. When the captain threatened his life, he had to pretend that being a scrubber was the lowest of the low. It was the only way his life would be spared. It was those moments, the moments when Mil'n was out of the confines of the channels, that he felt his most vulnerable. Most of the crew generally found scrubbers to be off-putting, but Mil'n was an oddball even for them.

During his meal cycles, he would listen to other crew complain about the working conditions and the abuse they got from the higher classes. They would vow to not do their jobs as well as they could, to make the ship less efficient in protest. Mil'n had once voiced his displeasure at hearing that—why would anyone not do their job as best they could? But he was soon scolded back into silence.

Now, as Mil'n finished up his channel, he saw the regulator talking to the six-armed Bracknoid engineer and a few others. Mil'n didn't care much for the regulator. He didn't trust any species that hid every inch of their bodies from exposure. His mother had once told him that the atmospherics of most ships would burn their skin if unprotected, but he thought it strange that such a fragile species would choose to work in a place so deadly to them—hence why most ships only had a few regulators.

The group whispered to each other when the regulator turned and looked directly at Mil'n, who waved back at him innocently. The regulator walked over to the channel, lowering his face so that his mask apparatus was right in Mil'n's view.

The regulator said in a growly, filtered voice, "Is there something troubling you?"

"No, sir. Just finish'n up 'ere," said Mil'n.

"Then why are you spying on us?"

"I ain't, sir, it's jus' where the channel ends," replied Mil'n.

The regulator stared at the scrubber. Though Mil'n couldn't read his expression through the mask covering his face, he somehow thought the regulator didn't trust him. He couldn't understand why. They had never interacted at all on board this ship.

Finally, the engineer piped in, "Leave Mil'n be. He's a good little scrubber. Just a bit off, you know?"

The others laughed, and someone said, "They all are." The regulator finally nodded and turned his back to the channel. Mil'n returned to his last polishing strokes, but his mind was preoccupied with everything he had heard. People often forgot how good scrubbers' hearing was.

Pola stared with wonder out the viewing glass on the bridge. The ship was stationary, but the asteroids were not. They slowly moved across her field of view, colliding with each other and occasionally the ship. "Incredible," she said.

"I never could convince you to come aboard during my tours," said Antonella.

"It just didn't interest me when I was younger."

"And what are your impressions now?"

"I never knew how good a view you had from the bridge," Pola said.

"In battle, you need to see in every direction."

"But it's ... beautiful," added Pola.

Antonella stepped closer to her daughter, lowering her voice so that the other crew on the bridge could not hear her words. "I sometimes come here and stare into the stars. The crew think I'm hunting for targets. But I just love the view."

Pola looked over at her mother. She felt a sudden heaviness in her chest. The Tsvezarians were supposed to be cold and arrogant people, but right now, Pola felt something different from Antonella. Was her mother opening up to her? Pola looked into her eyes, searching for the same level of emotion she now felt. *There is*, thought Pola as she saw a glimmer and wondered if this was the right time to talk to Antonella and open up to her. Maybe she would listen.

Bang! The bridge suddenly shook with an impact. A large asteroid had hit the Maiden broadside. The look in Antonella's eyes hardened once again, and she whipped around to glare at the new helmsman. "Any news from the engineer?" she growled.

"No, Captain, we're still dead in the water," the man replied.

Antonella gritted her teeth, then turned to Pola. "I'll be back. Enjoy the view," she said, and then stormed off toward the lift.

Pola stepped closer to the helmsman at his station. She smiled at him. He turned away, obviously uncomfortable with a Tsvezarian smiling at him.

The engineering crew mostly scattered when they saw Antonella storm in. The Bracknoid engineer did not, however, but turned to face her.

"I want my engines now!" demanded Antonella.

The engineer motioned with multiple arms toward the fans set up around the engine bay, ones blowing cool air on the pods that had been recently rebuilt.

"We need to let the welds cool down, Captain. Otherwise, they'll rupture," he replied.

"During the attack of the Shelling, we lost two pods. You were able to get them up in half the time," she said angrily.

"It's different, Captain. The shock wave broke the seams. We can't rush this repair."

"This is a level of incompetence I have not seen even in you—"Antonella began, but she was cut off by another thudding sound at the hull of the ship.

The engineer shook his head. "I know—asteroids. I promise, Captain, soon now."

Antonella felt a slight tingle down her spine. It would have been logical for her to assume that another asteroid had hit the hull. But this sound was slightly different, more metallic in nature. *Don't be foolish*, thought Antonella. She turned her attention back to the engineer. "Report to the bridge as soon as I have my engines back," she ordered.

He bowed his head deeply and quite appropriately this time.

Antonella had turned to leave when she was hit was a gust of wind from one of the fans. The regulator was working in front of it, and something struck her as odd. The smell. His smell. That tingle down her spine was back, and she did everything in her power to stride out of the engine bay as confidently as she had entered.

Antonella walked down the corridor. Some of her crew scurried away as usual when she passed, but she also noticed a few looks that lingered. She turned a corner and saw that no one was there. Off to one side was a maintenance hatch, one that led to the outer hull of the Maiden. With a glance over her shoulder, Antonella opened the hatch and squeezed herself in.

It wasn't easy going in the maintenance corridor. Antonella had to hunch over, constantly wary not to hit her head against scorching-hot pipes. Finally, she arrived at her destination, a viewing bubble that stuck out from the outer hull, allowing repair crews to see any deformation in the ship's skin.

But what Antonella saw nearly stopped her fluidic pumping organ. There were hundreds of invaders clinging to her ship, like Alerian moths on a stag's back. They were dressed in vac suits with magnetic shoes. More floated silently toward the Maiden, keeping away from viewing ports and making sure to stay in the blind spot of the bridge. *Thud!* She again heard the metallic noise that had triggered her initial reaction in the engine room. It was an invader landing on her hull and taking their position.

There was only a moment of doubt in Antonella as she tried to understand what was happening, but it all then became crystal-clear. This was the crew of the freighter. They were going to board the Maiden.

Antonella could feel her jaw clench, her back arch. She turned to head back to the corridor, vowing to kill each one of them. But suddenly, she stopped with a thought: *someone must be helping them from inside.* She shook her head angrily; it must be the engineer who had betrayed her, and she was now certain who was pulling his strings.

Antonella emerged from the maintenance hatch. She stood tall, hiding the anger that now coursed through her. If there were other spies, she could not let them know she knew of the impending attack.

As she turned to walk toward the lift to the bridge, there was a bone-rattling explosion. The deck shook, tossing crew aside, but once again, Antonella stood her ground. She knew those were breaching charges, as she had used many in her day.

Within moments, invaders dropped down into the corridors from the outer hull of her ship. They were a motley bunch, different races, all seven known genders. Several of her crew were overwhelmed immediately and then electrified. *Interesting,* thought Antonella, *they're not using lethal weapons.* Another of her crew, a Melthusian cook, ran up to Antonella with a look of terror across his face. "Captain! We're being boarded! What should we do?"

"Go and fight them, you coward!" she replied.

He stared at her, unsure. Antonella added, "Or you'll have me to deal with."

Terror and confusion battled in the man's eyes as he struggled between these two dreadful options. He finally turned and ran headlong into a group of invaders, uttered a pitiful squeal, and was immediately overwhelmed by them. Antonella continued as individual battles raged all along the corridor.

She had reached the lift to the bridge when she was suddenly dropped upon by two invaders from the mechanical works above. The first thrust an electric spark staff at her, but she easily sidestepped it. The second swung a battle club at her head but missed and impacted the corridor wall with a thud.

"Better!" said Antonella, every nerve in her body tingled with excitement. She lived for these moments. She grabbed this invader and drove him into the bulkhead, cracking his neck. The second invader dropped his electric staff and pulled a long blade from his belt. He swung at Antonella, but she avoided his attack.

"Was he a friend? The one I just killed," she said mockingly.

The invader grew enraged and ran at her. As he neared, Antonella bent a leg and crouched, letting his blade swing harmlessly over her head. With her other leg, she tripped the man, and he tumbled to the ground. Before he could right himself, she had taken his blade and impaled him in his chest. As he gurgled his last breath, she leaned over him and said, "You did well. There is no shame in your death."

The invader expired, and Antonella pulled the now-dripping blade from his chest. As she got to the lift, all she could think of was the safety of her daughter.

The door to the bridge opened, and Antonella stormed in. "Report! How many decks have we lost?"

But she stopped in her tracks immediately. Her Elite, all six of them, lay dead around the room. Her mind reeled at the impossibility of this. Even if a dozen invaders had made it onto the bridge at once, maybe one Elite would have been overwhelmed, but surely not all six. These were the best she had ever owned. But then Antonella saw it: the blade sticking into one of her Elite's back. She knew immediately what it meant. She turned to the helm.

The Bracknoid engineer stood there, with the new helmsman at his side.

"You filthy piece of stag shit," she growled at the engineer. "But I know you don't have the balls to have done this on your own. Where is he?"

The engineer moved aside, and the regulator stepped forward. A blinding rage surged in Antonella. She didn't try to hide it now, and she glared at the cloaked man. "Take it off!" she demanded.

The regulator slowly peeled away the wrapping around his neck, then pulled the mask aside. What revealed itself was the heavily sweating human face of her ex-husband, Lionel.

"How did you know it was me?" asked Lionel.

"I smelled you in the engine room. That sickly-sweet stench you humans have," she said with disdain.

"You didn't find it so offensive once," he said to her with a smile.

Antonella was overwhelmed with embarrassment. How dare he be so personal with her in front of the others. His lack of decorum was galling. But then she glanced around the bridge, disappointed that from the dozens of her crew there, only a few were under guard—the rest were obviously traitorous scum. She had no need to worry about how she appeared to them.

Antonella raised her weapon and took a threatening step toward Lionel. He was immediately flanked by a half-dozen invaders with lethal projectile weapons in hand. She could get one or two, but certainly not all of them. "You are and have always been a fool," she said to Lionel, her blade held aloft in front of her.

"And you have never been one. So please, put down your weapon," he replied.

Antonella did not hesitate. She threw her blade to the deck. It skittered across and came to rest at Lionel's feet. She knew there was no chance, and a meaningless show of resistance was below her standing. If she was to die, she would prefer it were with significant pomp and circumstance in front of an audience, even a hostile one.

"How long have you been on my ship?"

"Since the Melthusian homeworld," Lionel replied.

Antonella shook her head. She had taken on close to one hundred new crew members after the attrition of their last conquest. There were always checks done on them to ensure that spies or enemies did not get aboard, but if others were already in league with Lionel, then stowing away was not much of a challenge. He could easily blend in with the masses and pull strings in secret.

"And what did you offer my disloyal crew? Some promise of a new future? One where they could gain a status that birth had denied them?"

"Nothing quite so grandiose, my wife," he said.

"I am not your wife," she retorted. "You were nothing more than a passing fancy."

"You know that's not true."

Antonella wanted to say more but couldn't. He was right; Lionel had been more than a fling. She had loved him. They had met over a dozen orbits ago when Lionel's ship had been caught in a gravity well around a dark star. They were refugees from their own system, a few thousand humans crammed into a decaying vessel with archaic nucleonic propulsion. They were so backward that they didn't know that their circuit-based technology wouldn't work in zones heavy with dark matter. Only naturalized heavy elements were stout enough to function in this part of space.

A dozen or so scavenger-class tugs had set on them, cutting up the ship's hull, taking slaves. Antonella came upon them and chased away the others. Upon boarding the human ship, she found pitiful survivors clinging to life but nothing else of interest. She was about to put them out of their misery with a scuttling charge, but Lionel was their leader and confronted her, ultimately stopping their destruction. He negotiated with Antonella for his settlers' lives, and she was immediately impressed with their offerings of culture. It seemed that the humans' homeworld had forsaken all who considered art a necessity of existence. Barbaric.

Over the next orbit, Antonella had deposited colonies of them on a dozen worlds. These small pockets of humanity soon became havens for sculpture, painting, literature, and the culinary arts. They were renowned throughout the quadrant. But Lionel chose not to leave her side. They had bonded, and he became her husband. Though a husband had no chattel or political rights, he did become very important to Antonella as a figurehead.

But soon after Pola was born, their relationship soured. Lionel let his tongue slip at one too many social events; had spouted his views on the equality of the races, peaceful coexistence through mutual respect. He was ridiculed, and Antonella was forced to remove him from her family. And that was why, at this very moment, Antonella felt a pain unlike any she had ever experienced. Not only had he broken her spirit, but he had broken their deal.

"How dare you take what is mine," she said to him in a low growl.

"He's not, Mother," said Pola as she stepped out from the lift. "I am."

Antonella was stunned speechless. Pola strode onto the bridge. The engineer bowed his head to her in a most respectful way. Pola turned to address Lionel.

"You can tell her, Father," she said to him.

"I'd rather *you* did, my daughter. It would mean more," he replied.

Pola nodded in agreement, then turned to Antonella. "It was all my idea, Mother. I am the rebel who has taken your ship."

"Why?" was all Antonella could muster.

"Because, Mother, this is the beginning of a revolution."

Antonella burst out laughing. "Did you not wear a breathing apparatus in those mines? Did you poison your brain?" she said sarcastically.

"This is no joke!" barked the engineer. "We, the working class, are not taking any more of your abuse."

"Shut your mouth—" Antonella said but was immediately cut off by the man.

"We are not afraid of you anymore!" continued the engineer.

Antonella looked around the room. He was right. She saw no signs of deference, no lowered eyes, or fearful expressions. Those who had been her loyal crew for many orbits now looked upon her with the fortitude of character.

"We are taking your ship, Mother. We will use it to light a fire in this quadrant, one that will change everything," said Pola.

Antonella opened her mouth to respond, then closed it. She shook her head with deep despair. "Then, this is the end of civilization."

Pola motioned silently to an invader, and a squad of six surrounded Antonella. One even dared to place his hand on her arm, but Antonella was so shaken that she offered no acknowledgment.

"Take her to the brig," said Pola. "She will be useful in the bargains to follow."

The invaders bound her hands and led Antonella into the lift.

Antonella was led down the corridor by her invader escorts. As she went, those of her crew that had changed allegiances did not hesitate to show her their contempt, offered unkind words and gestures. She ignored them, but her spirit sank with every step. She had always thought herself a fair and just leader, one that had the respect of those beneath her. But now the veneer of this illusion had been stripped away. They hated her, and she no longer had any power over them.

It was quite a shock when she heard the explosion and then felt the deck below her feet give way. Surely some crew member was trying to kill her. Strangely, and at this moment, Antonella was grateful for that.

When the dust and debris settled, she stood up amid the corridor's wreckage, quite disappointed that she was still alive. Her escorts lay dead around her, most badly burned. She then saw what had caused the calamity. One of the heat-exchange pipes had ruptured below their feet—luckily just after Antonella had passed by. But it took only a moment for Antonella to realize it wasn't luck.

The scrubber Mil'n stood before her. For some reason, he seemed even shorter now than during their previous encounter, his eyes barely at the level of her suckling glands. He smiled at her through a crooked, soot-covered face. "It's amazin' when them pipes get clogged. Ain't it, Cap'n?" he said.

Antonella looked back at the pipes that had ruptured. If anyone could have sabotaged them, surely a scrubber could have. "You did this?" she asked.

"Are you pleased, ma'am?" he said.

Antonella had to clear her throat to keep her voice from cracking. "It will do," she responded.

He undid the bindings on her hands, led her down another corridor, and then off to a service alley.

"Where are we going?" asked Antonella.

"Best you don't know 'til we get there," he responded.

Mil'n led the way as they reached the alley's end, where a decking plate had already been removed. He jumped in and disappeared. Antonella followed, but much more cautiously. They were now in the confines of one of Mil'n's blessed channels. He moved easily, but Antonella struggled to stay in touch, now forced to slither on her belly like a serpent.

Finally, they reached the end of the channel. Mil'n turned back to her and put his hands over his lips, signalling for her to be quiet. He then looked to the metal grating that led to another chamber. Satisfied that the way ahead was clear, he pushed the grate aside and popped out of the channel.

Antonella was not quite so elegant and tumbled from the channel's mouth, landing with a thud on the deck plate. She stood angrily, preparing to lash out at Mil'n for dragging her through the soot, but cut herself off when she saw where he had led her.

They were standing in a maintenance airlock, one of the dozens positioned along the ship's length to allow crews easy access to make hull repairs in battle. Around them were the tools of the trade: portable welders, spare dark-matter-iron plates, and, most importantly, a half-dozen pressure suits. Antonella eyed them and then turned to Mil'n. "Before we do this, are there enough loyal men like you to take up my cause?"

"'Der are no loyal men like me," he responded.

Antonella's shoulders slumped with the weight of the realization of what was next.

Pola paced along the edge of the viewing glass next to the helm. She was cognizant that many eyes were on her right now, unsure of her skills as a leader. She made sure not to fidget or look worried. Her steps were purposeful, and her body language confident—a skill she had indeed learned from her mother.

Lionel walked up to Pola. "There's no sign of her."

"That is unfortunate," replied Pola. "We need her under lock and key, or things might get violent."

"I wouldn't worry. We've shackled anyone loyal, and there were barely two scores of them. She did a great job of pissing this crew off."

"My mother is like any captain in this Guild. Her power is built on a foundation of oppression."

Lionel smiled at his daughter. "You remembered."

"I remember *some* of the stories you told me of your homeworld, Father. I just hope we can change the course of our future to avoid the past of yours."

Lionel looked over his shoulder, then surreptitiously reached out and squeezed his daughter's hand. Pola knew he was proud of her, but she enjoyed the moments when he showed it.

Just then, the helmsman yelled out, "Port side, beam height!"

Everyone turned to look out the viewing window. Pola saw it immediately and pointed her father to the spot. Off in the distance, two people in vac suits held on to each other as they twirled away from the Maiden.

"They've spaced themselves," said Lionel.

"Looks like they're out of control," added Pola.

"Shall I send a party to gather them?" asked the helmsman.

Pola turned to him. It was not his words that struck her as odd, but rather his tone. There was a definite challenge in his intonation, as though he was testing her. Pola quickly glanced around the bridge. Every set of eyes were on her, every breath held in anticipation of her next order. Pola finally looked over at Lionel, but his face betrayed no emotion.

"There was no threat to her life, yet she killed six of our brothers in this escape, corrupted another of our crew," said Pola to the others. "I believe in justice and the rule of law. But we are the ones to write that law."

She slowly turned her back, so her gaze lingered only on the two, tumbling away from them into space. "I believe that justice should be swift and final for my mother and her accomplice," she said.

The helmsman understood immediately. He turned to the weapons crew. "Cannon five, single shot, wide dispersal." The crew jumped into action, and the lone cannon emerged from the port side of the hull. Crewmen worked the dials and levers until a positive lock was found on the target. The helmsman then turned his attention back to Pola. "Locked on target, Captain. What are your orders?"

Pola could feel the tightness in her chest, her breath becoming heavy. She wondered whether her mother had had these same sensations when in command. Regardless, she was ready for this. Though the method was quite unexpected, she had rehearsed this choice a thousand times in her mind and did not hesitate. "Fire," was all Pola replied.

A thunderous clap shook the bridge as the lone cannon fired into space, disintegrating the two vac suits in a plume of irradiated lead shot. The crew cheered, but Pola just turned to look at her father. To the untrained eye, he stared back at her with no expression. But Pola saw the edge of his mouth curl upwards, and it was all the validation she needed. She then turned back toward the helmsman. "Set a course for the Validian shipyards. We will punch a hole in the Guild fleet today and bring them to the table!" said Pola.

The crew cheered once again.

Antonella watched as the empty vac suits vaporized in the distance. She then watched as the Maiden's engines lit, and the ship quickly disappeared into the inky black of space beyond the asteroid belt. All things considered, she felt a surprising emotion over what her daughter had done. She was quite proud that Pola had the guts to kill her.

Antonella then sighed with the realization that she was now left clinging to an unremarkable rock in this very same asteroid belt, beside a lowest-of-class scrubber who had the audacity to save her life. "So, what now, Mil'n?" she said to him through their communications moist electrics.

"You remembered me name, Cap'n!" he said with pleasure.

"Should a captain not know the name of the most important member of her crew?" she replied. She could see Mil'n smile awkwardly at her through his helmet visor. Sarcasm was not a skill he possessed.

"I don't suppose you hid a skiff anywhere nearby?" asked Antonella.

"We don't need one, Cap'n," he said, then pressed a button on his suit forearm.

A moment passed, and a boarding barge hurtled toward them, stopping precisely a few arm's lengths from their rock. Antonella stared at the command deck screen on the barge, and her eyes lit up with shock. "Zaa!"

Zaa obviously saw Antonella's reaction from inside the barge and waved at her. Antonella then turned to look at Mil'n with absolute glee. "How did you know?" she asked.

"I served with Cap'n Zaa many orbits ago. Before you took her, Cap'n."

Antonella could feel the smile spread across her face, and she did nothing to maintain decorum in front of this lower-class crewman. Instead, she reached out and put a hand on his shoulder. "Let's get our ship back," said Antonella.

The man nodded to her, then smiled his crooked smile.

TO BE CONTINUED in Volume Two

CHAPTER 5

THE HARVEST

PART 2

Penny lay there on the couch, staring at a hairline crack on the ceiling. She did this often and for hours on end. It brought her comfort. She was certain that the crack had grown at least an inch in length over the weeks and months of her observation. However, there was no way for her to measure; the retirement home's ceiling was at least nine feet high, and she was barely five feet tall. Though sixteen years of age now, Penny felt she hadn't hit her growth spurt yet. Or at least she hoped she hadn't missed it. Not needing a bra was becoming embarrassing at school.

What also brought Penny strange comfort was the metronomic sound of the life support breather attached to her grandmother, Essie. The sound was not unpleasant—a gentle *whoosh* that reverberated throughout the room. The sound meant the machine was working. It also had a battery backup and would continue to cycle air even if the power went out. It made Penny feel good to know that her Grammy had a fighting chance to come out of her coma as long as air kept getting pumped into her lungs.

Penny glanced around her grandmother's private room, which had also been *her* home for the last ten months. Aside from the medical bed in which Grammy slept, there was a dresser, a full-length mirror, a small desk where Penny did her homework, and the couch where she slept. Penny kept the place tidy, as the staff didn't do much more than look after the residents. She dusted and swept up regularly, making sure to get under the bed as well. She knew Grammy liked a clean house.

After the big blow-up with her foster parents, Penny had moved in permanently. Frankly, they were glad she was gone, and Penny was happy to never have to see their ill-natured guard dog again. She wasn't fond of dogs—and theirs was a particularly mean one.

Essie was the only blood relative Penny had in the world. The home was going to kick Penny out six months ago, but after the previous administrator got arrested for stealing money from the residents, she became less of an issue. As long as Penny stayed under the radar and didn't make a fuss, the new bosses didn't care if she "visited" permanently.

Besides, the residents loved having her around. When not in school, Penny would spend time with them, bring them smokes and chocolates from the town bodega, and write letters to family that forgot them. All in all, Penny was relatively happy with the arrangement.

That is, except for the fact that she was looking for a way to end her own life.

Penny sighed as she looked over at the wall clock, which now read four o'clock in the morning. Another sleepless night. She had not slept a minute in close to three hundred days, and her life had become a blur.

The beginning of her insomnia was just an inconvenience. Penny tried over-the-counter sleep aids, but they did nothing. When a month passed without sleep, her school life started to suffer. She never had many friends and became irritable with the ones she did have, then finally pushed them all away.

At the three-month mark, she went to a doctor. Not the rejects Penny was certain worked here at the home, but a proper sleep specialist that state Medicaid still covered. They did all sorts of tests, and she was prescribed powerful sedatives, but all they did was make her groggy during the day. The doctor finally threw up his hands in failure, but at least she was in a medical journal now.

Penny had read dozens of these journals on sleep, and there had been other documented cases like her own. *Fatal familial insomnia*, they called it. She didn't understand most of what she read, but she learned that deep sleep was how the human brain cleaned the toxins that built up around the synapses. Deprive a person of sleep, and eventually, the poisons would build-up, and they would die. People like her could expect to live no more than thirty months.

That was too long by Penny. She could barely stand another day. There was only one thing keeping her from crossing into the afterlife, and that was Grammy. Penny couldn't stand the idea of Essie waking up to find no one beside her bed.

OK, thought Penny. She'd stick it out one more day.

Conrad walked past the open door to Essie's room. That struck Penny as odd. She had gotten to know most of the residents' habits over the months. Conrad was a sound sleeper, never having to get up to pee. Penny got off the couch and pulled on one of Grammy's old night coats to cover her pj's. The place was damn cold all the time.

She headed to the door and peeked into the hallway. Penny caught a glimpse of Conrad walking into his room, which was just down the hall. She liked Conrad. He had interesting stories, not just ones about family or friends that had gone. He and his wife had travelled the world, so he had great memories to share.

Penny headed into the hall and made her way to Conrad's room. The door was ajar, but she still knocked. When there was no response, she pushed it open and entered. "Conrad, you OK?" she asked.

He had his back to her and was looking at photos arranged on one of the walls. Penny walked over. She had to look up at him, as he was quite tall. "Conrad?"

Conrad turned to her, and she saw a strange expression on his face—a look of confusion. She had never known Conrad to be confused about anything. He was still the most tech-savvy person in the home, and that included the twenty-year-old orderlies.

"Who is this?" asked Conrad.

"Who's who?" replied Penny.

Conrad pointed to Elaine in a black-and-white photo. It was of them on their wedding day, walking out of the church as they were showered with rice.

"It's Elaine. Your wife."

Conrad furrowed his brow, shook his head in doubt.

"She died last year. Don't you remember?" continued Penny.

"I don't."

"You're joking. You told me a funny story about her last week. Don't you remember, when she fell into that river?"

Tears formed in his eyes. He then looked over at other photos, ones of his children. "I don't remember them either," he said.

Penny was immediately alarmed, "You want me to get someone? Maybe you're having a stroke like my Grammy!"

Conrad shook his head, "No. There's nothing wrong with me."

"But you're forgetting things," insisted Penny.

"I remember you," replied Conrad. "I remember that we talked about my time in Borneo a few days ago. That fever I got there; how sick I was. I even remember what we had for lunch, chicken fingers. Your favourite. I hate the breading."

He then looked over at the arrangement of photos on the wall, finally stopping on another colour photograph of Elaine, now in her seventies. "I don't remember who she is," he said. "I know that I should, but I can't and … it hurts like hell."

Penny turned to leave. "I'm getting the nurse," she began, but Conrad grabbed her arm and stopped her from leaving.

"No, don't …" he said, then wiped the tears from his eyes. "I'm tired, Penny. That's all it is. I need a good night's sleep, and I'll be better."

Penny felt a twinge of jealousy. What she'd give to have that option, to just choose to go to sleep. But she couldn't be angry at Conrad; he and most of the others didn't know about her condition. Finally, she nodded to him. "OK."

Conrad leaned over and kissed the top of her head. "You're a good kid, the way you take care of your grandmother. She's lucky to have you."

Penny nodded, then turned and left the room. She made her way down the hall back toward Essie's room, but then stopped. Something struck her as strange. Conrad once told her the motto he lived by: *There is no such thing as luck, only good planning that leads to predictable results.* She wondered why he would mention luck now.

Turning around, Penny headed back to his room. He wasn't there. "Conrad?" she called out, but she got no reply. She headed down the long hall and arrived at the front reception desk. The night nurse, June, was flipping through a magazine when she noticed Penny.

"Can't sleep again, hon?" June asked.

Penny ignored that. She only replied, "Have you seen Conrad around?"

"Conrad? No."

"OK …" said Penny, but then turned her head to look down another corridor.

"What's bothering you—" was all June could get out before they saw a body drop outside the front entrance. It hit the ground with a resounding wet thud.

June covered her mouth to stifle her scream. Penny just stared in shock at the pile of twisted limbs that now activated the front motion-sensing doors.

A crowd of residents had gathered as the sun rose in the distance. June and the other nurses kept them far back from the threshold of the front entrance. Penny was in the middle of the crowd. She had to crouch to see past all the residents clustered in front of her.

She saw several police cars with their lights flashing in the parking lot, two officers cordoning off the entrance from outside. She also saw a familiar face in a white lab coat peeking under the sheet that now covered the body.

An elderly African American resident, Rose, saw Penny amongst them trying to get a better view. "Penny! Don't look, child," she said.

"It's Conrad, isn't it?" asked Penny.

Rose seemed reluctant to answer for a moment, then replied. "Yes, dear. It's Conrad. Poor man. He was never the same after Elaine passed."

Conflicting emotions coursed through Penny. She was sad about what had happened to Conrad, wondering if she could have done something more to help him. But there was another feeling, one she wasn't proud of, which now overwhelmed her sadness. It was envy.

"Think it was quick? I mean, was he high enough?" asked Penny.

Rose scowled at Penny. "You are a twisted little girl," she said, then shoved her way through the others to get away from her.

But Penny was no longer interested in her opinion. She was tracking the man in the white lab coat as he entered the home again and made his way through the crowd. Penny gently pushed through the other elderly residents to keep up with him. As he made it to the hall, Penny moved to intercept. "Doc, can I talk to you?" she asked, but the man kept going. She was certain he heard what she said but was ignoring her.

Before she could catch up to him, he disappeared into the employee offices, locking the door behind him. But that didn't stop Penny. She'd been here a long time, and she knew a thing or two about the layout of the place.

Penny ran down an adjacent hallway, went through a service door leading outside, and then walked along the building's perimeter. She climbed through an open window that led to the employee washrooms. She kept a low profile and entered an office from its back door.

She shut the door behind her, then sat down at a desk. It was neat and tidy, with only a laptop and a few papers on it. *Screw him*, thought Penny. She put her feet up on the desk to make a point. Only a few moments later, the front door opened, and Dr. Joel Mattis entered his office.

"Jesus!" said Joel, startled at seeing Penny sitting there.

"It's not nice to ignore a child, Doc," she said.

A worried look crossed Joel's face. He glanced over at his laptop, but it was sitting on his desk, closed. "Not now, Penny," he replied. "I have a lot of paperwork to do."

"The death certificate for Conrad, right?" she asked. "What was the cause of death?"

"Gravity," he said cynically.

"You know what I mean."

Joel came around his desk. He was a young man in his thirties, fit. He grabbed Penny by the arm and easily hauled her ninety-pound mass away from the desk. "Get out of my office," he ordered.

"How's Mrs. Stein's treatment going?" said Penny. "You know, the non-FDA approved drug you're having her take. The one you swore her not to tell anyone else about."

Joel mumbled unintelligibly, caught off-balance.

Penny continued, "I overheard her. She comes in to talk to my Grammy, tells her everything. So, don't be mad at Mrs. Stein. She really didn't break a promise, if you think about it."

Joel sighed. "What do you want?"

"Tell me how Conrad died," she demanded to know.

"OK," said Joel. "He jumped from the roof. Sixty feet up, so he didn't have anywhere near the time to reach terminal velocity. He hit the ground shoulder-first, absorbing some of the energy before his neck broke."

"So, he felt something?"

"For a few seconds, yeah. I bet he felt a lot."

Penny shook her head in disappointment. She had thought about jumping off the roof many times but wasn't sure how it would work. Penny didn't kid herself—she hated the idea of suffering, and she was looking for a way out that was painless. A prescription drug overdose was an option, especially as she could easily get opioids in the home. But she had read horror stories on the internet about people becoming violently ill and throwing up, some choking to death. Jumping off the roof was her last best hope, and now she knew it sucked as well.

"You want to talk about this ... or something?" asked Joel.

"Or something?" replied Penny derisively. "That almost seemed like genuine concern there, Doc."

Joel shook his head; his disdain for Penny was palpable. He then sat down at his desk. "Always good talking to you, Penny."

"Why don't you get creative with my grandmother?" said Penny as she turned to leave. "Do something other than just keep her breathing."

Penny always thought her teacher's voice had a peculiar inflection. While many of her classmates would raise the tone at the end of a sentence, Mrs. Williams would start off low, peak in the middle of the sentence, then fade off almost to silence by the end. Penny found it funny and had to fight off many a chuckle, especially in English class, when she read Shakespeare. Penny wondered why no one else found it as funny as she did. But then again, she was more observant than most kids her age.

From her seat in the back row of the classroom, she noticed that the sneaker on Mrs. Williams's left foot had lost more rubber on the front than the back, while it was exactly the opposite on the other foot. Yet right now, as she walked in front of the chalkboard, writing a soliloquy, Mrs. Williams didn't seem to have any unusual limp or foot drag that would have caused such a wear pattern. Peculiar.

While the others sat oblivious to this, Penny also noticed a two-headed deer that casually walked up the row toward her desk. It was brown with white spots. One of the heads was clearly a stag, as it had early seasonal antler growth. The other head was a doe, which only had a tuft of brown fur on its head. As the deer made its way down the row, it bumped a desk, and a pencil rolled off and fell to the floor.

The boy that sat at the desk reached over and picked up the pencil; he nearly got clipped by the deer's tail. Penny laughed to herself, and a few of her classmates glanced over at her, then turned away again.

The deer arrived at Penny's desk, and the stag bent its head over and started chewing on the piece of paper that Penny was taking notes on. She smiled at it, and then the doe bent over in front of her. Penny began to rub its head. She had never touched a deer before and was surprised that the fur was coarser than she expected—it had a waxy feel. She surmised that it was probably a waterproof coating that kept it warm.

"Penny, what are you doing?" said Mrs. Williams from the front of the room.

Everyone in the class turned to look at Penny, who had her hand out and continued to pet the doe's head. Penny knew no one else in the room could see the animal. She could only imagine what she looked like, her hand petting the air in front of her.

Penny was certain the hallucinations were a side effect of her insomnia, which had started about four months earlier. She mainly saw animals, but not normal ones. She had seen a rabbit with six paws, a fox with no eyes, and several bobcats with porcupine quills growing from their backs. One time, she had seen a dark, human-like figure skulking in the halls of the home—but it also could have been a minotaur for all she knew.

"Just a fly, Mrs. Williams," replied Penny as she lowered her hand.

There was a chuckle around the room. Most of her classmates thought she was nuts, and to be honest, Penny agreed with them. Mrs. Williams knew about her condition and was sympathetic. She gave Penny a nod and then turned back to the chalkboard. When no one was looking, Penny pulled the paper from the stag's mouth, and the two-headed deer turned around, headed back down the row, and slipped out the classroom door.

Penny walked along the road back home. The retirement residence was situated at a dead-end street in a forested area. Though a beautiful setting, Penny could only imagine that the planner who had approved it in the 1970s must have had ulterior motives to banish the elderly into the woods so that people didn't have to see them. As she neared the parking lot, she heard a strange whimpering noise.

At first, Penny thought the noise came from another of her hallucinatory visitors, but then saw where it was coming from. Up ahead was a black man, probably in his late fifties, standing by his car in the lot. He was smoking, staring wistfully into the woods. As Penny drew closer, she could see the wet streaks down his face from tears.

"Are you all right?" asked Penny.

The man was startled, and he tried to quickly wipe away the tears from his face.

"It's OK. Everyone who comes here eventually cries," she said to him.

He laughed at that, nodded, then stamped out his cigarette. "I don't usually let it get to me," he said. Then his eyes narrowed with a realization. "You're Penny, aren't you?"

"Yeah, who wants to know?"

"Sorry, didn't mean anything by it," he said as he extended his hand. "I'm Eddie Emmery. My mother's Rose. She talks about you sometimes."

Penny took his hand and shook it. "Let me guess, stay away from that creepy little white girl?"

Eddie laughed again. "Yeah, something like that." Though he tried to put on a brave face, he finally sighed deeply. "A grown-ass man shouldn't be crying like this."

"What's wrong?" asked Penny.

"I just saw her. She didn't remember me."

Penny's shoulders twitched. "She forgot who you were?"

"Yeah," he replied. "She didn't know I was her son."

"Can I ask you something?" said Penny. "When was the last time she remembered you?"

Eddie tilted his head as he thought about it. "I was here a month ago. We had lunch."

"And she knew you then?" asked Penny.

"My mother was as sharp as the day she got her law degree. First black woman in the state," he replied.

Penny could feel her whole body tense up. She knew something wasn't right here. How could both Conrad and Rose forget the people in their lives so suddenly?

"It'll be OK," said Penny, but she started toward the home before he could respond.

It was dinnertime, and Penny knew where everyone would be. She walked into the dining hall and looked around. Rose wasn't there. *Strange*, thought Penny. Rose never missed a meal; she loved to gossip with the others. Penny exited the hall and quickly made her way to Rose's room. She didn't bother knocking this time but just opened it and entered.

Rose was there, sitting in her wheelchair by the window.

"Mrs. Emmery?"

She didn't respond. Penny walked up to her, and the woman whipped around, practically lunging at her from her chair. Her eyes were wild, her face gaunt, and her jaw crooked. She was frothing at the mouth. Penny recoiled and stepped away from her.

"Essie was right," Rose said in a low growl.

Penny was shaken, but she slowly built up her courage to approach. "Right about what?"

Rose put her hand to her head. "It hurts."

"Please, tell me what she said," Penny begged.

Rose took a deep breath, then looked into Penny's eyes. "Your grandma, she warned me it was coming. But I didn't listen. Now it's too late. Now they're all gone."

Rose closed her eyes. Her breathing became raspy and irregular. Penny slowly backed out of the room, trying to digest what she had just heard. All she knew was that she had to tell someone.

Joel straightened the papers on his desk. He didn't know why he did this. He wasn't particularly tidy in his apartment and wouldn't be surprised to find a slice of week-old pizza behind the couch if he looked. But for some strange reason, before he made an audio log, he felt he had to tidy up his desk. It helped him focus.

Now that everything was at a right angle on the desk, he opened his laptop and entered his password. The directory he navigated to had a separate encryption for which he needed to infrared-scan his face. He probably didn't need the second layer of security, but it made him feel better knowing that if someone took his hard drive, they still wouldn't be able to access the files in that directory.

Joel pressed the record button on the dictation software, cleared his throat, and then spoke as clearly as possible so the computer mic would pick him up:

"Doctor Joel Mattis, June seventeenth. I'm certain now; it's feeding on the memories of the people in this place. As far as I can tell, it started about ten months ago—well, at least that was the first case here. I've been trying to keep things quiet ever since. Conrad was the latest. About one week ago, he forgot he had children. There was no sign of Alzheimer's or dementia in him— his scans were perfectly clear. But still, he forgot they even existed. He killed himself last week, which means it probably finished with him. This is the first time I've been in a place while it's feeding. I'm so excited—"

But Joel cut himself off, paused the recorder. "Be professional, you idiot," he said under his breath.

Joel had dedicated the last five years of his life to this research, and his audio-logs were his legacy. He knew he needed to come across as professional; otherwise, people would think he was a crackpot. But then he felt a sudden onslaught of doubt. How could they not think he was insane? What man throws away a promising career in neuroscience to chase a monster?

Joel put his hands to the side of his head. "Get it right!" he said to himself. He had been out of sorts for the last few months, felt a bit frazzled. Maybe it was the stress of being the on-site physician for a large retirement home, or the fact that he was so close to a breakthrough in finding out what this thing was. Nowadays, he needed to refocus himself often. He took a deep breath and a moment later, started recording again.

"It's clear to me now that this creature can feed on memories. It can sustain itself with the energy found in people's minds. Once the patient has been harvested, they either die in their sleep, are left empty shells and kill themselves, like Conrad, or suffer neurological trauma like Essie Calder did—"

But Penny's startled voice cut him off. "Something ate my Grammy's memories?"

Joel turned around and was shocked to see Penny standing there. She had come in the back way like she had done previously.

"What the hell are you doing here?" he barked, quite embarrassed to have been snuck up on in his own office.

"I heard what you said," she said, looking stunned.

"You don't know what you heard, Penny. You need to get out of here."

But she charged him, slamming his chair back against the desk. Joel was surprised by the ferocity of her attack. "You need to tell me everything, or I swear I'll go to the administrator and tell him you've gone nuts," she said.

"No one will believe the sleep-deprived girl who lives with her comatose grandmother," he responded calmly.

Penny pulled out her cell phone. She pressed play on the audio recorder app. A scratchy but still understandable recording played. *"Doctor Joel Mattis, June seventeenth. I'm certain now; it's feeding on the memories…"* Penny stopped the playback.

Penny sat across from Joel. She could feel her heart flutter in her chest. Over the last half-hour, Joel had told her everything, and she wished he hadn't. This was the fourth retirement home Joel had worked at. He hid his medical credentials at first to keep a low profile, working as an orderly as he gathered what information he could. When the well went dry, he heard a rumour of a woman who forgot her whole family overnight at another home.

At that retirement residence, he became an assistant to the on-call doctor; and so it went until he became the ranking physician here. He had been tracking this thing across the country. He had been too late at the previous places, and he could only gather evidence on what had happened after the fact. But here he was amid a harvest.

Penny hated the word *harvest* to describe what was going on. As if human memories were food that could be consumed. It horrified her. But there was one thing Joel hadn't told her yet. "How did it start?" she asked.

Joel lowered his head, pausing before he answered. "My mother. She had early-onset dementia. It's the reason I went into medicine, into neurology specifically, so that I could find a cure for her."

Joel reached into his lab coat pocket. He pulled out a folded piece of paper. It was dog-eared and well-worn, as though it had been there for years. He handed it to her. Penny opened the paper and saw several crudely drawn symbols. "What is this?" she asked.

"My mother drew this just before she died. They're ancient runes—a language. I had an anthropologist friend tell me they were from an ancient central-African tribe. Hundreds of thousands of years old—from the time humanity evolved into our current form. The descendants of the tribes in that area still pass down stories of a creature that would 'eat the past.'"

A chill ran down Penny's spine as she realized his mother had been a victim. She folded the paper as quickly as she could and handed it back to Joel. "This is crazy."

"I need more information," he said. "I need to track it as it eats."

Penny felt sudden anger as she realized what he had just said. "You knew about this, this *thing*, but didn't do anything?" she said accusingly. "You let these people be harvested when you could've tried to stop it!"

"Listen, Penny, I don't think you understand—"

"You fucking asshole," Penny said. She got up to leave, but not before threatening Joel. "The residents are gonna know about this. I'm going to tell them!"

"If you stay out of my way, I can cure your grandmother."

That stopped Penny in her tracks. She turned to look back at Joel, her heart racing at the possibility. "You can do that?"

"Your grandmother suffered no brain damage. I faked the test results to show she had a common stroke. But her coma is psychological in nature. If I find out how this thing works, I can pull her out of it."

Penny stood there in stunned silence, her mind racing with the morality of his offer. Would she risk the lives of other residents for the chance that Grammy could be cured? But then she rationalized it. Would anyone even believe her if she told them what she knew? She'd probably get him fired, and herself kicked out for causing a stir.

"I have to keep my mouth shut?" she asked.

Joel nodded. Penny slumped down in the chair, realizing she had been bought and saddened at how easy it had been.

Joel's phone intercom chirped, "Dr. Mattis, code blue. Rose Emmery. Code blue."

Two attendants loaded a gurney with Rose's body into the funeral home wagon parked out front. There was a small crowd—friends of Rose and a few staff. The onlookers, many with raw eyes, slowly started to disperse. One by one, they walked away, leaving only Penny and Joel standing out front.

The two exchanged a look, and Joel shrugged. "It happens like this sometimes."

Penny was not impressed with his casual attitude; this was a woman's life, after all. Penny turned to head back inside when she saw her: a black woman, naked, standing a dozen yards away. No one else seemed to have noticed her, so Penny just shook her head, thinking it was another hallucination. That is until she saw the familiar runes that adorned her body.

"Doc," said Penny. "Do you see that woman over there?"

"What woman?"

Penny pointed him over to the spot.

"There's no one there, Penny," he replied.

"Then why do I see the runes you showed me? They're all over her body."

Joel looked at Penny with a stunned expression. He turned to look back at the location to which Penny had pointed. "I don't see anything. Are you sure?"

"She looks old," said Penny. "I mean, not age. She looks like she's from … another time."

"Penny, you sure this isn't from your illness?" he asked.

Penny was caught off guard. She had never talked to him about her insomnia.

He saw the expression on her face and continued. "I'm pretty observant…" he said. "You don't sleep, and hallucinations are common with your condition."

Penny nodded; what he was saying seemed reasonable.

"I showed you the runes," he continued. "And now you see them on some invisible woman?"

Penny thought on this for a moment, but then it struck her. "When did it all start here, Doc?"

"Less than a year ago."

"Be specific."

"It was with Mr. Hernandez. Last August, the fifteenth or sixteenth, I think," Joel said.

Penny did the math in her head. Ten months. Almost exactly to the day that her insomnia started. It wasn't hard for Penny to connect the dots; this woman was the cause of her problem. Then a strange feeling hit Penny, one she hadn't experienced in a long time—hope.

"It started at exactly the same time I couldn't sleep anymore," she said to Joel.

His eyes widened with surprise, then he nodded his head, like it all made sense. Joel looked over to where Penny had said the woman was.

"She still there?" he asked.

Penny glanced over, then nodded. "Looks like you need me to catch her, Doc," Penny said.

"I guess I do," he replied.

Remora watched the two of them, the man and the young girl. The male she recognized immediately. He was at the last hunting ground before she had finished the stock there. *Why was he now here?* she wondered. He could certainly not have followed her here. But then again, Remora knew that humans were clever, and they often surprised her.

More troubling, however, was the girl. Remora was certain the girl could see her. In all the hundreds of thousands of years of her existence, no one had ever seen Remora in the world where memories were made. Why this girl? Why now? Though it did concern Remora, it also felt strangely comforting to her. If someone could see her, then that meant she was changing.

But bitterness once again built up in Remora's gut. Her mind drifted back to the ancient times. That stupid, jealous girl didn't know what it meant when she drowned her sister. She was the first to kill without need, the first to kill because of desire or hate. And then Remora became because of her. And then Remora had to feed.

Remora looked past the man and girl to the building that she had been stalking. It was a sensible choice for her to feed in places like this. The old, they had lived the longest, had the most to harvest. Sometimes she took the good memories, leaving only the bad to punish them. Sometimes she took the ones they wanted to forget so that they felt gratitude and helped her find others to harvest.

But as Remora looked back at the young girl, she was certain another change was coming to this cursed species. When the sister had drowned Rain, humans became aware, for the first time, mindful that they existed in this world. Now another change was coming. They would soon be cursed with a connection that none of them would want.

Remora felt a great energy building inside her. She would bring their species to this era, and the world would never be the same. Remora just needed to feed so she could complete herself. To do that, she needed to stop the only threat that existed to her. *This child must die*, she thought.

TO BE CONTINUED in Volume 2

CHAPTER 6

THE BLUE PLANET

PART 1

There are thousands of them—tiny specks of light against the black expanse of space. Some are stars, others not. One pinpoint glows red, brighter than all its surroundings. A planet. We fly toward it, and an arid red surface becomes visible. Massive channels crisscross the terrain, scars on a bleak and inhospitable landscape of mountain and valley. The edge of the atmosphere strikes us, and we are pulled around this planet, view a sparse, ice-covered pole before being flung back into the inky void of space.

We are dragged by a great force now, a massive orange-yellow inferno that is a star. We hurtle toward it, feel the heat sear us. Our speed increases, and we round its bubbling surface, pass through a flare, and are flung into the darkness of space once again. The distant stars that pass by are no longer spots but now streaks of light that guide us on our journey.

In the distance, another point of light comes into view. It shines blue, looks pristine and beautiful, a shimmering orb in the vastness of space. But as we draw close, dark hues appear and stain the atmosphere, obscuring the landmasses and oceans below. We plunge into this planet through polluted and dust-filled skies.

Hurtling out of control, scars of an unknown civilization rush toward us in a terrifying blur. A desperate attempt to pull away fails, and we tumble, impact the surface, and are obliterated.

Peter Cole's eyes opened suddenly, and he gasped like a drowning man desperate for air. After a moment, he realized it had only been the nightmare at its visceral best. He could feel the sweat-stained pillow below his head, and he put a hand over his face and wiped the moisture from his eyes.

"Again," Peter said to himself in a raspy voice.

He tried desperately to hold on to the details of this recurring dream. Still, it faded quickly, leaving only a sickening feeling that whatever awaited him in the waking world was probably far worse.

As an alarm tone rang, Peter dropped his feet over the edge of the bed and sat up. He looked over at himself in the wall mirror, stuck out his tongue, and saw the white coating. He stood, was wobbly at first, then remembered there were consequences to lager. As Peter exited the darkened bedroom, he slammed his foot into a coffee table and grunted, "Fuck."

The light switch he flicked illuminated the mobile home where he had lived these last two years. He was slightly embarrassed as he looked around the place. A tireless and efficient worker when he was on the job, his domestic skills were lacking. There was a sink full of dirty dishes in the kitchen, empty pizza boxes and beer cans piled in the living room. He knew that a cluttered environment was not conducive to clear thinking, yet somehow, he just couldn't motivate himself to tidy up.

Passing through the living room, he was careful to step around the circuit boards and computer components he had laid out the night before. He noticed, then quickly unplugged, a still-smoking soldering iron. *Careless*, thought Peter. He could've burned the whole place to the ground. He had to fight off the disturbing thought that at least it would've been an easier way out.

Peter headed into the bathroom, one filled with custom-made shelves full of engineering and mathematics books. For that matter, every inch of space in the home had been optimized to store technical materials and electronics. There was a lone toothbrush in a cup, which he picked up. But first, he looked at himself in the mirror, rubbed his beard, and wondered if he could get away without a shave. No one would notice the little bit of stubble, he thought, especially with the bags under his eyes. His high-school guidance counsellor would have said Peter was intelligent and thoughtful, though if pressed, would also have admitted that a dark cloud always seemed to follow Peter around. He began to brush his teeth.

Peter emerged dressed in a white collared shirt and a pair of slacks. He locked the door to his trailer, one of dozens of other well-maintained mobile homes in this row. The park was part of a new way of thinking for many, downsizing. People had pride in where they lived, especially in this community, where a now-outlawed solar grid fed power, and evaporators provided water to the homes.

Moisture was not a problem in this part of the country. It was barely seven in the morning, and the relative humidity was already close to eighty-five percent. It had to do with the ever-present particulate haze in the air. The sun just couldn't cut through and burn off the damp. However, Peter and most other Floridians considered themselves lucky. There were parts of the United States where the air pollution caused droughts that prevented plants from growing at all.

Peter headed to his pickup truck. It had seen better days, with rust spots blending almost seamlessly into the burnt orange paint. He refused to let the truck go, as the ownership title was fully electric. The state government had outlawed the sale of electric vehicles to prop up the petroleum conglomerates, but people who had bought them before the ban could still use them. There was quite the aftermarket industry in keeping them going, but Peter had the technical skills to maintain his own.

Peter got behind the wheel, coffee in one hand, a necktie in the other. Rolling down the window, he heard the cicadas chirp. Insects were one of the few species that seemed to thrive nowadays. Even a Floridian entomologist would be hard-pressed to tell which of the nineteen varieties these cicadas happen to be. He put the truck in drive, and it glided off silently, out of the park and onto a nearby on-ramp.

Peter looked out toward the horizon as he drove. I-95 toward Titusville had changed a lot in the last ten years. In the distance, oil rigs sprouted from what was once the pristine green of the coastal Everglades. Massive pipelines shadowed the roads. Not a drop of black gold was to be overlooked these days. As an engineer, Peter was fascinated by the improvements in drilling technology that allowed even the deepest and most decentralized pockets of hydrocarbons to be harvested. But as someone concerned with

THE BLUE PLANET, PART 1

the rapid decline of the world's environment, he was also sickened by it.

Peter held his knee against the wheel while he knotted his tie. He turned his head to see a modern SUV cruise up beside him. The driver had a newspaper across his lap, with his auto-drive doing the work for him. The driver did, however, look concerned when he saw Peter steering the way he was. The man shook his head and mouthed the word *overtake* to his car, which dutifully obeyed. Peter chuckled to himself; he too would rather trust a modern AI to that of his own truck, which cruised along with only a million years of evolution to guide it.

After pulling off at an exit, Peter approached a property with an immaculately manicured lawn but surrounded by prison-like metal gates with barbed-wire tops. The gates automatically opened, and he drove onto the grounds, past whirling sprinklers which kept the lawn lush. There was a digital billboard, which flashed the words "Parents' Day" as he passed. A moment later, Peter pulled his truck into a parking spot amongst other shiny modern vehicles. As he got out, he heard a honk and had to jump back as a red convertible dashed into the spot next to his. Out from the car stepped Molly, fifteen years his junior and a rising star at the academy.

She noticed his startled expression. "Sorry, Peter, didn't see you."

"It's all right, Molly," he replied.

"I know what you're thinking," she continued. "DWA."

He shook his head; he didn't know what that meant. A mischievous smile crossed her lips. "Driving while Asian."

Peter chuckled. But then he suddenly felt a rush of blood to his cheeks and was concerned about how his laugh would be construed. He tried to backtrack. "No, I … I would never think that—"

Molly burst out laughing, then moved to straighten his tie. "Stay frosty, Peter. If little ol' me can throw you off, those parents are gonna eat you alive."

Peter knew she meant well. He smiled and nodded. "I'll do my best."

She finished with his tie, then patted down the creases on his shirt. "You'll need better than that," she said. Peter shrugged; he didn't understand. Molly headed off toward the compound with a grin. "I saw the Lowens' limo enter the grounds."

That was the last thing Peter wanted to hear. They had never come to one of these events before, but he had an inkling why they were coming now. He turned toward the main hall—a southern high school made to look Ivy League with tropical plants—and a knot grew in his stomach.

The lecture hall was well-appointed, with computers embedded in the desks and video touch screens on the walls. Peter stood at the lectern and looked at the two parents in the room, Richard and Sandra Lowen. They were sitting at the surprisingly comfortable student desks, with padded seats and armrests that nested neatly into ergonomically designed workspaces. No expense spared here.

Peter knew they were one of the wealthiest families in the state. He tried to recall what they did but could only remember that they had made a fortune selling "meals ready to eat" to the Chinese when their civil war started. The look on both their faces was of tempered tolerance. The same could not be said of their sixteen-year-old son, Jimmy, who stared blankly at the holographic display on his smart phone. An AI video had captured his attention—artificially generated entertainment was all the rage now.

"This is your final decision?" Sandra asked, a frown creasing the corners of her mouth.

"I'm sorry, but it is," replied Peter.

"I don't think you realize how important this is," she continued. "He's not getting a C on his transcript. That's an unacceptable blemish."

"I understand your concern, Mrs. Lowen, but—"

"He's going to Princeton, Mr. Cole," she said, cutting him off. "Where my husband and I, and all the Lowens, have been educated."

Sandra looked over at Richard, who nodded proudly. Peter measured his response as carefully as he could. "The term assignment accounts for fifty percent of his final mark. Unfortunately, James put very little effort into his, whereas other students spent hundreds of hours on theirs."

"What does Mars have to do with science anyway?" asked Richard accusingly.

Peter looked at the man, not quite sure if he was joking. He was never good at reading facial cues. Though nowhere near the entrance threshold of the autism scale, Peter had been known to miss more than a few winks or subtle nods.

"We don't mean to belittle your expertise, Mr. Cole," interjected Sandra. "But frankly, if this is some attempt to regain past glory, I can understand your motivations but not accept them."

Peter was taken aback by that accusation. He opened his mouth to respond but couldn't.

"We want you to assign another topic to our son," added Richard. "Something, I assure you, he will invest the time and energy to research, given that it's … something relevant."

Peter's eyes narrowed. "Relevant?" That got Jimmy's attention, and a sly grin crossed the boy's lips as he continued to watch his hologram.

"Mars has roughly the same landmass as the Earth," said Peter. "It has similar atmospheric chemistry and large sustained polar ice caps made of water ice."

Richard and Sandra exchanged a look, but Peter didn't let them interrupt this time. "The geological process of our two planets are surprisingly similar. There are river basins, volcanoes, canyons, evidence of flowing water and water ice. There's a tilt in its axis, giving Mars seasonal variability and indication of changes in climate."

"That's all good and fine—" said Sandra.

But Peter continued breathlessly. "At some point, there was a runaway greenhouse effect in the atmosphere, and the CO_2 content cascaded, probably snuffing out any life that clung to its surface. So, in a very real and definable way, studying Mars is like seeing the future. A future we'll have if we continue destroying our planet."

There was an awkward silence. Sandra stood up, followed by Richard, who cleared his throat, so Jimmy knew it was time to go.

"A very passionate dissertation, Mr. Cole," said Sandra. "But we'll be discussing this with Dean Mitchel, as I'm sure you'll understand." She turned and walked off. Jimmy glanced at Peter, shrugged apologetically, and then continued after his mother—his eyes back on his device.

Richard walked up to Peter and lowered his voice. "They say you're a good teacher, and you were a gifted scientist, which means you deal in facts. And the fact is, sometimes you eat the bear, and sometimes the bear eats you. And if I'm not clear enough, Mr. Cole—my wife's the bear." Mr. Lowen turned and left, leaving Peter grasping the edges of the lectern.

Peter hated the texture of the floor. It was a mixture of spilled beer and peanut shells, which would both crunch under and then cling to his shoes. What he did enjoy, however, was the neon light fixture that hung behind the bar: a cowboy lassoing a buxom cowgirl. Though he thought the subject matter was amusing in a kitschy kind of way, it was the neon that interested him.

He knew the science, how the glass was sealed with neon atoms inside it. There were electrodes at either end of the tube, one positive and one negative. When the tube was exposed to a high enough voltage, positive particles would go to the negative terminal, and vice versa. Along the way, they would collide and make small explosions of energy that the neon atoms would absorb, then release to maintain their neutral state. These photons of energy would give the lights their glow. That was the physics, but Peter could appreciate the beauty as well—he would stare at it for hours.

What he was not as big a fan of was the holographic jukebox in the corner, which now played a twangy Patsy Cline tune to a few couples slow-dancing on the scratchy floor. It wasn't the song that bothered him but rather the holographic display unit in the jukebox that projected a life-sized, 3D Patsy. In the last five years, there had been an explosion of gimmicky holographic technology that had reached the consumer level. It was cheap, generally an eyesore, and everywhere.

As Peter took a swig of his beer, CNN played silently on the massive flat-screen TV beside the neon light fixture. A report began with an image of a rocket on a launchpad, one that was familiar to Peter. "Bill, turn it up," Peter said to the bartender.

Bill looked over at the screen and shook his head. "Naw, man. Not tonight."

"I'm a paying customer," replied Peter, then motioned to the empty stools on either side of him. "One you can use right now."

Bill paused, then reluctantly went to the television and turned up the volume. The newscaster's voice filtered in over the country song. *"NASA continued its dismantling of civilian operations by transferring all planetary research units to Military Space Core control. This shutters the last civilian-run department at the agency…"*

Peter gulped down what was left in his bottle, then slammed it down on the counter. Bill gave him a stern look, and Peter raised his hand apologetically. The image on the screen changed to that of an aircraft carrier for the next report: *"In international news, Russian President Popov criticized the United States for its continued military operations in Iran. The State Department subsequently condemned the deployment of two Russian aircraft carriers to the South China Sea, as tensions continue to rise over the Russian occupation of key Chinese territories ..."*

Peter lowered his head in disappointment. Though the geopolitical news concerned him, it was the NASA story that cut deep. "My tab still good?" asked Peter.

Bill turned off the television, then took the empty beer bottle away from Peter. "Go drink at home," replied Bill. "I don't need your business that much."

Peter nodded. Bill was right to ask him to leave, as his mood would only continue to ferment with more alcohol.

Captain Rick Landry stood beside the passenger door of his Humvee in the early-morning haze. This one had recently been painted blue, though he noticed a fair bit of desert yellow bleeding around the seams. The door insignia had the original NASA meatball, but it was now positioned over a sword-and-shield emblem. Rick liked the new symbol; it honoured the past, which was something he thought important. It also made sure to point to the future and the new mandate of NASA.

He had been part of the Military Space Core for the last ten years. His own unit was once part of the disastrous United States Space Force, which had been hastily put together with little thought to the purpose. Luckily, wiser heads prevailed in the subsequent years, and the MSC was commissioned with a clear mandate to protect America's space interests. The recent merger with NASA was only the next logical step in a unified mission.

Rick turned and watched as Lieutenant Rahim Richardson gave mission instructions to two marines, one man and one woman, by the Humvee parked behind theirs. Rick had worked with Rahim for many years, and there was no other man he enjoyed working with more. What he wasn't happy about was that Rahim could beat him in a forty-yard dash. Rick always joked that Rahim had an unfair advantage, as his father was once

THE BLUE PLANET, PART 1

a linebacker for the Bears. Rick rarely made excuses, but this one was too good not to use.

Rahim finished giving orders to the marines, then walked over to the driver's side of their Humvee, nodding to Rick. They both entered their vehicle and drove off, with the other Humvee close behind. A massive hangar building loomed in their mirrors as they drove away.

"They clear on the mission?" Rick asked.

"Clear as mud, Captain," Rahim replied.

Rick offered him a puzzled look, and Rahim grinned. "I don't even know what it is."

"Our mission," elaborated Rick, "is not to spook him. Or the general will have both our asses."

"Copy that," said Rahim, then continued, "You know anything about this guy?"

"Enough," replied Rick.

Their Humvee arrived at the base's main gate, passing a sign that read Kennedy Space Center. Rick looked out toward the street and noticed a crowd of people outside the centre. "Shit," he said, then pointed it out to Rahim. On the other side of the gate were a few dozen protestors. Many held signs, some of which read, No Wars in Space!

Their Humvee was pelted with eggs and tomatoes as it exited the armed checkpoint. Rahim had to swerve to avoid hitting a protestor who jumped in front of the vehicle. "Idiots," grumbled Rahim under his breath.

Rick looked back to make sure the other Humvee made it through, which it did. Rick was neither surprised nor concerned with what had just happened. It was now a regular occurrence. The two vehicles entered the highway, and traffic parted for them. The vehicle AI laws meant that autonomous vehicles were programmed to automatically allow military, police, and rescue services. The driver didn't have a choice anymore.

Rick wasn't a fan of this level of automation. He preferred human control, even if it meant imperfect execution. Though proficient with complex computer systems, he was a country boy at heart and didn't quite connect to the omnipresent artificial networks until he joined the forces. Rick did like the fact that they made great time on the highway even though it was the early-morning rush hour. He'd take any advantage given to him.

Rick checked the GPS tracking on his cell phone as they travelled and saw that they were close. He told Rahim to take the next exit, and they steered off the main road and entered the familiar mobile home park. Rahim looked around as he drove down the paved private road. "Not what I was expecting."

"Yeah," replied Rick. "These new parks are high-end now, have their own community centres and gyms."

"I wonder how much they cost," questioned Rahim with genuine interest.

Rick looked over at him, surprised. He was worried Rahim was thinking of leaving the force.

Rahim saw his expression. "I'm not retiring, just curious."

"None of my business," Rick said unconvincingly. He didn't like it when his real emotions slipped out accidentally, even with someone he considered a friend.

Rahim grinned at him. He didn't press.

Rick motioned to Peter's unit at the end of the road, and they parked and got out. The second Humvee arrived moments later and blocked in Peter's truck. Rick looked over at the two marines that had joined them. Smith and Philips were their names. They were new to his unit but had served together and spent time on Moon Base Alpha, so he knew they were good in low-gravity environments. He motioned to them silently, and they took up positions on either side of the mobile home, drawing their pistols.

Rahim was first to the door and was about to knock when he saw it was ajar. He pushed it open. The lights were on inside, but they both entered cautiously. Rahim put his hand on his sidearm,

THE BLUE PLANET, PART 1

but Rick shook his head. They continued into the living room, paying special attention to the electronics laid out on the floor.

"A bomb?" asked Rahim.

Rick shook his head; he recognized some of the components. "These are control systems, probably for a solar panel."

They continued and heard a voice coming from the bedroom. The room was dark. A news report played from a radio sitting on the dresser: *"The levees were finally overwhelmed, flooding the abandoned downtown core of New Orleans. The administration continues to deny any link to the melting of the polar—"*

Rick turned off the radio and then hit something with his foot, which skittered away. Rahim turned on the light, and they both saw an empty whisky bottle lying on the floor. They heard a moan, and there was Peter, half-undressed, lying face-down on the bed. He tried to roll over but was obviously still somewhat drunk.

Rick could feel the blood rush to his cheeks as he saw the state Peter was in. "Let's sober him up," he said to Rahim. They grabbed Peter by his arms, hauled him to his feet, and then dragged his dead weight out of the bedroom. In the bathroom, they unceremoniously dropped him into the shower. He was just starting to stir, mumbling to himself in confusion. Rahim turned on the water, ice-cold. Peter was shocked; he twitched and coughed at the rude awakening. He struggled, but both men held him down.

"What the fuck," shouted Peter, now fully awake.

Rick and Rahim held Peter in the stream until he started shivering. Rahim turned off the water, and Peter slumped against the back of the shower. Rick grabbed a towel and dropped it on him, and then they left him in the bathroom.

Peter sat on his couch, hands still tingling as he held a steaming cup of coffee. He had done cold-water emergency training and understood the effects of hypothermia, but he knew he wasn't in the shower long enough to drop his core temperature. *Curious,* thought Peter.

"This is impressive," said Rick from across the room.

Peter looked over at him. Rick stood in the living room, examining a wall covered in photographs, diplomas, and commendations. "Masters in Aerospace from MIT, a doctorate from USC, Exceptional Bravery Medal ..." read Rick. His gaze then landed on a blown-up photograph of Peter in a flight suit in front of a blue-and-white NASA training jet. "Where did you do your flight training? Kennedy or Canaveral?"

Peter didn't respond; he just took a sip of his coffee.

"Maybe we should start off at the beginning, Captain," Rahim said from the kitchen, having just topped off his own cup.

Rick nodded. "You're right." He then turned to Peter. "Let me introduce us. I'm Captain Rick Landry, and this is Lieutenant Rahim Richardson. We're Military Space Core—"

"I know who you are," interrupted Peter. "Why the fuck are you in my home?"

Rick paused and didn't immediately respond. Peter did his best to track both marines' expressions, though he couldn't tell if they were hiding hostility or not. What he did notice, however, was that Rick often looked to Rahim before he spoke.

"All right," said Rick. "The Russians are launching a mission to Mars in four months. The complement is a half-dozen of their top scientists, as well as a squad of Spetsnaz. The best of the best."

Rick let that bombshell hang in the air for a moment.

Peter did his best to hide his emotions. A thousand questions churned in his mind, all piling up and about to spill out. The only thing keeping him steady was that he could imagine Rick's displeasure at waiting for his poker face to break.

Luckily for both, Rahim let them off the hook. "Peter, we're here because we need you back on the team."

Peter was sure now. Rahim was the peacemaker and could probably be reasoned with. He put that piece of information away for the moment; he wasn't quite ready to play nice. "I'm not interested," said Peter.

"You're teaching now, right? At a prep school," said Rick.

Peter couldn't sense any sarcasm or condescension. But then again, he rarely could. He nodded in reply. Rick didn't look at Rahim this time; he stood above Peter. "All those trust-fund kids. Can't imagine it's much of a challenge."

"The youth are our future," Peter replied dryly.

"But still, all that training going to waste. You're not as smart as they said you were."

Peter put his cup down, not impressed. "It's time for you guys to go—"

"I thought you'd be grateful for a chance to redeem yourself," added Rick. "To make amends for what you did."

Peter rarely got into fights at school. He was never the first to throw a punch. But now he could feel his blood pressure spike, and he stood up. He knew his odds against two trained soldiers, but he had boxed in college; he knew enough, so at least one of them would leave with a bloody nose. "I did nothing wrong," said Peter. "And I sure as hell don't owe you people anything."

Rahim stepped in between them. "Hey, let's take it easy—"

But Peter pushed forward so that he was nose-to-nose with Rick. "Get the fuck out of my house."

"You get to go up," Rick said coolly.

Peter felt a tingle start at the top of his head and work its way down his neck, then to the rest of his extremities. If it had been any other day, he would've thought it was a stroke. But right now, it was just pure shock. "What did you say?"

Rahim nodded reassuringly to Peter. "We land four weeks after the Russians. You get to go to Mars."

Peter backed away from Rick. His mind was racing with questions. Was it some elaborate joke to make him look like a fool? But then Peter realized he was doing a good job of that himself, standing there in his T-shirt and underwear. "I ... I need to get dressed," he said, then rushed off to the bedroom.

Peter picked up clothes from the ground and smelled a collared shirt he found. He cursed under his breath, wishing he had done laundry recently. He grabbed a golf shirt from his closet and some khaki slacks, then finished with a pair of deck shoes. *Shit*, he thought to himself. He looked like he was going antiquing. Peter grabbed his cell phone and wallet and headed back into the living room.

Rick and Rahim were gone. There was a terrifying split-second where Peter thought it was perhaps all a dream, but then he saw the two Humvees parked out front. He exhaled with relief and exited the trailer. Peter froze when he saw the two marines standing on either side of his door. By this point, they had their sidearms holstered.

"Four against one isn't a fair fight," Peter said dryly.

"Just protocol," replied Rick. "Dangerous times we live in."

Peter noticed the tomato and egg stains all over their vehicle. He knew exactly what it meant. "Yeah, imagine if those protestors had weaponized onions."

Rahim laughed out loud. It was genuine. Peter smiled at him, then got into the back of the Humvee.

The main hangar building at Kennedy Space Center was one Peter knew well. They called it the VAB—the Vehicle Assembly Building. It had been built in the 1960s and was designed to mount the pre-built space vehicles on the crawler that would transport them to the launch site. It was a massive building, over five hundred feet high and covering eight acres. Back in the day, it was home to the Saturn V and the space shuttle. In recent years, it became an ad-hoc factory to build spaceship components.

What wasn't familiar to Peter, however, was the military security that now patrolled it. The last time Peter had stepped inside was two years earlier. They had security then, too, but it

THE BLUE PLANET, PART 1

was subtle: white-shirted NASA guards who were more helpful than threatening. Now, as they approached the employee entrance, Peter was surprised to see scores of heavily armed marines in combat gear, patrolling.

Peter knew there would be changes when the military took over, but he had naively hoped those changes would only be skin-deep. If this was on the surface, he didn't want to know what lay beneath.

As they arrived at the new guard-post entrance to the VAB, Peter's heart quickened with anticipation. He had been the chief designer on the Mars exploration missions. His office was on the top floor of this hangar. From the balcony here, he could look down and see the landing craft being built. When Peter was fired, they had just started to lay the groundwork—to install the mounting brackets so that the hull could be secured. His mind raced with the possibilities of their progress as he was searched for entry.

Peter was certain that the mission purpose had changed since then. If he ignored any delays because of that, they might have completed the superstructure and mounted the engine pods in the last two years. Maybe, if they were really pushing it, the flight control surfaces would have been roughed out. Regardless, there was no way the timing Rick had enticed him with could have been true. Peter was damn good at his job, and he knew how long things took. They couldn't be aiming to launch in five months.

Which is why what happened next was so much of a shock to him. As Peter and the others entered the hangar, he saw before him a completed Mars landing craft. There were still dozens of technicians working on it, but he immediately knew that this spaceship, at least structurally, was nearly complete.

Peter stared at it in awe. The landing craft was a marvel of engineering and design. It looked like an enormous armoured beetle, with black heat shields covering its smooth top surface. Also visible were the hefty landing-gear struts tucked under its body, which could retract completely when in orbit. The craft could transport fifteen personnel, gear, and even a planetary exploration vehicle if necessary. Though he noticed a few design tweaks to the control surfaces, in every other way, it was his.

Rick saw his look. "The Artemis," he said.

"Is it operational?" asked Peter.

Rick didn't respond but only continued to the freight elevator. Peter turned to Rahim with the same question, but Rahim just smiled in his disarming way. They got into the caged freight elevator, and it started to go up.

Peter pressed his face against the wire mesh as it rose. He was filled with a mixture of anticipation and dread—anticipation to once again pick up his life's work and dread over who he knew was waiting for him.

The conference room was packed. Around the large oval table was a variety of military brass and civilian managers. Rick entered first and took a seat, then Rahim led Peter in and made the introductions. Peter knew all the civilians. One way or another, they had worked for or with him. The military personnel were mostly new, except for one face he wished he didn't know.

"Peter," said General Alan Zimmerman.

"Shit," Peter let slip.

"You were hoping that I was reassigned, weren't you?"

"Yeah, I was," Peter admitted.

The general grinned and shook his hand anyway, making sure to offer an overly firm grip. Rahim cleared his throat, then motioned to the last person for Peter to greet. "I think you know Dr. Melissa Ramirez, our administrator."

The general wasn't who Peter dreaded meeting. It was Melissa. They had been in a relationship, and he had loved her. When he left NASA, they ended it. There was a small part of Peter that wondered whether it was the trip to Mars that had brought him here or the chance to see her again. Regardless, he refused to let whatever baggage he was carrying to get in the way now. "Administrator," he said to her. "Congratulations."

"Well, I deserved it," she replied with no hint of arrogance.

Peter smiled. There was so much more he wanted to say. The squeak of a chair got his attention, and he took the seat that Rahim had pulled out for him.

General Zimmerman sat across the table from him. "Thank you for accepting our offer, Peter," he said.

"I haven't accepted anything, General."

Concerned faces around the table exchanged uncomfortable looks.

Even Peter could feel the tension in the room. Over the years, people had told him that one of his most undesirable traits was that he held a grudge. And right now, Peter was holding on as tight as he could.

"Right," said General Zimmerman, who then motioned to Melissa. At the podium, she activated a holographic display that projected from the middle of the table. The display showed the entirety of Mars. She zoomed in on a mountainous part of the western expanse.

"The Chryse Planitia," she said, and then faint infrared images of the Martian subsurface appeared, highlighting a section of undefined dark material inside a mountain range. "After your mission was scrubbed, a classified operation took its place."

This was not a surprise to Peter. There had been a half-dozen confirmed human landings on Mars in the last ten years. The first was by NASA, followed soon after by the Russian Space Agency. A new space race had erupted between the two countries, and Russia, now fat with the spoils of taking half of China, had been looking to regain the lead. When the NASA coup was announced, Peter assumed it was to weaponize NASA's assets and complicate the Russian plans on Mars.

"Our satellites found massive deposits of alloys under the surface of this mountain."

This was a surprise to Peter. He leaned into the table to get a better look. "Alloys? Not metals?"

"Alloys," she replied, and Peter knew what this meant. Metals could be natural; alloys were manufactured. He nodded for her to continue.

"The pathfinders," said Melissa, as the holographic image changed to show several robots around the mountain, "recorded unusual magnetic fields. What we didn't know was that the Russians found these two years before us on a previous expedition."

"Now they're sending another?" asked Peter.

Melissa paused. She looked over at the general, who nodded for her to continue. This was obviously highly classified information. "They've lost contact with their people on the surface. They're rushing a rescue mission. We need to get there a year earlier than we planned and find out what's gone wrong, what those alloys are. We've had to cut corners to make the launch window; we used independents to do some of the work …"

Peter's back muscles tightened as he now realized how the lander was completed this fast. He had no problem with the Boeings and Raytheons of the world involved in space programs, as they knew the proper protocols. But after many deaths and the failure of several private space entrepreneurs, level heads realized that NASA was best equipped to lead interplanetary space missions. Leave the puddle jumps to the private sector, but deep space was still NASA's domain.

Melissa continued. "You designed the Artemis, our systems and protocols. We need you back, back to—"

"Fix what we screwed up," interjected the general.

Melissa opened her mouth, but then just nodded in agreement.

Peter leaned back in his chair. All eyes were on him now. This had been a lot to take in, and he had many detailed technical questions to ask. But as he looked around at the military personnel, one concern had risen to the top. "Who are we sending?" asked Peter.

Melissa nodded, understanding where he was going. "There will be special forces, but their purpose will be to—"

"I don't care," interrupted Peter. "I won't be part of any mission to set up a military outpost."

"We've picked up weapons fire from the surface," said the general. "A lot of it."

Peter turned to look directly at him. There were many things about the man that made Peter's skin crawl, but he did appreciate how blunt he was. General Zimmerman never sugar-coated things or lied to Peter. He used truth as his weapon.

"It's a shit show up there," added the general.

Peter wrestled with how to respond. If something had gone horribly wrong on Mars, and the Russian crew was fighting amongst themselves, they'd need the marines for protection. Peter finally had a compromise he could stomach. "Do I have your word that we're not going there to start a fight."

The general nodded. "We won't start the fight. But if we must, we'll finish it."

Peter took a deep breath. Over the years, he had taken many classes on stress management. What he found always focused him was a deep breath, followed by a long exhale. Others might have found it strange for him to do it in mixed company, but it always seemed to work. As Peter exhaled, he nodded to the general.

Rick walked the R&D facility's long central corridor, labs and offices branching off on either side. The last few months had been a blur. Not only was he the general's liaison to the engineering and technical staff, but he would also be leading a highly trained group of space marines on Mars. What troubled Rick somewhat was that he had to grudgingly admit that Peter was very good at his job. He had reorganized the engineering teams into smaller problem-solving task forces, and there was a real momentum building on the technical front.

What Rick couldn't understand was the morale change. It had been terrible over the last few years, and Rick wasn't blind to the fact that a lot of lifelong NASA employees weren't happy with their new mandate under the MSC. They had lost some good people, but the bulk had stayed on. The grumbling that the engineers and technicians had been doing on the Artemis project disappeared almost overnight when Peter got back on the job.

Maybe it was the fact that Peter was one of them, that they trusted him, thought Rick. It surely couldn't have been his charming personality. Peter really rubbed him the wrong way. They had tried to start fresh at a team-building bowling night but got into a yelling match when Peter questioned the score his team had recorded. One of his bowlers had added wrong— and whether it had been intentional or not, Peter just wouldn't let it go. Rick couldn't understand why it was such a big deal.

Rick knew a friendship with Peter was impossible, especially since he and Melissa were in a romantic relationship. They had met when he was assigned to the space centre to set up the new command structure after the president had announced the reorganization. They hit it off and started dating. Luckily, this was before he was assigned to the Mars mission, as that would have been a conflict of interest. As it was, their relationship wasn't a secret, but they tried to keep it as low-key as possible while working. Knowing Melissa as he did now, Rick couldn't understand what she had seen in Peter.

Arriving at the last laboratory that branched off the hall, Rick placed his hand on the security scanner, and the door opened for him. The lab was full of computers and high-tech equipment. Dr. Carlson was bent over a microscope, examining a blood sample. Rick walked up to him, but Carlson just raised a palm, while keeping his eyes pinned to the reticle of the microscope. He was made to wait until Carlson was done.

Rick wouldn't have tolerated this behaviour from any other person—military or not—but Carlson was a unique case. He reported directly to the general. All Rick knew about Carlson was that he had known the general for over twenty years. Rick wasn't even sure what Carlson's specialty was. He had medical, biological, and technical expertise, though the details weren't public. Rick got the impression that the less he knew about Dr. Carlson, the better.

"The physical," said Carlson, with his eyes still on the microscope.

"What?" replied Rick, but then he noticed a folder on the workbench. He picked it up and saw a comprehensive medical report.

"I'd look at the blood work-ups," continued Carlson.

Rick flipped the pages and landed on what Carlson was talking about. Rick had basic battle-site triage training, but he knew immediately what he was looking at. Carlson finally looked up at him from the microscope. "Interesting, wouldn't you agree?"

"I don't know if that's exactly the way I'd put it," replied Rick.

"Which is why you have me around, Captain," said Carlson, who then turned back to his microscope.

Rick stood there in silence, not exactly sure if their meeting was over or not. After a few more seconds, he was sure. Rick took the report and left.

Peter stared at the digital board, which stretched across the entire room. It was covered in schematics, plans of the interconnected systems of the Artemis. He looked tired and pale, his shoulders hunched from fatigue. Behind him sat a half-dozen engineers at tables covered in computers and data pads. Peter moved his digital cursor over the screen. "The line splits off here ..."

Engineer Ellie Yung, who Peter had worked with on the original power systems design, stood up and moved to the screen. She touched it with her hand and repositioned a block on the drawing. The data on the screen changed in real-time. "If we run the conduit through here," said Yung, "it'll draw power from life support."

Cirus Leed, a new member of the team, had his feet up on the table. He shook his head, disapprovingly. "That's the dumbest idea I've ever heard."

Yung looked over at him and raised her hands questioningly. Leed continued, "That junction can't handle the power."

Back and forth it went between the two of them, each trying to one-up the other with a fancy bit of technical reasoning.

Peter stood back and let them go at it. Over the years, he had learned that people need to have their ideas heard. That was one of the main reasons his subordinates liked working for him; they knew they had a voice. But now, his patience was wearing thin. Just as he was about to end the debate, a young military officer entered the room quietly in the back and took a seat. Peter stared at the officer as the others continued speaking over each other.

"Get it? Fizz, then boom," said Leed dramatically.

"It's rated at a thousand amps," replied Yung.

"For a static load. This isn't."

It was when the officer pulled out his data recorder that Peter finally reacted. "Who the hell are you?"

The room fell silent. Everyone turned to the officer, who was surprised by the attention. It took a moment for him to compose himself. "Uh, the political attaché, sir."

"And you're here to do what?" asked Peter.

"Observe," he responded.

Yung, who was familiar with the military procedures, looked over at Peter and nodded, as if to say, *it's OK*. Peter ignored her guidance, however, and turned back to the officer. "Do you have a degree in electrical engineering?" he asked.

"No," the officer said.

"Science, then?"

"No, sir," he replied.

"Then get the hell out of my meeting," demanded Peter.

The officer stared at him, stunned. Peter had no intention of backing down. The young man had no choice and slowly packed up his gear, then headed to the doorway, looking quite upset.

Melissa was there at the threshold, having seen it all transpire. As the officer passed her and disappeared into the hallway, she looked at the engineers with a sharp expression. People immediately straightened in their chairs, and even Leed dropped his feet from the table. She was the big dog, after all.

Melissa turned to Peter. "That's gonna cost you."

Peter agreed. He knew who was going to hear about this, but frankly, he just didn't care. He looked back at the screen and shook his head. "If it wasn't for the weight of all that military hardware …" Peter then changed the schematic. He stared at it for a moment, then realized he might be on to something.

Melissa sat at her kitchen table. There was a partially eaten meal on a plate in front of her, surrounded by dozens of technical documents. She couldn't remember the last time she hadn't worked over dinner. If there wasn't a report or study in front of her, she wouldn't know what to do with herself. It had always been like this for Melissa. She was an overachiever. NASA was full of them, and to be the best of the best was always her goal.

She had Carlson's report in hand and had lost her appetite. "This isn't good," she said. "Does Peter know?"

Rick entered the kitchen and took her dish. He shook his head no, then took the dish to the sink to wash it.

"I guess I'll tell him in the morning," Melissa added.

"The general said he'd handle it."

She put the report down. "That's not the protocol."

Rick grabbed a beer from the fridge and sat down across from her. "His order was very clear. Peter is not to know until he tells him."

Melissa was aware of many of her own personality traits. One of her least favourite, and one many overachievers had, was a healthy dose of paranoia. It was what kept her sharp. And now, Melissa felt a twinge in her gut—the type that told her something didn't feel right. "This could jeopardize the mission," she said.

"I've got my orders."

Melissa was about to say something but changed her mind. She had been with Rick for over a year now. She loved him, but she also knew he could be a stubborn son-of-a-bitch. He was so different from all the previous men in her life. Men like Peter. Tortured men. Rick was the most self-assured person she had ever met. His self-confidence and belief in the chain of command infuriated her at times, but it also centred her and gave her a foundation that was comforting.

Rick finally broke the silence. "Why didn't you tell me about Peter when we started seeing each other?"

She was taken aback for a moment, and then her defensive instinct kicked in. "Have you told me about all your girlfriends?"

"This is different."

"No, it's not."

Rick paused for a moment, then a grin slowly crept across his face. "No, I guess it's not."

She appreciated that Rick accepted indisputable facts when they were presented to him.

"He was a long time ago," Melissa said. "We were good for a while, then we weren't. Not much else to say, really."

"You didn't tell me about him until the general said he wanted him back on the mission. So, it wasn't relevant then, but it is now?"

"What are you getting at?"

"We have to put our lives in his hands up there," he said. "I've tried to connect with him, but we just don't get along. I need to know what type of man I'm dealing with, so if things go to shit, I know I can rely on him."

Melissa thought about this for a moment. She was impressed. He had never once shown her this level of doubt or concern about anything in all their time together. "The only thing I can say is that I have very good taste in men."

Rick looked surprised by her answer. He opened his mouth to respond, but then closed it. Melissa could see him weigh what to say next. Finally, she burst out laughing, and Rick's face went red. He got up from the table and fooled her by moving to plant a kiss, but pinching her backside instead. She yelped in surprise. It was going to leave a mark, but Melissa grinned; it was worth it.

The cockpit of the Artemis shook with a tooth-chattering intensity. Peter and Rick were in the flight seats, wearing pressure suits, fighting the controls. The rest of the crew—Rahim, Carson, Yung, and Leed—were strapped into the jump seats behind them, holding on to their armrests for a modicum of support.

Flames licked the exterior surface of the windscreen, and a sound akin to a burning blowtorch filled the cockpit. The green tactical displays were almost unreadable due to the vibrations shaking the Artemis.

An alarm sounded, and the stick trembled in Rick's hand. "It's sluggish," he said.

"Bring the nose down two degrees," Peter replied.

Rick worked the flight controls, and another alarm sounded, this time with a maddeningly calm computer voice: *"Hull temperature rising to threshold."*

Rick adjusted a toggle on the control panel. "Stabilizer's not responding. Do we initiate the abort procedure?"

Peter read the data screens. "This doesn't make sense. There must be a sensor error. Let me trace it ..."

The cockpit suddenly jolted, as though the Artemis was a stone skipping across water. The flames through the windows grew in intensity, and the burning sound became deafening. "We're hitting the atmosphere. I'm losing it," said Rick.

Peter worked his computer system. "Hold on, I'm almost there ..."

"Hull temperature critical," reported the ship.

Rick didn't wait any longer. He flicked a series of switches. "I'm pulling us out."

"No, don't!" yelled Peter, but the cockpit suddenly lurched, and then everything went completely black. A silent moment later, the lights turned back on.

Peter pulled off his helmet, and Rick saw the furious expression across his face. "Just once, I'd like to survive one of these," he said accusingly to Rick. Peter then looked over his shoulder at the rest of the flight crew. "You guys wanna live too, right?"

Before any of them could respond, there was a *whoosh* sound, and air rushed in as the hatch opened from outside. A technician appeared—this cockpit was part of a massive multi-axis simulator.

Carlson and the others quickly exited. Peter brought up the rear, leaving Rick stewing on his own. As Rick finally undid his belts, General Zimmerman stuck his head through the hatch.

"Permission to come aboard," requested the general.

"Always," replied Rick.

The general climbed in, which wasn't easy, as he was a barrel-chested man. He closed the hatch behind him and squeezed himself into Peter's seat. "Fifth drill in a row you've failed."

"I'm not used to having my actions questioned," replied Rick.

The general considered that for a moment, then pressed several buttons on the control panel. Rick knew what he was doing: cutting off all the internal microphones. Now they couldn't be heard from the control room. "We've lost contact with the surface," said the general. "It's doubtful we'll get it back."

"I understand," said Rick. "Has there been progress with the chemical data?"

"Some."

Rick wrestled with a decision, one directly tied to his commander's personality. Rick knew his history well. General Zimmerman had a stellar reputation. He had served in several combat zones as a non-com, then worked his way up the ranks until he was put in charge of a key sector in the Iranian invasion. That's when he got his first star. The next logical step for him was a senior role in the central command. He had different aspirations, though, and maneuvered his career to lead the MSC.

Rick remembered when he first reported to General Zimmerman's unit. The only question the general asked him was what flavour of ice cream he liked. Without a second thought, Rick replied that he didn't eat ice cream; it made people soft. The general promoted him the next day. Since then, they had worked closely together, and especially on this mission. But Rick wasn't blind to the general's weakness as a leader. The man rarely offered up his reasoning. He was in charge, so he could do that, but even Rick occasionally wondered if he knew the whole story at any given time.

Rick had finally made his choice, and he knew the general wouldn't be happy. "I'd like permission to brief the team on these developments."

General Zimmerman looked at Rick for a long silent moment, betraying no emotion. Rick was surprised that he took his time to answer; he normally wouldn't even consider such a request.

"No ... it's too risky," the general finally replied.

"They're going in blind, sir."

The general's next response was immediate. "Which is why you're there, son. Or have I overestimated your ability to complete this mission?"

"No, sir!" replied Rick, though internally, he was kicking himself for even bringing it up.

The general put a hand on Rick's shoulder to soften the blow. "If the Russians have assets in here, this all falls apart," he said. "The only tactical advantage we have is surprise. It's a risk, but a necessary one."

Rick had pushed as far as he could. "Understood, sir."

"Any other concerns?" asked the general.

"What's your decision about Peter?"

"An unexpected opportunity."

Rick nodded. The general squeezed his shoulder in a fatherly way, then got up. He headed to the hatch and opened it, but then stopped. "Besides," said the general with a dry smile, "Peter was right about the sensor error."

Melissa walked the VAB's upper-level hallway. Very few people worked up this high because it unnerved them. Peter's office was the only one on the whole floor, which was probably why he chose it. She arrived at his door, which was marked with the strange designation C-57D. She made a mental note to ask him about that one day. The door was open, and she walked in.

The office was empty, and Melissa thought she had missed him. She knew the next day would be a game-changer for Peter. She didn't know what the general's final decision would be, and that made her anxious—so much so that she had a desire to see him beforehand.

Melissa was about to leave when she remembered to check his favourite place. She walked through the office, passed through a storage room, and emerged to an open-air balcony that jutted out from the structure. From here, she could see the entirety of the VAB in one view.

Peter was there, leaning up against the railing and looking down. Melissa saw what he was observing: in the distance sat the Artemis, with technicians working on it through the night. A large, heavily armed surface vehicle, much like an armoured personnel carrier, was being loaded into the cargo bay. As Melissa slowly approached, she could see him shake his head with displeasure at the sight of it.

"I'm sure you won't mind when it's hauling your ass across the Martian desert," she said.

He turned with a twitch of surprise.

"Didn't mean to startle you," she said apologetically.

"You didn't."

"Liar," she said with a grin.

Peter stared at her silently for a moment. His unreadable expression and long pauses could unnerve some, but Melissa knew him, knew it was just his way. She also could read him, and she could tell there was something important he wanted to say to her.

"What can I do for you?" was all Peter asked.

Melissa was disappointed in that, but she continued. "General Zimmerman wants to see you in his office at nine sharp."

"About?"

"I don't know."

"And you came all the way up here to tell me that personally?"

"I wanted to stretch my legs," she said, then looked down over the railing at the vertigo-inducing view. "And to ask you why the hell you have your office here."

"The air's better," he said with a thin smile. Peter then looked over at the Artemis with an expression of wonder across his face.

She knew it was his baby, his life's work. "I sometimes forget how important this is to you."

"I've dreamt about Mars my whole life," he said. "Did you know that this year will be the closest Mars will be to Earth in sixty thousand years?"

"Of course, I did."

"Now who's the liar," he said. Peter then looked up as if he could see through the hangar roof above him. "Sometimes, I feel like it's pulling at me."

Melissa was no longer in love with Peter. She was sure of that. But she *had* loved him, and she still cared for him. There it was again, an unexpected desire to somehow comfort him. Which is why she felt she had to say more. "I'm sorry about how things ended, Peter. Between us. I don't know if I ever told you that."

"You didn't have to," he said. "My opinions weren't good for your career. I got that."

"If you had just taken the time to hear what they had to offer—"

"They turned NASA into a weapon, Melissa. Exploration was replaced by conquest. Science by fear. It's against everything you stood for."

"And how would you know that?" she said. "You never bothered to ask what I stood for."

He stared at her blankly for a moment, and then a grin slowly crept across his face. However, that's all she got from him—no *mea culpa*. Unlike Rick, Peter was not one to admit his errors. She was disappointed in him for that.

Melissa finally turned to leave. "And yes ... I had to compromise on certain things. Had to be practical and look at the bigger picture."

"You mean like why you're with Rick?" he blurted out tactlessly.

She stopped, and once again remembered why they hadn't worked as a couple. "You are such an asshole."

"I know," was all Peter said in reply.

Melissa shook her head and left.

A sprawling city is seen from thousands of feet above. Black plumes of smoke rise from factories that cover the concrete expanse of the structures below. Slowly, dark shadows appear from hundreds of objects that hover in the air.

The shadows move erratically over the surface, like angry wasps swarming for food. More and more of these shadows become visible. They coalesce and cover the cityscape in darkness.

Suddenly, there is a horrendous roar—the ground trembles and heaves. White light flashes across the horizon, and then a powerful, hot wind blows over the landscape, blasting the surface until all signs of civilization are swept away, leaving only dust.

Peter shuddered awake in bed. It had been another nightmare, but this one was much worse than the other. Though his breathing was raspy and his heart racing, he desperately tried to remember it. The details were disappearing quickly, leaving Peter suffering the emotional toll but not able to digest it.

He looked over at the clock, which read just after three in the morning. Peter sighed. He was exhausted but knew he couldn't fall asleep again. He got up to get dressed.

General Zimmerman's office was comfortable but not inviting. The chairs were plush but angular and lacking armrests. The walls and desks held pictures of his family, but they were interspersed with combat photos of some of the worst fighting the last few wars had seen. He welcomed visitors but didn't want them to stay long.

Peter sat across a massive oak desk from the general. He had Carlson's report in hand, and he was paralyzed by what he had just read. It took every fibre of his being to finally speak. "Diabetes?" said Peter.

"Type two, but modified, as there's no genetic history in your records. Dr. Carlson says it's in the early stages. He did, however, say you would have been experiencing some symptoms. Sleepless nights, tingling nerves, muscle pain … irritability." The general grinned. "Though that's hardly out of character for you."

Peter was still shell-shocked, and the general's words took seconds to register. The symptoms were indeed there. "I, uh, I guess that's it for me, then. I can't go."

"Not so fast," replied the general. "You've got this mission back on track. We're going to make our launch window."

The general got up and walked over to sit on the corner of the desk across from Peter. "I hate to admit it, but you're a resource I need on Mars as much as I need here."

"I don't understand—"

"See the doctor in the morning. We'll make this work," said the general.

Peter sat there, digesting for a long moment. He got up and began to head to the door.

"Though," added the general, "I'd appreciate if you'd let my political officers sit in on the occasional meeting."

"Yes, sir," was Peter's reply.

Peter stood in Carlson's lab, outfitted in his pressure suit less the helmet. Dr. Carlson adjusted a microcontroller mounted to his left shoulder with various instruments from his workbench. Melissa observed from the side. Carlson walked away to get something, and Melissa saw her chance.

"I couldn't say anything," she whispered to Peter.

"Another compromise?"

She opened her mouth to argue the point, but Carlson returned before she could. Peter gave her a self-satisfied grin that he had gotten the last word in.

Carlson held up a smartphone-sized digital device. He pressed a button on it, and there was a clicking sound. Peter winced in pain from his shoulder.

"That was the intra-muscular needle embedding itself in your arm."

"It wasn't pleasant."

"It's not supposed to be," said Carlson. "The shoulder-mounted unit will continuously monitor your blood sugar and administer insulin as needed."

"I thought the commercial versions weren't rated for extreme environments," Melissa said.

Carlson looked insulted. "This isn't commercial. I designed and built it myself. It can handle any environment." He entered a series of commands on the handheld device and pointed it at the suit. The lights on both units flashed in unison. "It's now calibrated," said Carlson. "Don't mess with the settings."

Peter moved his arm and shoulder around, then nodded with satisfaction at the way it felt.

Just then, Yung rushed in with Leed right behind her. Both looked quite upset. Yung handed Melissa an electronic data pad and pointed out the concerning figures. "The ion batteries aren't holding their charge under load. We really need the type-forty power cells."

"You know those are too heavy," objected Leed. He then turned to Melissa. "She's inducing the current too fast, frying the separator films."

Yung shook her head. "You are such an arrogant ass. I told you that's not the issue—"

But Carlson cut them off. "This is fascinating, really. Do it somewhere else."

Melissa took one final look at the data pad and handed it to Peter. "This is your baby ... if you're up to it."

"I am," he said, then turned to Carlson. "Doctor?"

Carlson sighed, then entered a command on the handheld device. Peter winced again as the needle was retracted from his shoulder. "You may now remove the suit."

Peter nodded, and then he and the others left.

Carlson packed up his equipment. The man was meticulous; he made sure every one of his instruments made it back into its holder and carrying case. Rick entered a few moments later, making sure they were alone. "Does it work?" he asked.

"Of course, it does," replied Carlson.

The workbench was now cleared—that is, except for the handheld device that controlled the insulin unit in Peter's suit. Carlson looked down at the device, then at Rick. He walked away with his other equipment, intentionally leaving the device on the bench.

The Artemis was a buzz of activity, with technicians crawling all over the cockpit, performing tests and finishing their checklists. Leed had a panel open as he spliced his data pad into the wires that led to a control station. Yung was at the display for that very same station, with Peter hovering over her shoulder. "Initiate the charge," Peter said.

Leed entered a command on his data pad, but nothing happened. "*Nada.* No conductivity."

"Maybe the switches in the fuel-cell bay are closed," Yung said to him.

"That was on your checklist," Leed replied.

"Since when does a control-system checklist include power functions?" she asked sharply.

Leed opened his mouth to argue the point, but Peter got in the middle before it could escalate. "If this is gonna be another pissing contest, let me put some newspaper down."

They both turned to him, surprised—he usually let them fight these things out. Peter raised an eyebrow, waiting for their response. Leed looked over at Yung, who nodded sheepishly at him and then turned back to Peter. "I'll go check the fuel cells," said Leed.

"And I'll take another look at the code on this panel," added Yung.

"Isn't it great when we all get along?" Peter said sarcastically, his point made.

Leed expertly slid down the ladder that led to the access passageway and went on his way. Yung opened the panel on the main console, tapped in her data pad, and started digging around the jumble of code. She glanced up at Peter at one point. "So, you gonna do it?"

"Do what?"

"Christen the Artemis," she said. "You know, hit its snout with a bottle of something expensive."

"And waste the booze?"

"I thought you stopped drinking," she said. He shrugged, and so she continued, "Come on. It's bad luck if we don't."

But before he could respond, an explosion rocked the whole ship, knocking Peter and Yung off their feet. Blistering alarms sounded, and the computer's voice echoed in the cockpit: *"Fire in fuel-cell bay."*

Peter got to his feet and scrambled down the ladder to the passageway. Yung was right behind him. They ran down the full length of the Artemis as other technicians scurried past them, coughing and hacking. Peter arrived at the hatch first. Smoke billowed out into the passageway. He grabbed an extinguisher from an emergency box, then turned to Yung. "Get a fire crew in here!"

"Don't go in there, Peter. Those cells are too volatile!" she pleaded.

"Ellie ... they need to know what they're up against ... go!"

She paused for a moment, then reluctantly turned and left him.

Peter moved into the smoke, trying to cover his mouth with the collar of his shirt. Exposed electrical panels sparked, and small fires burned throughout the room. Peter used the extinguisher to knock out the fires, but then started hacking badly; the air was thick with poisonous chemicals from the burning wires and circuit boards.

A surge of flames burst out from a conduit, and Peter had to dive out of the way to avoid it. He fell to the deck plate. As he tried to right himself, he saw a foot through the smoke haze. Peter knew it was Leed lying there unconscious. He tossed aside the extinguisher and grabbed Leed by the foot, dragging his dead weight back toward the hatch. He then hauled Leed over his shoulder, cursing at how heavy the man was.

Peter passed through the hatch and then shimmied down the passageway. Leed wasn't moving, and Peter was terrified the man was already dead. Then he saw one of the emergency hatches that led to the exterior hull. Every second counted, and it would take at least another five minutes to maneuver Leed out through the cargo bay. *This is the quickest way out*, thought Peter, though he knew the inflatable emergency ramps hadn't been installed yet.

Peter pulled the plastic panel off the hatch switch and hit the escape button. The hatch blew open, and Peter tumbled out with his human cargo. He fell ten feet to the concrete floor and landed with Leed right on top of him. Peter gasped in pain. He was winded, might have even broken a rib or two, but he managed to get to his feet. He dragged Leed by the shoulders away from the Artemis.

Just then, Yung arrived with the fire crew in tow. As the crew headed up the cargo bay ramp into the ship, she ran over to Peter. "How is he?" she asked.

"He's ... not ... breathing," Peter said, barely able to speak through the pain.

Yung jumped into action. She flipped Leed onto his back, opened his mouth, and tilted his head back. She started chest compressions. Peter was impressed with her force, considering how much smaller she was than him. Yung clamped her mouth onto Leed's and forced air into him. His chest rose and fell with each of her breaths. Over and over, she repeated the compression and breath cycle until Leed coughed and gagged. He was alive.

"Well done, Ellie," Peter said.

She wiped away the spit and soot from her mouth. "Make sure to tell him I did this. He'll be pissed."

Peter sat on a bench in the unisex change room. He was singed and badly bruised but otherwise unhurt. Peter hated electrical fires. He had been through one before; it was how he got his bravery medal from NASA. Three years prior, he and two other crewmen were in a prototype surface vehicle, one barely a quarter the size of the military APC. They were doing rough terrain testing when the driver lost control on a hill, and the vehicle rolled over.

It had burst into flames as an electrical fire started in one of the drive system's power cells—fusion cells very similar to those that would now power the Artemis. The driver had broken his back and couldn't move. Peter dragged him to safety outside the vehicle. He then went back for the other crew member, but flames had surrounded the exit where the man was trapped.

Peter was quick-thinking that day. He realized he could create a foam explosion with the compressed nitrogen tank used in the air scrubber and the aluminum hydroxide used in the CO filter agent. It wouldn't work on a regular fire, but it would do the trick on an electrical one. He set off his improvised fire retardant and doused the flames. The other crew member survived as well.

What Peter remembered most from that event was the nauseating smell of burned wire coatings. It was a sickly-sweet stench that stuck in his nostrils for weeks after the accident.

Peter now raised his newly charred hand to his nose. He had washed it three times already, but it still smelled like burnt wire. He cursed under his breath as Rahim walked in.

"How's Cirus?" Peter asked.

"He's stable, but the burns are pretty bad," said Rahim. "You saved his life."

"Ellie saved his life. I just hauled his ass out."

"Still," continued Rahim. "You both did well."

Peter nodded, but he knew Rahim could see the demoralized look in his eyes. "How are you doing?"

"I'm fine."

Rahim raised an eyebrow. "Don't kid a kidder, Peter."

"What do you want me to say?" asked Peter. "Just another day at the office?"

But before Rahim could respond, the general stormed in. Rahim only had to see the look on his face to realize he needed to leave. He saluted the general and was gone.

"What the fuck happened out there?" said a seething General Zimmerman.

"It looks like a switch in the fuel-cell bay overloaded," replied Peter.

"I was told we had that problem licked."

"On paper it is. Some of the systems haven't been tested," Peter explained. "We shortened the checklists. We're marginal; we need more time to test."

"You don't have it. And now the whole goddam mission is in jeopardy!"

"I know that," said Peter.

"What you don't know is the shit I had to eat to get you back," added the general. "You pissed off a lot of people before you left. With the letters to Congress, the interviews on CNN … you told anyone who would listen that the military couldn't be trusted to run NASA. So, when I had to go to those very same people and tell them that I was putting you back in charge, they thought I had lost my mind." The general leaned over so that his face was right in front of Peter's. "And you know what, maybe they were right."

General Zimmerman turned and strode out of the room.

The launch pad observation deck overlooked a still-untouched pocket of swampland. As Peter looked out over it, he was comforted by the fact that at least here, they wouldn't be drilling for oil or gas.

In the distance stood the launch gantry with a massive rocket on the pad. It was so tall that it no longer comfortably fit inside the VAB. The rocket awaited its payload, the Artemis, but it was still an impressive sight to behold, especially in the fading evening light.

Peter heard a car drive up to the parking area where his vehicle was. Moments later, familiar footsteps approached, and then Melissa joined him at the overlook railing. "You weren't picking up your phone," she said.

"Turned it off," he replied. "How'd you find me?"

Melissa motioned to a light pole with a security camera mounted on it. Peter nodded, remembering there was no real privacy here. He turned his attention back to the rocket in the distance. He appreciated that Melissa let him enjoy the moment, and he didn't say anything. It was finally his choice to break the silence. "At four times the thrust of a Saturn V, it's still barely enough to get the Artemis into orbit. Hard to imagine all the energy stored up in that rocket—"

THE BLUE PLANET, PART 1

"This wasn't your fault, Peter," Melissa said.

"Of course, it was," he replied. "I modified the protocols to speed up delivery. I cut down design time for manufacturing purposes. I let us take shortcuts when I knew they were dangerous. The kicker is, I don't know if I'm more upset that a man was nearly killed or that I failed in my mission."

"Probably a bit of both," she replied earnestly.

He nodded, agreeing with her. Melissa grabbed his hand, which surprised him. "All I mean is, you're not perfect. None of us are. We can only do our best in any situation, and then hope that our best was good enough on the day." Melissa then looked over at the lift rocket in the distance. "Maybe this was just too much of a load for any one man to carry ..."

Peter knew she meant that the responsibility might have overwhelmed him. And maybe she was right. Maybe it was unreasonable for him to be the saviour. But then he felt a strange tingle down both sides of his face. It was like his cheeks were suddenly burning. Was this an effect of the illness? Alarmed, he put his hand up to his skin, but it felt fine. Peter often had these moments where his nervous system reacted peculiarly. When he was faced with a big decision or a revelation.

"Holy shit," said Peter.

"What is it?"

"Get everyone in the conference room."

Melissa looked at her watch. "Now? Why?"

Peter didn't respond. He just turned his back to her and headed to his car.

The topographical hologram of the Martian surface was projected once again from the boardroom table. Three landing sites were marked with national flags. The Russian landing site was closest to the mountain. The American landing site was over twenty kilometres away in a protected valley. But a third landing site was also marked, this time with a simple holographic X. It was only a few hundred meters away from the Russian landing site.

Rick blew air over his lips, felt astonished by the images. "It's too dangerous."

Peter walked over to the hologram. "It's our only chance," replied Peter.

Yung, sitting around the table with the others, raised her hand. Peter nodded to her.

"You want us to land the Artemis a stone's throw from the Russian landing craft?"

"Yes," said Peter.

Carlson snorted derisively. "That way, it'll be easier for them to shoot at us."

"We're beyond design tolerance," Peter continued. "We need more powerful fuel cells but can't take the extra weight. If we don't bring the armoured personnel carrier—"

"We need to be close enough to travel on foot," realized Yung.

Peter then turned to Melissa. "It's too much of a load to carry."

She nodded to him, finally understanding what had happened.

Rick shook his head. "That vehicle is our only tactical advantage. We land that close to the Russians, and they can tear the Artemis to shreds before we can do anything about it."

"Yes, they can," replied Peter.

Rick opened his mouth, then shut it. He was about to say something else but then changed his mind. Finally, he just raised his hand. "Can you repair the Artemis in time?"

"It'll be tight. But we can do it," Peter replied.

"Well, then," said Rahim, "I guess we're only short a mission specialist."

"No, you're not," Melissa answered.

Everyone in the room turned to look at her. Rick immediately understood what she meant. "Oh, no ... no way. We're two weeks from launch," he said.

"And no one else is better prepared to go than me," she replied with certainty.

There was a long, silent moment as people wrestled with their thoughts. Melissa didn't need their approval as she was in charge, but she wanted to know. Peter finally looked at Melissa and told her that he agreed. She turned to Rick. He felt stunned by what was happening but realized he had no choice to get on board. Hesitantly, he nodded.

Melissa closed her notebook and stood up from the table. "I'll wake the general and tell him the good news."

As she and the others gathered their things and headed out, Peter and Rick were left staring at each other from across the table.

General Zimmerman stood on the observation deck overlooking the launch site. Like all the launches NASA had executed since the takeover, no civilians or press were allowed to be present. Of course, there were rumours amongst conspiracy theorists and the like, but this was always a clandestine mission—off the books.

The lift rocket with the Artemis now mounted to it fired its engines. Flames erupted from the tunnels that channelled the blast away from the gantry, and an ear-bursting roar swept across the Everglade swamps as the rocket lifted off and slowly gained altitude.

The general watched it rise with a look of satisfaction across his face. He then looked up to the night sky, toward a bright light already orbiting overhead.

The American mothership, the Leto, awaited the docking procedure. It was an enormous cylindrical structure, nearly three hundred meters in length. The bulk of the Leto was made up of four unique interlinked modules: habitation, power generation, life support, and cargo. They all rotated around the command centre, which was the heart of the ship.

The Artemis, now in orbit, approached the Leto. Thrusters fired on the Artemis to slow and rotate it until it matched the spin of the Leto. Massive grapples on the Leto extended and took hold of the Artemis, attaching it to the undercarriage.

The Leto's propulsion engines ignited in a blinding burst of white light, and the ship and its precious cargo left Earth's orbit.

CONTINUED in Chapter 7

CHAPTER 7

THE BLUE PLANET

PART 2

The Leto approached Mars. Though the ship was massive, it was nothing more than an insignificant grey speck against the planet's brilliant red surface. Other than a few navigation beacons, the Leto's hull was dark. As it drew closer, lights began to flash across the superstructure. One by one, the modules came to life. An antenna on the central command module repositioned itself until it pointed toward the planet's surface. Screens lifted along the length of the habitation module, exposing the interior.

Inside the hibernation chamber were dozens of rings. They were ten feet in diameter and several feet wide, and they spun vertically like tires on a highway, held aloft by magnetic fields emanating from the deck plates. The fields weakened, and the disks slowed. They lowered to the deck until they rested, motionless. One by one, the pods split down their lengths and opened to reveal steaming chambers within.

Inside one of the rings lay Peter, a web of cables and sensors attached to his body. His eyes opened, and he jolted up, gasping for air—was it another nightmare? Peter found the breathing tube down his throat, panicked, and yanked it out. Shaking, he leaned over the edge of the pod and threw up a viscous gel. Now able to breathe on his own, Peter calmed. He leaned back in his pod and saw the others around him wake, but they lay peacefully in their cocoons.

Peter had always thought the location of the galley was a mistake. He wasn't involved in the design of the Leto; it had been built six years before he joined NASA. It was the third ship in the Mars fleet and the largest, able to house and transport close to thirty passengers. Its designers rationalized that the crew would spend a significant amount of time in the galley and that it should be as close to the bridge as possible, in case there was an emergency.

The downside of this was that the galley was in the command module down the ship's centre axis, around which all the other modules rotated. If one was in the outer modules, such as habitation or storage, they would experience close to three-quarters of Earth's gravity. As they moved down one of the four connecting tunnels toward the ship's axis, they would slowly lose gravity and be weightless by the time they arrived on the bridge. Peter understood why the designers selected this location—for safety reasons—but it wasn't the best choice. With the aid of the spinning disks, the gravity felt during hibernation was close to Earth normal. It would be a shock to one's system to function in zero-G, especially after a long time in an induced coma.

And now, as Peter floated in the galley, his stomach churned. His queasiness was not helped by the fact that he had to ingest the contents of the toothpaste-sized tube of gel in his hand. It was an electrolyte concoction meant to replenish his body after the two hundred and five days in hibernation. Again, Peter understood the importance of the gel, but he dreaded the flavour. *They could have made this taste less like shit*, he thought. Stalling to ingest his tube, he looked around the room, where Melissa, Rick, and Yung also floated. Carlson handed each of them their own specialized gel, meant to work best with each one's individual body chemistry.

Peter watched as Yung became the first to try hers. Though she made a valiant effort not to react, a sour expression made its way across her face, and she had to cover her mouth with her hand so as not to spit it up. Peter looked down at the unopened tube in his hand with trepidation, then caught a glimpse of Melissa staring at hers in a similarly wary way. She smiled at him and shrugged.

"How's the neighbourhood?" asked Peter, trying to deflect.

Melissa looked quite happy for the distraction and let go of her tube. It floated there in front of her. "I'll get the latest scans," she said.

She touched a screen embedded in the wall, and a three-dimensional holographic image appeared in the centre of the room, showing Mars from orbit. Everyone gathered around it as Melissa worked the controls.

"This is us," she said as a three-dimensional Leto appeared orbiting Mars. She then panned past it to a lower orbit. "The first Russian base ship." Melissa studied the data associated with the ship. "Zero power output. Looks like its orbit is decaying."

"It's been here two years," added Rick. "It's out of juice." He proceeded to squeeze the contents of the entire tube into his mouth. It was not lost on Peter that it didn't seem to bother him.

Melissa zoomed out to a higher orbit. "There she is—the Vladivostok."

Peter leaned in to get a better look at the live data stream from the Russian ship. "The electromagnetic fields are really low. It's unmanned."

Melissa touched her control screen, and the image changed to that of the surface, where two Russian landing crafts were separated by a few miles of rocky terrain at the base of a now-dormant volcanic mountain.

"Their landing crafts are on the surface." She sounded surprised. "There's a massive radiation field on the opposite side of the mountain."

"Radiation from what?" asked Rick, suddenly alarmed.

Yung floated over to Melissa. "May I?"

Melissa floated aside so that Yung could work the control screen. New reams of data appeared holographically in front of them. Yung shook her head like she couldn't believe what she saw and motioned to several locations in a line on the topographical map. "Looks like they used tactical nukes along this ridge."

"Nukes? Why would they do that?" asked Peter.

Yung shook her head, thought on it for a moment, then realized. "For some reason," she said as she highlighted the ridge's edge with a digital marker, "they tried to collapse the mountain range into this ridge."

"Great. Just great," moaned Carlson. "Is there more good news, or can I go back into my pod now?"

Rick ignored him and looked at Melissa. "Any idea why they'd do that?"

"None," she replied. "But there's one way to find out."

Rick nodded. "OK. I'll brief the others." He pushed himself off the wall and floated to the aft hatch of the galley.

Carlson turned to leave as well, but Yung grabbed him by the shoulder. "Oh, no," she said. "I need your help to double-check the re-entry calculations."

"Not my department," he replied.

"Well, I'd like a safety check, and since you've got actual skin in the game this time, maybe that's reason enough for you to be helpful?"

Carlson sighed, then nodded, and the two of them floated off toward the forward galley hatch and the bridge.

Peter leaned into the hologram and tried to gather more details, but the resolution wasn't great. He shook his head and wondered aloud, "What are you guys doing down there?"

But then he heard a slurping sound, and then a gag. He looked over to see that Melissa had consumed her tube.

"Come on. You're the last one," she said to him.

Peter took his tube in hand again. He stared at it. He hated taking medicine, but finally, he forced it down his throat with one continuous gulp. He was wrong; it tasted worse than shit.

Rick could see the surface of Mars below. Though he rarely took a moment to enjoy the scenery during a mission, this view was one that was worthy of a pause. Strapped into his command seat as he was, the Artemis was positioned so that the front screen looked directly down on the planet with an unobstructed view. It was summer now on Mars, and the atmosphere looked clear, with no dust storms to be seen. There were many different shades of red on the planet: a lighter orange tinge above the equator, a darker rust-red below. Both sides were capped by white ice-covered poles, though the northern one had shrunk considerably because of the season.

Though there were rough spots with many of the simulations, Rick wasn't nervous about the landing. He was confident in his abilities. On his third landing on Moon Base Alpha, one of the thruster controllers had jammed open on his shuttle, and it spun. He was a co-pilot on that mission, and nothing his captain did could turn off the thruster or counter the rotation. They had quickly lost control and would spiral into the surface. Rick calmly requested control from the captain. The man was out of options and relinquished the stick. It wasn't that Rick was a better pilot than his captain; it was that he did more training than anyone else. While others would do the minimum number of hours to stay certified, Rick would do two or three times that amount in the sims. He had practiced the very situation they were in. Though he couldn't fix what was causing the malfunction, he knew that he could force the shuttle in the opposite direction and counter the rotation if he was gentle with the stick and applied opposite thrust. As he did so, the spin rate slowed, and he managed a controlled crash just off the landing pad. They had lost the shuttle, but the crew had survived. All in all, it was a good day. And now, as Rick looked toward Mars, all he could hope for was another good day.

He felt motion to his left and turned to see that Peter had strapped himself in. Once set, Peter turned to him and nodded. Rick flicked a switch on the control board and up came an image of the crew in the jump seats behind them. He could see that Melissa, Yung, Carlson, and Rahim were all strapped in. There was a palpable tension amongst them, and Rick remembered that none of them had ever been in space before, let alone attempted a planetary landing.

"All right," Rick said into the intercom. "We ready to go?"

"I need to pee," joked Rahim.

That brought a grin to Rick's face; he appreciated Rahim's attempt to reduce the tension. "You'll lose your deposit if you soil your suit," replied Rick.

"Then I'll grab a cup, Captain," Rahim said.

Yung's face brightened, and she slapped Rahim playfully on the knee.

Rick switched on the pilot communications line so that only he and Peter could hear each other. "Ready?"

"As ready as we'll ever be," replied Peter.

Rick flicked a series of toggle switches on the control panel. There was a judder and then a metallic groan. He looked over to one of the other display screens, which showed the undercarriage of the Artemis as the docking clamps were released. They were free of the mothership.

"Firing thrusters," said Rick, and the Artemis gently moved away from the Leto. Another series of thrusts rotated the Artemis, so the heat shields now faced Mars. He could no longer see the surface directly, and he had to rely on display images from the dozens of cameras around the exterior of the ship.

Peter scanned his screens. "Temperature and pressures nominal."

Rick flicked a switch on his panel. "Ion shields charged. Beginning descent."

There was a slight vibration that slowly grew in strength. The first flames became visible as they licked the exterior of the viewscreen. The ship had hit the upper atmosphere of Mars.

Rick pressed a button on his panel. "Autopilot engaged," he said and removed his hand from the stick. The ride was a bumpy one, but the vibrations maintained their intensity and didn't seem to grow. Rick clenched his left hand over and over, keeping it loose.

There was a beep, and Peter noticed a yellow indicator on his display. "Cut throttle two percent. We're getting stress readings in the aft bulkhead."

Rick adjusted a digital dial on his panel. The ship lurched to one side, and a blistering alarm filled the cabin. Carson could be seen lowering his face shield through the viewing monitor, obviously not confident with their chances.

"Reading a hull breach in the cargo bay," said Peter. "Wait, the bay pressure is still OK."

"Go manual?" asked Rick.

"Yes."

Rick flicked the switch and put his hand back on the control stick. The vibrations had increased steadily, and now it became a concerted effort to read the data screens, as they were shaking badly.

"I can vent the bay's atmosphere so that we don't decompress on entry," suggested Rick.

The ship lurched once more, and the familiar alarm shrieked again.

"It's a fault code. A sensor or switch has failed," Peter replied calmly. "Bring the nose up, get us out of the heat."

Rick felt his eyes start to water, doubt creeping into his mind. "Are you sure?"

"Hull stresses critical," voiced the computer as the flames outside the viewscreen glowed a blistering orange.

"It's affecting the descent rate," stressed Peter. "We're going in too steep."

Rick could feel the simulated feedback of the stick fighting his hand. Every instinct he had was telling him to follow his gut, just like he had on the moon. "This doesn't feel right," he said.

Peter turned his head as far as he could while strapped in his seat. He and Rick made eye contact. Peter didn't say a word, but something in Rick changed at that moment. It wasn't just the look in Peter's eyes, but more accurately, the look behind them. For the first time since they had known each other, Rick saw the spark of genius that others had always said was there.

"Understood," said Rick, and then he quickly made the adjustments to the controls. The vibrations slowly reduced, and the cabin alarm stopped. Carlson, visible on the screen, raised his helmet's face shield and exhaled.

The tremors through the hull were considered normal now—just the regular buffeting caused by the atmosphere. Rick was impressed by the stresses the Artemis had been put under. Though the Martian atmosphere was only one percent of Earth's, at this speed, it was still enough to rip the landing craft to shreds if they weren't careful.

"We're approaching target altitude," reported Peter.

Rick activated the landing sequence, then removed his hands from the controls. The ship would do the rest. As the Artemis cut through the atmosphere, the thrusters activated, and the craft rolled. Rick was momentarily disoriented as the surface disappeared, replaced by the sky through the front screen. The Artemis now plummeted toward the planet with its landing gear facing down. They continued like this for several minutes, and the flames through the viewscreen were replaced by the buffeting Martian air. Rick could see that the air brakes had extended on one of the monitors. They were massive baffles that captured just enough air to reduce the craft's speed.

Peter counted off their altitude, "One hundred meters, ninety, eighty," and Rick looked at the monitor, which showed their targeted landing site. He noticed a series of large boulders.

"Adjusting landing zone, minus eighteen meters," he said as he worked a rotary dial. Though the computer had automatically chosen the safest location to land, it still took a human eye to pick out any dangerous rocks or terrain that could tear into the hull. Judgment calls were still needed, and that pleased Rick considerably.

"Thirty, twenty..." continued Peter.

Rick saw four plumes of flame flash across one of his monitors, but they were expected. "Descent rockets firing," he reported.

There was nothing much else Rick could do at this point, but he still scanned the camera images, on the lookout for the slightest hint of trouble.

"Ten meters," said Peter.

The camera images were obscured by dust as the Artemis neared the surface. A series of green lights appeared across the control board, and Rick called out, "Landing gear extended and locked." There was a split second of silence before the Artemis touched down, and then the ship sank slightly as the landing gear flexed on impact. "We're down," Rick said as he scanned the screens. "All systems green."

"Shut her down," said Peter, and then they both flicked switches and turned off the flight systems on the Artemis.

The lights brightened in the cockpit, and Rick looked over his shoulder at the rest of the flight crew. Melissa was the first one up from her seat. She looked over at Rick and smiled at him. Her look quickly changed to excited anticipation, and she scurried down the access gangway to the back of the ship. Rick turned his attention back to his controls, though he felt he had to say something to Peter. "Thanks."

Peter turned to him with a questioning expression. Rick continued, "You were right about the error."

"It's my job to be right," replied Peter.

Rick stared at him. He couldn't tell if Peter was being combative or just impolite. But before he could press the issue, Melissa's voice came in through the intercom: "You two need to come and see this!"

Moments later, Peter and Rick arrived at the viewing window, which overlooked the hatch to the cargo bay from above. Melissa was there but didn't turn to them, as her gaze was fixed on something outside. "What is it—" Peter began to ask, but then cut himself off when he saw what she was looking at.

A few hundred yards away was the Russian landing craft from the Vladivostok. There were multiple tears in its hull, including a massive one on the port side, big enough to drive a car through. The metal was bent outward as if an explosion had come from inside the craft. The ground around the Russian ship was littered with newly formed craters, a destroyed surface vehicle, and a single cosmonaut lying motionless and face-down in the dirt.

"Jesus," said Rick.

"Not much of a rescue," added Peter.

Melissa turned to Rick. "I'm very glad to have you boys along for the ride," she said, then turned and headed back inside.

Rick made sure to give Peter a lingering *I told you so* look before he followed. Peter turned his attention back outside. He shook his head, concerned.

This had been a mission of firsts for Peter. Though he had taken a low-Earth-orbit commercial flight years ago, it had only reached the edge of space. The resurrection of his career at NASA had given him the opportunity to not only go into high Earth orbit but also into deep space. It was a privilege that thousands trained for, but only a select few would have the opportunity to do—at least without going the commercial route, fraught with shady companies and a Wild West mentality.

As Peter put on his pressure suit helmet, he felt humbled by the experience of this mission. This was a strange sensation, as he was never humble about anything. He was also quite pleased with the advances in suit technology over the last five years. Trips to Mars had necessitated developing lighter, more durable, and more flexible pressure suits. The one Peter was now wearing was half the bulk of the designs from the turn of the century.

The helmet itself was an example of elegant design. It had a wraparound face shield, which meant that Peter had a nearly two-hundred-and-eighty-degree field of view. He could also access critical systems like temperature control or communications with just the movement of his eyes. The only part of the kit he had any concern about was the automated insulin device. It was not that he didn't think Carlson was talented or smart enough to build it, but he knew intimately well that new technologies, no matter how well-thought-out, needed to be thoroughly tested. And Carlson's device hadn't been.

An alarm buzzed in Peter's earpiece, and he knew he didn't have time to dwell on that or any other nagging doubts. He was about to take the next great step, one he never thought he would have had the chance to do. Peter clicked the final clasp on his helmet and took a deep breath. He then exited the staging area and entered the cargo bay.

Melissa was there. She turned and nodded to him, and he could see the grin across her face. She was as excited about this as he was. Assembled throughout the rest of the bay were Rick, Rahim, and a dozen MSC marines, all in their own pressure suits. The marines were a diverse bunch: men and women, all armed with low-gravity assault rifles that fired depleted uranium slips.

Peter was not a fan of weapons in general, but he did marvel at the technology. Each clip on the gun could hold seventy-three shells in a casing that would only hold twenty 5.56 millimetre rounds on Earth. They could do this because the uranium shells were shaped like sticks of gum and were only 1.8 millimetres in thickness. They packed the same punch, and an individual could carry many more rounds.

Rick stepped up to the cargo bay door and turned to address the group. "All right, you've all been briefed. Let's do this slowly and by the book. I'll take point, and Lieutenant Richardson will bring up the rear." He then spotted Melissa and Peter. "Civilians are to stay back twenty meters at all times."

Melissa gave him a thumbs-up, and Peter followed suit, though he felt silly doing so. Rick then turned toward the cargo bay door and hit a red palm button on the bulkhead. Lights whirled, and a warning klaxon sounded. The door slowly opened upward. The first thing Peter felt was a push to his back, but he knew it was just the air rushing out of the bay to equalize the pressure.

The ramp extended out with the whirl of the electric motors, finally touching Martian soil about twelve meters from the ship. Rick led the way, and three squads of four followed him, with Rahim the last to go. Melissa and Peter waited until the marines were all off the ramp and then edged their way to the threshold.

Peter's heart was pounding in his chest. The closest he had ever come to this feeling was when he had done a solo skydiving course, but even that paled by comparison. He watched as Melissa gingerly walked down the ramp. When at the bottom, she delicately put her foot down on Martian soil, then looked up at Peter.

"It's good," she said to him with a broad grin.

Here I go, thought Peter. He took a step from the landing of the cargo bay onto the ramp, but in his excitement, he didn't judge it properly. The gravity on Mars was about a third of what it was on Earth. With the suit, the weight Peter felt was closer to eight-tenths of Earth's. That meant his step had a lot more spring to it, and he missed the edge of the ramp. Peter tumbled head over heels, slipped off the edge of the ramp, and fell about five feet to the Martian surface, landing headfirst.

He was stunned, but only for a moment. The next thing Peter thought about was how fine the Martian soil was as it pressed up against his helmet visor. Most of the surface of the planet was covered in a finely grained iron oxide. It was why dust storms could engulf the whole planet. The grains were so tiny that even the low-density atmosphere could churn them up. It was also the reason why complicated mechanisms needed constant maintenance, as the stuff got into everything.

"Peter! Are you all right?" asked Melissa.

Peter lifted his head and saw her standing above him. "Yeah, I'm fine," he said.

She grabbed him by the arm and helped him up. Melissa dusted off his visor and quickly checked his suit for tears. He should have been terribly embarrassed, but all he could do was grin at her like an idiot.

"What's so funny?" she asked.

"One *not so* small step," he said.

Melissa paused for a moment, then burst out laughing.

Peter turned and saw that the marines were well ahead of them. "We gotta catch up," he said, then grabbed Melissa by the hand and pulled her along. As they sprinted to close the gap, he was much more mindful of his longer, more powerful steps.

Up ahead of them, the three squads of marines had fanned out with their weapons raised, crouching and moving cautiously through defensive positions. They were now only ten meters from the Russian craft. As Peter and Melissa drew close, the marines split up and circled the ship. Many crouched and aimed their weapons as two—Smith and Philips—broke off from their squad and approached the tear in the hull, Rahim flanking the opening from the side. Peter had a lump in his throat as he watched them. They were moving carefully so as not to get caught on the jagged metal. Smith and Philips entered the opening, weapons raised and then disappeared from sight.

Another of the marvels of the new suit technology was that the communication tech was directional in nature. It would play from different locations in the helmet and lead the listener to the sound's location, just like one's ears would on Earth—which was why Peter twitched ever so slightly when a new signal cut into his suit's com. It was Rick's voice. "Over here!"

Peter and Melissa turned and saw Rick kneeling beside the Russian cosmonaut who was lying face down. Rick waved them over, and they quickly joined him. As Rick stood up, he motioned to the body. "What do you make of that?"

They both saw what he meant; there was a massive tear in the suit, one that led from the helmet's base all the way down to the waist. Melissa knelt and pulled the tear apart. The suit was empty.

She examined it more closely. "The material has been torn from the inside," she said.

"What does that mean?" asked Rick.

"Xenomorph," replied Peter, tongue firmly in cheek.

"What?" asked Rick, not getting the reference.

"Ignore him," Melissa said. She then stood up and twisted around, looking for something. She saw another suit some distance away, toward a valley northeast of their position. She pointed it out. "What do you see?"

Peter looked over, and with a blink of his left eye, brought up the magnifying feature in his suit visor. He scanned the area and saw another suit lying there, as well as metallic debris, though he couldn't make out what exactly it was. "Looks like they were headed in that direction," said Peter.

Just then, a general com signal cut in, one broadcast to everyone simultaneously. It was Rahim's voice: "Be ready!"

Everyone turned toward him and saw that he had aimed his weapon into the opening, obviously sensing something coming from inside. A tense moment passed, and then Smith and Philips emerged, their weapons lowered.

"Report," said Rick as he and the others gathered at the opening.

"Ship's empty," replied Philips.

Smith added, "It's screwy. Some of it has been taken apart, careful-like, while some's been ripped to shreds."

Rick surveyed the area around the Russian craft, then looked back toward the Artemis. He finally turned to Melissa. "I think we've learned all we can here."

Melissa digested this for a moment, then glanced off toward the valley where the other Russian suit had been seen. "We follow the breadcrumbs," she said.

Rick nodded and turned to Rahim. "Send two back to guard the Artemis, the rest with us."

Rahim immediately motioned Smith and Philips to head back to the Artemis, and then he took point. "Rest on me."

The marines followed him, with Rick, Melissa, and Peter bringing up the rear.

Peter was awestruck by the terrain he had seen in the last few hours—the rust-red hills framed by a harsh yet beautiful landscape of jagged rock outcrops and windswept plains. Now, as their column travelled through a narrow valley, they approached a blind corner at the base of a foothill, a mountain looming beyond it in the distance.

Over the last few months on Earth, Peter had learned the geology of the planet. He knew it mostly consisted of rock, with minerals containing silicon, oxygen, even small traces of metals. Tholeiitic basalt was what they called it—rocks created by ancient magma. He had been practicing his categorization of the different geological features as they went, which was why he recognized that one particular rock stood out from the rest. It was about the size of his hand, and oddly shaped: rough and weathered on one side but flat and smooth on the other.

Peter knelt to examine it but didn't initially disturb its location. He saw that the flat side was perfectly smooth and uniform. *Too perfect*, he thought. He felt his heart quicken with the possibility that it could be artificial. Peter reached out and grabbed it with his gloved hand, and he suddenly felt his whole body electrify, as though a wave of energy was passing from his body directly into the ground.

The reaction was instantaneous. The ground under his feet heaved and split open in giant steaming fissures, knocking him onto his side. The outcrop of rocks around him crumbled and fell, nearly crushing him. A howling wind swept across the valley, and he was consumed in a whirlwind of dust that obscured everything. Peter closed his eyes in terror, as it felt like the whole planet was being torn apart around him.

"Peter!" called out Melissa.

He opened his eyes to see her standing above him. "Are you all right?" she asked.

Peter looked around. Nothing had changed; not a single pebble had been disturbed. Gone, however, was the rock that he had picked up. "What … what's happened?" he asked with a mixture of shock and confusion.

"Nothing's happened," Melissa replied. She helped him to his feet. "I heard you yell. Saw you had fallen. Are you hurt?"

It took a moment for Peter to compose himself, but then he replied, "No, I'm fine. I just … saw something. But it's gone."

"Maybe it's your sugar level," she said, then looked over at the readout of the insulin device on his shoulder. "It's reading nominal."

"I'm fine," he said. But at the look of doubt in her eyes, he added, "Really."

Melissa nodded to him. Both their coms cut in simultaneously with Rick's voice: "Is everything OK?"

They turned and saw that Rick was stopped some twenty meters down the path, watching them.

"Peter slipped," Melissa responded. "He's fine."

"Don't fall too far behind," Rick said, then disappeared around the corner. Melissa took Peter's arm in her own and led him along as they tried to catch up.

"Thank you for not saying anything to him," said Peter.

"Just take it easy, OK?" Melissa replied. "I know Carlson is confident in his little device, but I think you might be pushing yourself a bit."

"I'll take it under advisement," said Peter.

"Which means you won't do anything different, will you?"

Peter just smiled at her, and she shook her head with a look of bemusement.

As they rounded the corner of the foothill, they saw the marines in defensive crouches, aiming their weapons toward a target in the distance. Peter and Melissa ducked down and made their way forward.

"What is it?" Peter asked Rick.

"You tell me."

Peter then saw what had caught their attention. In front of them was a large clearing that ended at the base of the mountain, one with rugged foothills surrounding the area. The clearing was littered with the signs of a battle: military crates, discarded weapons, explosion craters, and three more cosmonaut suits. A defensive perimeter of barricades had been established around the wreckage of another landing craft, but they appeared smashed.

"The first Russian landing craft," said Peter. "Looks like they built defences around it."

"Doesn't look like it held up too well," Rick said.

"But against who?" asked Melissa.

Rick shook his head; he didn't know. He then used hand signals to motion to Rahim and the others. The marines quickly dispersed through the clearing, guns aimed and fingers on triggers. It took only a few minutes, but Rahim's voice chirped through the com: "Area is secure."

Peter, Rahim, and Melissa entered the battle site and split up. Russian machine guns littered the ground. Rick picked one up and checked the clip, which was empty. "They didn't go without a fight," he said.

Peter scanned the area for clues. "Their pressure suits are empty, and there's no blood. It doesn't make any sense."

Before Rick could respond, they heard Melissa saying, "Guys, over here." Peter and Rick turned to see that she had moved to an exposed section of the rock face at the base of the mountain, behind the wreckage of the landing craft.

"What is it?" asked Peter as they joined her.

Melissa slowly reached out to touch the surface of the rock. It disappeared the second her hand reached it, revealing a six-foot-square rectangular opening whose interior was completely shrouded in darkness. She pulled her hand back, and the rock façade reappeared.

"What the fuck?" said Rick in amazement.

"Is it a hologram?" asked Peter.

Melissa tapped a series of commands on the computer screen on her forearm, then aimed it at the rock. After a few seconds, she checked the data from her scanner. "No power signatures. It's no hologram."

Peter picked up a baseball-sized rock from the ground. He rolled it through the opening, and the rock passed through the façade and disappeared inside. His ambient sound sensors picked up the noise as the rock bounced several times on a hard surface.

"Seems solid enough," he said.

Melissa gave him her approval. Rick keyed his communicator. "Rahim, round up the men, we're heading inside the mountain."

Smith stood guard at the end of the ramp to the now-closed cargo bay. He paced back and forth, eyes scanning the area around the Artemis, paying specific attention to the Russian landing craft in the distance. His expression was stoic, but there was a nervous energy about the man as he kept squeezing his hands on his weapon.

On the opposite side of the Artemis, Philips patrolled. Keeping her eyes on the clearing behind their ship, she saw a dust devil spiral up a few hundred meters away, but it quickly dissipated. Philips used her com: "Adam, you see anything on your side?"

"Nothing here but us chickens," he replied.

She kicked at the ground with her boot, and a plume of fine dust flew up, staining it red. "Tell me another one."

"So, these two jarheads are walking down the street. One sees this dog, right—"

"What type of dog?"

"It doesn't fucking matter what type of dog," he replied. "The dog's licking his balls, so he says to the other, 'Man, I wish I could do that.'"

"Are they terrestrial marines, or MSC?" she asked.

"Jesus, Gail, you gonna let me finish the joke or not?" Smith barked, agitated.

"Hey, it's all about the details," she replied, her head on a constant swivel, checking her corners, looking for anything out of the ordinary.

"Fine, they're MSC. So, the other marine says, 'You better not. That dog might bite you!'"

"Shit joke," said Philips.

"You ruined it," he replied.

"Maybe," she said, but then saw movement back at the Artemis from the corner of her eye. However, it was only a moment of excitement until she realized it was just Dr. Carlson at one of the viewing windows. She gave him a thumbs-up, then continued to scan the area. "Give me another," she said into her com.

Carlson didn't bother waving back and just stared at Philips from the viewing window in the maintenance bay. He then picked up what he had come for: an electrical wire spanner from one of the toolboxes. Carlson left the room, having to duck his head at the hatch. He passed the power-cell bay and made his way down the long corridor that led back to the ship's bow. He then climbed the steps into the cockpit.

Yung was sitting in Peter's seat, working the computer controls. She was studying a detailed three-dimensional scan of the mountain. What was an undefined mass from orbit now looked like a maze of tunnels deep inside.

"What do you make of this?" she asked Carlson.

He looked over her shoulder at the screen and shrugged.

"Some of these tunnels are at right angles," Yung said. "Others are positioned to lead into larger chambers."

"So?"

Yung shook her head at him. "There are kilometres of them crisscrossing through the mountain. These sure as hell aren't natural, and the Russians couldn't have built them."

"Little green men, then?" Carlson said dryly.

"I'm not joking."

"There must be some sort of interference from the nuclear radiation," said Carlson. "I'm certain there are no tunnels in this mountain."

Before Yung could reply, a garbled audio transmission cut in from Rick. "Artemis, we've found an entr ... into the mountain ... heading in—"

"You're breaking up, Rick," replied Yung.

"Too much interfere ... losing cont—" said Rick, but then his signal cut out.

Yung crossed her arms over her chest and offered Carlson an insolent expression. Carlson ignored her, turning his attention back to an electrical panel that needed repair.

Rick led the way as his team moved into the tunnel that sloped down at a gentle three degrees. The tunnel was roughly six-foot-square per his estimation, which meant the bulk of the marines had to hunch over as they moved. The walls were perfectly smooth, made of black, obsidian-like stone. The confines unnerved Rick. He wasn't afraid of dark places or claustrophobic in any way, but the combination of the two agitated him in this case.

As they walked in a long, spread-out column, Peter came forward and got his attention. Peter turned on his forearm flashlight and pointed it at the wall. The light was completely absorbed by the surface, with no reflection at all. Rick knew that even black rocks on Earth reflected some visible light, so this was obviously an unusual material.

"What's it made of?" asked Rick.

"I have no idea," replied Peter, who then dragged his gloved fingertips across the wall. "It looks like stone, but there's something strange about it ... a texture I can't see but can feel."

"Whatever it is, it's not natural," added Melissa.

Rick nodded, then continued along the tunnel. He shone his suit's flashlight in front of him, and the beam only illuminated a few meters where it should have cast light for at least a dozen. The group moved on silently, the only sound the crunch of their boots on Martian dust that had blown in through the opening. Rick knew what that meant. The opening they passed through was nothing more than an illusion. *But why?* he thought. *Why hide it?*

Rick realized they were out of the tunnel when he couldn't see anything on either side. "The tunnel's ending. Move out slow," he said into his com.

The group emerged into an enormous black chamber. Rick could just make out walls that seemed to stretch off into the distance from either side of the tunnel's mouth. As his team spread out, he could only track their positions by their suit lights. It was like they were moving through a thick, invisible fog. Rahim had ventured out the farthest and was starting to disappear. "Rahim, back up. I'm losing sight of you," said Rick.

Rahim took a few steps backward and again came into view. He was looking at his suit's forearm display. "My scanner can't get a read on the size of this ... chamber," said Rahim.

"It's like a stealth material," added Melissa. "An anti-radar coating. Any signal we send out gets absorbed."

Rick realized she was right, and he told her so. He made a mental note to remind her how damn smart she was when they were alone. "Everyone, turn your suit lights to maximum intensity," said Rick. One by one, everyone upped the gain on their lights. Huddled as they were, Rick had to squint a bit from the blooming effect.

Peter then pointed to something in the distance. "Look over there."

THE BLUE PLANET, PART 2

Rick saw what had caught his attention. It was a faint greenish glow, like a vertical cloud of mist floating in the distance.

"You see that too, right?" asked Peter.

"Yeah," Rick said, then turned to Rahim. "Mark the start of this tunnel, then drop a light every ten meters."

Rahim reached into his pack and pulled out a pencil-sized glow stick. He cracked it, then dropped it at his feet. It was bright enough to illuminate the entrance to the tunnel they had just come through.

Rick spoke into his com to the others. "Follow me. Stay in sight of those around you. We're not here to rescue our own asses." He received barks and other affirmative replies from the marines. He then looked at the digital compass on his suit display, chose a path toward the glowing mist in the distance, and started off.

Philips noticed them first: two shadows across the ground that were oddly shaped, elongated and twisted. They seemed to dance around each other, moving across the red Martian soil about twenty meters from her position. She looked up immediately but didn't see anything in the sky. When she looked back, the shadows were gone.

Philips activated her com. "Adam, you see anything?"

"Haven't seen shit in two hours," he replied. "You?"

She paused for a long moment before answering, "No ... nothing."

Yung rested her head in her hands as she read data streams scrolling across a monitor in the cockpit. Feeling tired, she blinked her eyes and tried to refocus several times. When she looked back at the data, the screen flickered and then went fuzzy for a moment. She rubbed her eyes with her hands, and when she looked back, the screen was back to normal.

Carlson entered the cockpit, a steaming cup of ramen noodles in his hands. He saw the data she was looking at. "Will you give up on it, already? You're not going to learn anything else with scans from here."

Suddenly, all the screens in the cockpit started to flicker and grow distorted.

"What's going on?" asked Yung.

Carlson put his cup down, went to Rick's station, and adjusted the console. "There's some kind of interference," he said.

"The Russians?" asked Yung.

The whole cockpit shook with an impact from above. Both looked up to the bulkhead, then saw it flex with another blow, one that shook the cockpit badly enough to knock the cup of ramen to the deck, splattering it all over Carlson's shoes. Before either could say anything, there came an ear-splitting metal screech.

Smith heard the screech as well but couldn't tell which direction it came from. He raised his weapon, scanning the horizon around the Artemis. There was nothing out of the ordinary at the Russian landing craft either. He then saw a shadow appear to his side, so he whipped his weapon around, ready to fire, but it was only Philips.

"Jesus! Be careful," she said.

"Sorry," he replied. "What the fuck was that noise?"

Philips was no longer looking at him. She had instead turned her attention toward the Artemis. Smith turned to see what had caught her attention, then slowly raised his head to look upward.

Rick was walking at a steady pace, one eye on the mist they were approaching, the other on his directional compass. The others were spread out behind him. They had been walking for about a half-hour but didn't seem to be getting any closer to the target. He was just about to stop and reassess when he saw it: a faint light on the ground just ahead of him. He approached and when he saw what it was, he felt a sinking feeling in his gut.

Melissa came up behind him. "What's wrong?" she asked, then saw what he was looking at and picked it up. It was a glow stick. She looked back along the way they had come to see the faint glow of the last beacon they had dropped. "Did we go in a circle?"

"Then where's the tunnel entrance?" he said.

Peter joined them. "Why have we stopped?"

Rick turned to tell him, but then saw one of his men disappear right in front of his eyes— pulled into the darkness in the blink of an eye. Rick wasn't the only one to have seen it happen, either, as Rahim immediately raised the alarm.

"We lost Blair!" he shouted.

Everyone turned to look where he had been, but all they heard were the man's screams—a guttural and painful wail—in their coms, and then his lights faded away into nothingness.

Rick knew they had to act quickly. "Form a perimeter!"

The reaction of the marines was immediate and decisive. They spread out, forming a circle around Rick, Melissa, and Peter. Several crouched to offer a smaller target, and all raised their weapons, searching for something—anything—to shoot at.

It was a reflection—a blurry image that crossed over the glass of Philips's visor for a split-second. Something was out there, and now it was gone. She shook her head like she couldn't believe it. "Did you ... did you see that?" she asked Smith.

"Yeah, something on top of the Artemis ..." He swung his weapon from side to side, searching. "I mean, was it one or two?"

"I don't know," replied Philips.

But then the shadows returned, passing over the hull of the Artemis. Smith didn't wait this time. He opened fire—*ratta-tat-tat*—but Philips pushed his gun up, and the rounds sailed harmlessly into the air.

"You'll hit the Artemis," she barked.

"Yeah, right, sorry."

And then they heard it: a deafening squeal—a sound like that of a bald eagle but much more piercing. They both searched but couldn't see where it came from.

"Fuck …" said Smith.
"Yeah," replied Philips.

The same blistering squeal echoed inside the mountain chamber, but there were dozens of iterations. Some marines had their hands to their helmets, instinctively trying to block out a sound they couldn't.

"What was that?" Melissa asked Rick.

He paused, stuttered uncharacteristically, and then said, "I don't know."

The marines twisted around and searched for targets, but nothing was visible in the inky black. A loud thud came from one direction, as though something heavy had hit the ground. Everyone turned, and another marine from the opposite side was pulled away by an unseen force, then disappeared into the darkness.

"We lost King!" yelled out the closest marine.

"King—sound off!" Rick yelled into his com. There was only a gurgling gasp, then silence in return.

Rick and the others twisted around, searching for the marine, then caught a glimpse of another trooper as she disappeared from the opposite side a moment later.

"Montese!"

This time, they all heard the marine call for help, but then her voice was suddenly smothered and went silent.

"Does anyone have a target?" yelled Rick, but he only got negative replies.

Rahim turned to him. "We gotta do something."

Rick raised his weapon. "Controlled bursts, rotate direction!" He began firing.

Within moments, all the other marines opened up as well, creating a wall of deadly uranium projectiles hurtling out from their group in every direction. There were dozens of intense bursts of light, and Peter and Melissa huddled together, both looking helpless.

"They're all around us!" screamed one of the marines.

Suddenly, a clawed hand—massive, red, and chiselled—appeared from the darkness. It wrapped itself around a marine's neck and pulled him away. The marine got off a few rounds, and his muzzle flash briefly illuminated an enormous red torso.

"Did you see that?" Peter asked Melissa.

She nodded her head. "I think so…"

A marine near Peter had his legs pulled out from under him. He grabbed desperately for the ground but couldn't find purchase. Peter took his hand and pulled with all his might, but the man was torn away from him. His screams receded as quickly as the lights of his suit were swallowed by the dark.

"Fall back!" ordered Rick.

The remaining marines, six of them, collapsed their perimeter while firing blindly around them. Rahim picked up a fallen weapon and handed it to Melissa. She pulled the bolt back and immediately fired off a few rounds. The muzzle flashes were just enough for those around her to see two enormous, clawed legs suddenly appear above a marine and grab his shoulders. The man was then pulled upward and disappeared.

"They're coming from above!" screamed Melissa.

"Just fucking perfect," said Rahim in frustration.

Curses and confused chatter filled the com lines as the last few marines backed into Rick and the others. They had to shoot upward as well, limiting any effect they might have had.

Yung and Carlson huddled around the video feed monitors in the cockpit. Yung adjusted the camera settings, but the images were badly distorted.

"What's going on out there?" asked Yung.

Carlson pointed to one of the monitor screens. "There they are!"

The grainy image was of two impossibly large flying objects, which circled around the Artemis like birds of prey. A look of wonderment crossed Carlson's face.

Philips grabbed Smith by the arm, saying, "Come on!" and dragged him underneath the ship, just as something very large swooped by in a blur, narrowly missing them. They huddled, back-to-back beside a landing gear strut, gasping for air.

"What the fuck are those things?" said an exasperated Smith.

Philips didn't answer. She looked stunned; she couldn't take her eyes off the two shadows that circled the Artemis's perimeter.

Smith cursed and rambled, "… not fucking human!"

"Get a hold of yourself!" yelled Philips.

That cut off his tirade, but she could still see his head jerk, eyes darting from side to side. Philips put both hands to the sides of his helmet and brought hers so close that their visors touched. "Remember when we were training in Arizona, when I got freaked out by those tarantulas? Remember what you did?"

"I told you I'd shoot the fuckers."

"And I was good," added Philips.

"These are a lot bigger than spiders," he said.

"Then, we'll use more bullets."

Smith liked the sound of that. He nodded at her.

A marine fired his weapon expertly: first horizontally, then up at a forty-five-degree angle, then back to ground level. When his clip ran dry, he hit the release and popped in a fresh one. "Last clip!" he called out. Another marine then yelled out the same; they were all running out of ammunition.

Rahim turned to Rick. "I think we're out of options."

Rick nodded. He reached into his pack and pulled out a gray cylinder, the size of a coffee thermos. He twisted it a half-turn, then pulled it apart to reveal a small display screen at its centre. Peter saw the device and moved over to him. "What is that?"

Rick entered a code on the screen. "A detonator," he said in a rather matter-of-fact way.

Melissa joined them. "Rick, what're you doing?"

He turned to her with a desperate look in his eyes, looking like he wanted to say more, but then continued setting the detonator. "It'll take down half the mountain," he said.

"This is insane," said Peter.

But Rick continued, "I'll give us two minutes. Maybe some of us can find the entrance."

"It's suicide!" Peter argued.

Rick looked at him, grimly. "I'm open to suggestions."

Peter twisted around, searching frantically for another option. All he saw were the muzzle flash and brief glimpse of what had attacked them. One by one, the marines started to call out that they were low or out of ammunition.

Rick twisted the cylinder another half-turn, and the data screen went red. Peter grabbed for the device, screaming, "No!" but Rick shoved him away. Peter tumbled backwards. He got to his feet and was about to lunge at Rick when, from the void, a clawed arm reached out and grabbed onto his waist. Peter yelped in pain. Melissa took his hand, but Peter was pulled away and disappeared into the darkness.

"Peter!" she screamed.

The gunfire from the marines started to slow. Rahim turned to Rick. "You'd better do it now!"

Rick pressed the red screen, and the timer started counting down from two minutes. He turned to the last of his marines. "Run!"

They just stared at him, surprised, until one replied, "Where?"

Rick shook his head; he didn't have an answer. He then looked back at the timer, which read one minute and thirty seconds. Melissa stepped up to him, and he looked at her with pleading eyes. He wanted her to go.

"I'm not going anywhere," she said, then grabbed his free hand.

Rick looked at Rahim, who shook his head. "It's been an honour serving with you, Captain."

The last of the guns went silent. The timer was down to the last minute—sixty, fifty-nine, fifty-eight—when suddenly, a brilliant white light flashed out from behind them. They all turned to it in shock. It seemed to push the darkness aside, flowing over them like a wave. Rick dropped the cylinder, blinded by the light. The rest fell to the ground, and they were completely engulfed in a flood of brilliant white.

Smith and Philips inched their way along the underbelly of the Artemis until they reached the edge. The shadows were gone. Smith took aim and nodded at Philips; he was ready to cover her. She stuck her head out from under the ship and got a clear look for the first time.

Two creatures circled in the air. Each was twelve feet tall, with powerful limbs ending in razor-sharp metallic claws. Massive wings extended from their backs, and long, thick tails ended in black, scorpion-like tips. They were reddish-gray, with smooth, angular bodies.

"Gargoyles ..." said Philips in amazement.

"What?" replied Smith.

Philips motioned for him to look, and he stuck his head out from under the ship. They had gargoyle-like features, but instead of being made of flesh, they looked like they were chiselled out of stone. Though similar, both creatures had distinct features—one with an elongated face, the other a much rounder one.

"Naw, man," said Smith. "These things look like demons."

Suddenly, one of them saw Philips peeking out from below. It dived with lightning speed at her, and she retreated under the ship.

The ground shook as the creature landed. It was too large to fit underneath the Artemis and could only reach in with its sharpened, curling nails. Smith fired a burst from his weapon, and the creature launched itself into the air and disappeared once again. The other landed on the opposite side of the ship. Smith swung around and fired again, but only hit the dirt. "I had it!" he howled in frustration.

Philips activated her com. "Artemis, we are under attack. Please assist." But she got only static in return. "Artemis …"

Carlson heard a few broken syllables from Philips' transmission. He adjusted the settings on the communication control panel, but it didn't make the signal clearer.

Yung entered from the gangway. "I couldn't see them at the hatches. They must be under the ship."

"There's some type of interference," said Carlson.

"What the hell are those things?"

Carlson turned away from the console, rubbing his jaw. "Big is what they are."

"We need to warn the others," Yung said to him.

"I think we have our hands full right now."

Yung opened her mouth, then closed it. She couldn't argue that point.

The first sensation Peter had was that of warmth. He grew up in Florida and had always been a fan of high heat and humidity. Mars had a wide variety in temperatures due to the thin atmosphere, which wasn't good at retaining solar heat. The surface temperatures varied from negative one hundred and forty degrees Celsius in winter at the polar caps to around thirty-five degrees at the equator in summer. The temperature when they landed was around twelve degrees, but that was outside, in direct sunlight.

When they entered the mountain chamber, the temperature plummeted into the negative fifties. Their suits could easily handle temperatures as low as negative one-eighty, and their power packs could keep them warm for over thirty hours without a recharge.

The integral suit heaters, however, left a few spots that were always a bit cold. Specifically, the balls of the feet and the elbows were continually chilly. It was also a dry heat, as the suit worked very hard to keep moisture away from the wearer's skin. All in all, Peter was often uncomfortably cold and dry in his suit.

But right now, as Peter straddled the line of consciousness, he felt warm and moist. What finally brought him out of his sleep was a more localized feeling of warmth: a hot spot directly against his right cheek. As he opened his eyes, he realized he was lying down and saw Melissa hovering over him, her hand to the side of his face. In those few moments of confusion, his mind drifted back to a time when they were happy together after spending a week on a beach in Miami before the city was shuttered for the coastal flooding season. Peter could feel the blood rush to his face, and a smile spread across his lips. *Are we on the beach again?* he wondered.

"Welcome back," she said to him.

He wanted so much to stay in this moment, but then he saw Rick appear over Melissa's shoulder. The reality of his situation hit him immediately, and Peter sat up. He was on a stone slab in the centre of a smooth-walled rectangular chamber, one with four entrances, each framed by a massive stone door that could be slid out of the way. The room was cluttered with equipment and dimly lit by electric lamps. There was moisture and grime all over the walls, and the room had a sauna-like feel, looking like it had been lived in for a very long time.

Peter moved his hands to his face in a panic, suddenly realizing he didn't have his helmet on. A woman in a Russian space suit stepped forward and handed Peter his helmet. She spoke in English with a thick Russian accent. "You will not need it here."

Peter stared at her in confusion. She motioned to several jury-rigged air scrubbers hooked up to power packs in each corner of the room, blowing moist air.

Peter turned to Melissa. "What's going on?"

"These Russians," she said. "They saved us …"

It was then that Peter noticed who else was in the room. There were seven Russians throughout, armed with their own assault weapons. Some were in well-worn space suits, others in much newer-looking ones. Rahim and three other marines sat together, unarmed, with two Russians standing guard over them.

Peter then felt a twinge of pain. He noticed his suit bottom was pulled up so that his torso was exposed, which was wrapped with a blood-stained bandage.

"You were injured, Peter," said Melissa. "We were worried you wouldn't wake …"

Olga spoke as clearly as she could. "I am Olga Tershenko. These are my comrades." She motioned to the first, a small, bookish man wearing spectacles. "This is Dr. Yuri Kirov, a survivor from our first expedition."

Yuri nodded to Peter but never actually made eye contact with him. He fidgeted as he rubbed a smudge on his filthy spacesuit.

Olga continued. "This is Captain Dimitri Simonov from my mission."

Dimitri was a man with fiery red hair and broad shoulders. He stepped up to Peter with an angry glare. "They thought we were dead. Now you have stirred them up again!"

"Dimitri!" Olga said to him. "This is not helpful. They did not know."

Dimitri shook his head in frustration but slowly calmed. He then nodded to Olga with an apologetic look on his face.

Peter turned to Olga. "What happened to us?"

Olga, Dimitri, and Yuri shared looks amongst themselves. None of them knew where to start. Finally, Olga looked at Yuri. "It does not matter anymore. Tell them."

Yuri took off his glasses and wiped them with a dirty rag. "My mission. It awoke something. An alien being that was in hibernation. We were attacked like you were." He then motioned around the room. "The few of us that survived stripped our landing ship for life support equipment, and we turned this chamber into our home. We have been in hiding since then. Unfortunately, our comrades, and now you, have suffered the same fate."

Yuri shuffled over to the far wall, one which was purposefully kept clear of people and equipment. "Their technology is quite remarkable," he said, then touched the smooth surface, illuminating with glowing, hieroglyphic alien characters. "I have deciphered their systems and have a rudimentary understanding of their language."

What played across the entire wall was a recording, though unlike anything Peter had ever seen. The images were ghostly—like a living painting, in muted colours, reminiscent of impressionist artwork from the nineteenth-century masters. Peter and the other Americans all stared in shock as they saw who their enemy was for the first time: the giant winged creatures, a half-dozen of them. They circled and pounced on the marines.

"This is what attacked us?" asked Peter. "These are the things killing us?"

Yuri nodded, then used his hands to zoom the image to a specific part of the recording. "Though their intention is not always to kill."

Peter looked back to the wall, where a creature pulled a marine away from the others with its claws. It flew some distance away and then pinned the man to the ground. As the marine struggled, the creature impaled him in the back with its tail.

Melissa gasped, covering her mouth as she watched.

On the screen, the marine stopped moving, and the creature stood back. It took only a few moments, and then the suit swelled and tore open from the inside.

"A parasite!" Peter said with alarm.

"No," replied Yuri. His eyes sparkled as he looked at the images. "They do not use us as hosts, or for food. It is a complex chemical transformation that takes place, but the best analogy I can use is that we are nothing more than raw material for them."

As Peter looked back at the image, the marine emerged from the tear in the suit. He was no longer recognizable as human but was more a mass of glowing flesh. The transformation was incredibly fast, with the mass reformed and reconstituted into a version of the creature, this one only smaller in size.

"It is a juvenile," added Yuri. "It will attain full size in a matter of hours."

The new creature spread its wings and took off with its comrade, both circling each other in a balletic dance. Yuri touched the wall, and the image froze on the creatures. There was a stunned silence, even amongst the Russians who had seen this before.

It was a coordinated attack. The first creature landed on the ramp side of the Artemis. Smith and Philips retreated under the centre of the ship, but then the other creature landed on the opposite side. Both creatures reached underneath the Artemis with their clawed arms, but when they couldn't reach the marines, they swung their tails, hitting the landing gear and damaging the undercarriage. As soon as the marines had a fix on them and fired, the creatures flew up and away, only to return a few moments later and do it all again.

"We're gonna run out of ammo," said Smith.

Philips nodded and then added, "They're also gonna punch a hole in the ship with those tails."

"What do we do?" asked Smith.

Philips looked out toward the ramp in the distance. "We make a break for it."

"Are you fucking crazy? We've got no cover out there."

"You got a better idea?"

Smith bit his lip in frustration. He didn't.

Yung worked the cockpit scanner controls—the same system she had used to scan the mountain. She studied the data reams carefully. Carlson saw what she was doing and hovered over her shoulder.

"What do you have there?" he asked.

She pointed to the data sets as she spoke. "This interference, it's coming from them. They have a natural electromagnetic signature. The farther away they are, the weaker it is."

There was a loud thud above them, then another. Carlson's eyes lit up with an idea. He moved to a control panel at the cockpit's rear, where he started to push buttons and flick switches.

"What are you doing?" she asked.

"Switching battery power to the ion shields."

Yung's eyes grew wide. "That'll electrify the hull."

"Exactly."

"If the marines are touching anything conductive down there—"

"Let's hope they're not," said Carlson, then threw the main switch.

The hull of the Artemis sizzled and glowed with an electrical charge. The creatures, who were perched on top of the superstructure, were instantly electrocuted. They squealed in agony, but then launched themselves into the air and flew away.

Carlson moved to the communications panel. "Smith, Philips—are you there?"

"Jesus H. Christ!" yelled Philips. "Where have you guys been?"

Yung leaned over to speak into the mic. "The interference is coming from those things."

"We gave them a pretty good jolt," added Carlson.

"Nearly fucking got us as well!" said Smith.

Yung shook her head disapprovingly at Carlson, who just shrugged in reply.

"Are they gone?" asked Philips.

Yung glanced out through the viewing screen, then at the multiple camera monitors. "We can't see them," she replied. "What can we do to help?"

"We're not moving until we have cover fire," said Philips.

Yung and Carlson immediately looked at each other, a standoff over who was to go. Carlson folded his arms across his chest. "Seniority," he said.

Yung sighed, a resigned expression across her face.

Peter gingerly got up from the slab and turned to Yuri. "They're obviously intelligent. Maybe we can reason with them?"

"We have attempted, but to no effect," replied Yuri.

"We need to try again—"

Rick took an angry step toward Peter. "Don't you get it? They killed my marines. We need to wipe these fucking things out!"

But Rick was roughly shoved back by the Russian guards. Rahim and the other American marines quickly jumped to their feet. "Leave him be!" barked Rahim.

The Russians raised their weapons at the Americans, and the two sides glared mistrustfully at each other. Peter turned to Olga. "We are not your enemies."

There was a long silence as Olga digested all that had happened. She looked at Dimitri, who nodded in agreement.

Olga turned to her soldiers. "Give them back their weapons."

Her men stared at her, unsure, but a final sharp look from her did the trick. The Russian soldiers gave the marines back their guns.

Rick checked his clip, then slammed the bolt shut. "Can we kill them?" he asked.

Olga nodded. "Direct weapons fire … if you can hit them." She turned to Yuri. "Show them your toys."

A smile crossed Yuri's lips. He went to a storage crate and pulled out a silver disk, about six inches in diameter. There was a look of pride across his face as he spoke. "They have a sensitivity to light, but they have multiple eyelids to protect them from dust and sunlight, like camels. These incendiary charges will stun them."

"That's how you saved us," said Melissa, connecting the dots.

Yuri nodded and handed her the disk to examine.

"Well, that's something, at least," said Rick. "Let's go kill these fuckers."

Dimitri shook his head. "A pointless discussion. There are too many, and we cannot kill them all."

Olga turned to Rick. "If they have not attacked your landing craft, then we need to get to it, make it to orbit."

"Fine. Let's contact the Artemis," said Rahim excitedly.

"We do not have the signal strength from inside the mountain," said Dimitri. "There is too much electrical interference from these things."

Rick glanced over at Yuri, but the Russian just lowered his eyes and avoided his look.

Olga rubbed her face, looking exhausted. "If we could get to our ship in orbit, we would be able to launch our missiles and destroy this cursed place …"

"What?" said Peter, alarmed by that notion. "Why would we do that?"

Dimitri sighed loudly. "These things. They are preparing to leave."

"And go where?" asked Peter.

There was a moment of silence as the Russians looked at each other; they knew the answer. Olga finally nodded to Yuri to deliver the final bad news. He touched the display wall again, and an image of a familiar blue planet appeared—Earth.

With no surface vehicle inside it, the Artemis's cargo bay was practically cavernous by spaceship standards. Yung, now dressed in her pressure suit, had a machine gun in hand. She opened the cargo bay door and braced herself as the air rushed out. She cautiously moved to the edge of the ramp and raised her weapon. "I'm in position," Yung said into her com.

Carlson's voice came in through her helmet speakers. "Smith, Philips … move *now!*"

THE BLUE PLANET, PART 2

Smith and Philips heard the transmission, but it was distorted by static.

"Shit, the interference is back ... we'd better hurry," said Philips.

"Get your ass going," replied Smith. "I'll cover you."

Philips crouched, braced herself, then ran out from the cover of the Artemis. She scanned the horizon, keeping her weapon trained on anything that looked like it might move. "Looks clear," she said as she reached the base of the ramp. Hearing that, Smith ran out and followed her path. As Philips made it halfway up the ramp, Smith arrived but stumbled at the base, cursing to himself. Philips turned to go down and help him, but he waved her off, saying, "Go!" Suddenly, the two creatures appeared in the sky above them.

"They're here!" Yung yelled from the threshold of the cargo bay hatch.

Philips looked up but couldn't track the creatures, as they were moving too fast. "Well, then, fire at them!" she yelled into her mic.

Yung fired on automatic, but the gun jumped in her hands. One of the rounds hit the ramp near Philips's leg, and she rolled to the side to evade the round. It was lucky she did, as the first creature narrowly missed her with its clawed legs.

Philips righted herself and hustled her way into the bay.

"I'm so sorry!" said Yung about almost shooting her.

"No worries," replied Philips, who then dropped her own spent weapon and grabbed the one Yung was holding. Philips began to shoot at the second creature, which was targeting Smith as he made his way up the ramp.

"Move!" Philips yelled at Smith. The second creature evaded her volley and collided with its mate in mid-air, knocking the first creature to the ground with a thud. Smith, now midway up the ramp, saw his opportunity. He pulled out a grenade from his pack and threw it at the dazed creature lying on the ground below him. The grenade exploded, shattering the creature into pieces resembling rock more than flesh.

"Take that, bitch!" yelled Smith excitedly.

But the second creature lunged at Smith and landed on his back. Smith struggled, but it easily held him down. From above, Philips aimed at the creature but couldn't fire without the possibility of hitting her man. "Fuck!" she yelled out in frustration.

The creature looked up to the hatch and then down toward its comrade's remnants on the ground. It was enraged, eyes flickering with anger as it bared its metallic teeth. With an ear-piercing squeal, the creature tore Smith in half with his clawed legs.

"No!" screamed Philips from the cargo bay as she saw her friend die.

Yet Philips and Yung had no time to mourn as the creature lunged up the ramp. They fell back into the bay, stumbling over each other. Yung got to her feet and slammed the button, and the hatch started to lower. Yet the creature was determined, and it ducked underneath. A groan came from the honeycombed aluminum as the hatch was hung up on its chiselled back. It moved into the cargo bay, and the hatch closed behind it.

"Holy shit," said Yung as she stared at the monster in front of her. The snake-like hiss was heard as air began filling the bay. The creature moved into the centre, forcing Philips and Yung to either side. Philips raised her weapon and took aim, but Yung yelled at her, "You'll breach the hull!"

"What the fuck do you want me to do, then?" asked Philips.

Yung had no answer but just stared at the creature. It was a tight fit in the bay, and the creature had to crouch with its wings folded on its back. It swung its head from side to side as it tracked the two women who circled it.

In the cockpit of the Artemis, Carlson watched a distorted image of the cargo bay on a monitor. He could see a grainy mass lunge at Yung, then impact the bulkhead as she scurried out of the way.

THE BLUE PLANET, PART 2

"Shit," said Carlson to himself. "They're going to ruin my ship."

His mind made up, he finally turned and left the cockpit. He did not head toward the cargo bay but instead to the maintenance room at the back of the ship.

Philips took aim at the creature's bobbing head. "I gotta take the shot!" she said in desperation.

"OK," replied Yung. "Just don't hit anything critical."

"Everything in here is critical!" replied Philips.

"I know!" said Yung as she slid away from another swipe from the creature's tail.

The creature sensed hesitation and had lowered its head to lunge at Philips when the inner hatch opened. Carlson appeared in the threshold, startling the creature. But only for a moment. It now turned to lunge at him, but Carlson calmly raised an unusual-looking silver handgun and fired. A dart flew out of the barrel of the gun, embedding itself in the creature's chest. It took only a moment, but the creature's head slumped forward. It stumbled and collapsed onto the deck, then shook and writhed in agony. Philips and Yung stared at it, shocked, and then turned to a grinning Carlson with equal disbelief.

Peter was certain that the tunnel they now hunched their way through was at least a foot smaller in height and width than the one they had entered. The Russians had shown them scans of the mountain, revealing hundreds of similar tunnels in a three-dimensional web throughout the interior. There was some debate over their purpose, but Peter believed the tunnels had something to do with ventilation. The atmosphere inside the mountain had a significantly different composition. Outside, the carbon dioxide levels reached ninety-six percent. Inside, they were down to twenty percent, with the corresponding increase being in nitrogen. It was still a lethal concoction to humans, but the Russians believed it was somehow an advantageous mixture for the creatures.

Dimitri carried a hand-held scanner with a display screen. The Russians had patched it together from parts of their ship. They had told Peter it measured the electromagnetic waves emanating from the creatures.

"We are heading northeast through an ancillary tunnel," said Dimitri. "It will not be far now …"

As Peter went along, he stumbled and grabbed the wall for support. Melissa moved to his side. She checked the reading on the insulin panel on his shoulder. "Your insulin's fluctuating," she said. "You should go back to the chamber and rest."

"I'm OK," replied Peter. She gave him a look, and he feigned a smile. "I'm not missing this," he said, then squeezed her arm reassuringly.

They continued along and reached the opening to the large chamber.

"This is where we rescued you," Olga said. "But from the opposite side." She disappeared into the darkness, and the rest followed her. Olga then pointed to the green glow about a hundred meters in the distance. It had grown much brighter now.

"They ignore us … unless we get too close to this," Olga said.

Dimitri pulled up the scanner. The radar-like image was rudimentary, but it revealed a massive alien ship in the centre of the chamber. It appeared silver in colour—a cigar-shaped cylinder, perfectly smooth, with no external features. It hovered impossibly on its rounded end. A large, glowing conduit fed power to it and what appeared to be a stone control panel at its base.

"Their ship emits the same EMF they do," said Dimitri. He then pointed out the creatures flying around the massive ship like wasps buzzing. One of the creatures landed on the ship's surface, which then became fluid, like liquid mercury. The creature was absorbed and disappeared inside. Dimitri lowered the scanner. "This activity is new. I believe they are preparing it for launch."

"Have you tried to get inside it?" asked Peter.

Olga replied with a heavy-hearted expression across her face. "One of my crew touched it. He was absorbed immediately. We assume he was turned into one of them."

Suddenly, an alarm sounded from Dimitri's scanner. He looked at it and saw a flickering image heading right toward them. "Back into the tunnel!" yelled Dimitri.

The group retreated into the tunnel. Dimitri stood his ground and opened fire to buy them time, but then fell back as well. A creature landed at the tunnel's mouth, shaking the ground with the impact, then reached in with its massive clawed hand. Dimitri stumbled and fell. It grabbed hold of his leg, and Dimitri lost his weapon as it started to pull him out. Rahim dove forward and grabbed Dimitri's hand. "Hold on!" he yelled to the Russian.

The creature was too large to enter the confines of the opening. It lowered its head, and Rahim's suit lights illuminated it from up close. It had the familiar chiselled, angular face, but also evidence of an injury—a deep gash along its jaw that looked like a crack running through stone. The creature dug its free claw into the tunnel rock, gashing it, then pulled back toward the void of the large chamber. Rick picked up Dimitri's dropped weapon and opened fire. The sound was deafening in the confines of the tunnel. The creature shifted its body from side to side, avoiding the rounds while still holding on to Dimitri's leg. It had almost pulled him out, and Rahim with it, when Peter and Melissa leapt forward and took Dimitri's other hand. The three pulled with all their might, and Dimitri screamed in pain as he was stretched.

But this was enough to have distracted the creature. Rick kept firing, hit the creature in the shoulder. Stone chips seemed to fly off at the impact point. It squealed in pain and let go of Dimitri, leaving a claw-print stain on his suit leg where it had held him.

As their balance was upended, Peter and Melissa fell back. Rahim, still with a hold on Dimitri, yanked him away from the opening and into the relative safety of the tunnel. They tumbled over each other and landed in a heap, with a panting and exhausted Rahim on top of Dimitri.

"You can get off me now, my friend," Dimitri said to Rahim.

Rahim rolled himself off, and Dimitri patted him thankfully on the helmet.

Melissa leaned against the wall, gasping for air from the ordeal. "That one was determined," she said.

"*Rubetz,*" said Olga in Russian. Then she translated, "Scar ... we have seen him many times. He is most likely their leader."

Peter got to his feet. "These things are ... incredible," he said. He walked over to where the creature had dug its claw into the ground. There were deep gashes in the stone. Peter moved his hand over them, and he had a strange sensation, as though he could still feel its body heat. The sensation quickly changed, intensified, and Peter felt a searing pain from the wound to his torso. He fell to his knees.

It was an incredible city seen from high above. Crystal towers rose into the air in a dense, alien urban sprawl. Massive bridges spanned rivers, and earth-moving machines tore up hillsides to clear space for growth. Dense grey smoke spewed from enormous, obelisk-like factories that cut swaths into the forests of blue and green foliage. It was an industrial civilization, unlike anything seen before, one full of energy and purpose.

The air above the city hummed, and the crystal towers began to vibrate at their resonant frequency. Hundreds of silver cylindrical ships—identical to the one seen in the mountain chamber—appeared in the sky. Waves of energy emitted from the ships, and there was a rumble that shattered the glass of the structures.

The ships landed and, once again, hovered only feet above the ground. Thousands of creatures emerged from the liquid-like skin of the ships. They flew off in every direction, flowing over the landscape like locusts.

Crystal buildings that once stood proudly along the boulevard lay smashed, some glowing with reddish-brown flames. A creature landed, dug its claws into the surface, and left markings identical to those in the tunnel. It approached another, much smaller being from behind, a Martian.

The Martian turned suddenly, its teardrop-shaped eyes widening as it faced the creature. It was androgynous, bipedal, with features reminiscent of a human, distinguished mainly by the reddish colouring of its skin and the ridges along its spine. The Martian screamed in terror at the sight of the creature. It tried to run. But the creature lunged, pinning the Martian to the ground with its clawed legs and impaling its writhing prey with its tail. The transformation had begun.

Once again. Melissa found herself looking down at Peter. He had his hands to the side of his helmet as he shook his head from side to side. She could read the expression on his face, that of agonizing pain. She knew Peter had trained to get ready for the mission, but he was also fragile. He often complained about a sore back or neck, an ankle or wrist during their time together. Peter wasn't a klutz by any means, but he got injured a lot, especially when playing his favourite sport, tennis. At times, he also didn't take the best care of himself. He ate too much sugar, drank too much beer. It was no great surprise when she found out about his diabetes.

With Peter, as with many of her previous relationships, she always seemed to take on the role of the nurse, and she would take care of whatever ailed her partner, be it physically or emotionally. Melissa didn't mind that; she had grown up in a large Latin family with an overabundance of empathy. As a child, she had a habit of taking in stray cats and dogs, nursing them to health, then finding them new homes. Her parents were shocked when she didn't go into medicine but instead chose engineering and the sciences. Yet her choice was not without reason. Deep down, Melissa was tired of taking care of others. She found her career at NASA invigorating, as it was all about the mission, not the individual. That's why her relationship with Rick seemed to work for her now. He didn't need to be coddled or supported. And Melissa found that refreshing.

"Peter, are you OK?" she asked.

Her voice seemed to do the trick, and Peter opened his eyes and stopped thrashing. He looked up at her in confusion but slowly seemed to regain his senses. "Yeah, I think so …"

"What happened?" asked Melissa.

Peter saw Rick and the others. His expression darkened somewhat, and he got to his feet. "You might be right," Peter said to Melissa. "I need to rest."

Once again, she read his expression and knew he wasn't being quite honest with her. "What is it that you're not telling me?" she asked.

"I think I should head back," was all she got in return, and then he headed off. She saw the concerned looks exchanged amongst the others, and then Rahim, Dimitri, and Olga followed him.

Rick turned to Melissa when they were alone. "Are you all right?"

"Yes," she said, then reached out and put her gloved hand on Rick's arm. "Thank you for asking."

"Listen," Rick said. "Be careful with Peter, OK?"

"What do you mean?"

"I'm concerned about him."

"So am I."

Rick shook his head. She could see he was struggling with something. He wasn't the overly talkative type, and sharing about pretty much anything wasn't in his nature. But Melissa also knew how to pry him open, even if it was a dirty trick. "If there's something I need to know that could jeopardize what we're doing here, then as the leader of this mission, you need to tell me," she said.

Rick stiffened. She had pulled rank. "All I'm saying," he continued, "is that there are things you don't understand about Peter."

"Then explain them to me," she pressed.

Rick looked off toward the mouth of the tunnel where Scar had attacked, then back at her. His gears were obviously turning. "It's just a feeling," he said. "I think Peter is a liability on this mission. He should be treated that way."

Melissa opened her mouth to question that, but Rick walked off after the others.

Philips, now with her helmet off, slammed Carlson against the bulkhead of the cargo bay. She jammed her forearm across his throat and leaned in. "You knew about these things!"

Carlson struggled to breathe and pushed back, but he couldn't budge her. Yung put a hand on Philips's shoulder. "He can't answer if he can't breathe."

Philips took the hint and reluctantly released Carlson. He gulped a few breaths of air, then composed himself, straightening his shirt. "We've had contact with a Russian," he said.

Yung's eyes lit up. "And you didn't tell any of us?"

"Un-fucking-believable," added Philips.

"We only had fragmented information," Carlson said, defending himself. "A few details about their physiology."

"Bullshit," said a still-seething Philips.

Carlson ignored her comment and moved to examine the motionless creature on the deck. It looked even more like it was made from stone as it lay there perfectly still. He put his hand to it, then shook his head. "A shame," said Carlson. "I was hoping it was only unconscious."

Philips whipped around with an enthused expression. "You killed it?"

"Unfortunately," Carlson said.

The alien ship glowed with energy from the power conduit. The stone control panel at its base was covered in the familiar hieroglyphic symbols, which appeared and disappeared seemingly randomly.

Scar, hunched over with his wings folded across the back, stared at the panel. When not enraged, Scar's face was expressionless and calm, almost noble in appearance. Scar touched the control panel with the tip of a clawed hand. A three-dimensional image appeared of the network of tunnels that crisscrossed through the mountain. Now Scar put a clawed hand flat against the stone. A pulse rippled from the point of contact through the image, as though Scar was sending a radar wave out. It took only a moment, but a small speck of light appeared on the stone.

The image field narrowed, then zoomed through the translucent maze but finally stopped at a single chamber. Inside were ghostly figures, those of the humans. Scar was interested in one, with a glowing dust print in the form of a claw. Scar had left a homing beacon on Dimitri's leg.

Scar touched the wall, and it went black. He turned and looked at the now-dozen of its compatriots calmly crouching around. A few turned their heads, uttering shallow grunts at each other. It wasn't a language, however. Some motioned toward the ship with outstretched arms and upturned heads. It was a telepathic conversation, a debate, in fact.

Finally, Scar squealed in anger, and all the faces turned again. Those with dissenting views now bowed their heads to Scar. Three creatures stepped forward from the group. Unlike many of the others whose bodies seemed unblemished, these three were covered in battle wounds, with cracks and chips all over their stony façades. These were the old guard.

Rahim walked through the Russian chamber. He passed several Russian soldiers sleeping against the walls, while others sat somberly and ate their rations. Rick and the remaining marines cleaned and reloaded their weapons. But what caught Rahim's attention was Dimitri. He was crouched in the corner near a small scrapyard of equipment. Rahim watched him carefully as he assembled a light bomb from various recycled components.

Without looking up, Dimitri addressed him. "You are welcome to join me."

Rahim sat down on a crate across from Dimitri. "Thanks … was curious how you made them," he said.

Dimitri kept his attention on the intricacies of the bomb he was building. Rahim's gaze landed on a dog-eared photo of a woman and child that Dimitri had laminated and adhered to his suit's right forearm.

"Your family?" asked Rahim of the photo.

Dimitri nodded. "To remind me what I have to fight for."

"That's a good idea."

"We Russians are full of good ideas. Just not good luck," Dimitri replied.

Rahim grinned at him and nodded. Dimitri quickly glanced up at Rahim. "And you," he said. "A family?"

"No. Not yet." Rahim paused for a moment, reflecting. "I didn't want to have someone I had to leave at home, someone that would worry about me." But almost immediately, he regretted having said that. "I'm sorry, I didn't mean to imply that *your* family's worried."

Dimitri inserted a timer switch into the bomb housing. "No need to apologize," he said. "I know they are worried. But in the end, it is a worthwhile risk." Dimitri then looked Rahim over. "Well, you are not ugly. When we are off this planet, you will come to Moscow with me. I will introduce you to my wife's sister. She is a terrible cook."

Rahim stared at him for a moment, seemed to hesitate. "Well, maybe if she had a brother."

Dimitri opened his mouth, then closed it—the implication of Rahim's sexuality visibly washing over him. Dimitri's eyes narrowed, and his jaw clenched, and Rahim laughed out loud at his discomfort. Dimitri went red in the face, but then shook his head and smiled at Rahim.

Dimitri forced the partially finished light bomb into Rahim's hand and then grabbed another housing. "Watch me and do as I do," and Rahim turned his housing over, just as Dimitri did.

Peter was feeling the effects of the last twenty-four hours on his body. He was certain it had nothing to do with his illness. Dr. Carlson's device was working admirably. He was cognizant enough to realize that the dizziness and general feeling of being unsteady on his feet probably had more to do with the two visions he'd had. They troubled him.

The first was of the very ground underneath his feet being torn apart. The second was more specific, of the creatures destroying a civilization and attacking a being that looked somewhat human. It also wasn't hard to connect these two visions to the dreams he had on Earth. But it was all still a jumble in his mind, like a puzzle he didn't have all the pieces to. He put aside these thoughts for the moment, as he had more pressing matters at hand.

As Olga and Melissa joined him at the stone slab, Peter unrolled a Russian map of the terrain that Yuri had given him.

"I'm not even going to bother telling you to get some rest," Melissa said to him wryly.

"I'm glad," Peter replied in earnest, having missed her subtle jab.

"What do you have for us?" she finally asked.

Peter pointed to the map. "There are three viable routes back to the Artemis from here," he said, then looked at Olga. "The most direct was the path you guys nuked. We can't go that way anymore."

Olga nodded. "When we arrived, we thought we had a chance to trap them inside the mountain, but we didn't know the extent of their tunnel network. It was pointless in the end."

Peter nodded, then pointed to another path. "This was our route to the mountain from the Artemis," he said. "We can try and head back the way we came, but it's exposed, not much cover to aerial attacks." He then pointed to the third and final section of the map. "This route will take longer, but the terrain offers more cover from rock outcrops."

Olga studied the map for a moment. "I think our chances are about equal on either path," she said, but then shook her head with doubt. "But any time we have moved in large groups, they have seen us as a threat and attacked."

"What if it's one at a time?" asked Melissa.

"They will most likely ignore us," replied Olga.

"Great," Melissa said. "Then we go one by one. It may take two or three days, but we'll sneak our asses out of here."

Yuri's voice cut through Melissa's optimism as he arrived with Dimitri's scanner. "We do not have the time," he said. "I have analyzed the data you brought back. Their ship is powered by some unknown gravitational force they have learned to harness. What I do know is that it takes time to recharge, and they have been steadily feeding it through the conduit at the—"

"Please be more succinct, Doctor," Olga said impatiently.

Yuri sighed, then continued. "Their ship is nearly ready to launch."

That got everyone's attention. Rick and the others stopped what they were doing and gathered around. Yuri walked over to the display wall and brought up the alien symbols. They changed every few seconds, like a countdown.

"Six hours ... I believe," said Yuri.

There was a prolonged silence. Rick seemed to take the news particularly hard. He shook his head and looked straight at Yuri, who wilted under his glare.

"We have to stop these things," said Olga. "No matter what the cost."

"Then we'll risk moving all at once," Melissa added. "Fight our way to the Artemis."

Rahim shook his head. "It might be destroyed, for all we know."

"I volunteer to go and see," offered Dimitri.

"What if you don't come back?" asked Olga. "Do we send another, then another?"

"What choice do we have—" said Peter.

But he was promptly cut off by Rick. "We can contact the Artemis from here."

Everyone turned to look at him. "How would we get through the interference?" asked Melissa.

Rick paused for a moment, as though he was convincing himself of something. "Yuri can send a message to our Pathfinder," he finally said. "It will boost the signal to the Artemis."

"He'd need our frequencies to do that," added Melissa.

There was a long silent beat, and then Peter took a step toward Rick. "He has them … doesn't he?" asked Peter.

Rick nodded. Melissa's eyes grew wide as she understood what Peter meant.

Olga grabbed Yuri and threw him against the wall. Images and symbols appeared from the inadvertent contact on the surface. "You warned the Americans!" He squirmed under her grip, but she slapped him across the face. "How much did they pay you?"

Yuri's gaze darted around the room, like a trapped animal looking for an escape. He mumbled unintelligibly but didn't deny it.

Melissa turned to Olga, still shocked. "I didn't know," she said. Melissa glanced at Peter, then back at Olga. "We didn't know."

Olga let Yuri go, turning away in disgust. Dimitri walked up to Yuri and glared at him so that his meaning was clear. "You are very lucky that we still need you alive."

Melissa looked at Rick. "You knew this was waiting for us?"

He nodded. "We had no idea how powerful they were. We thought … *I* thought we could handle them." Rick then touched

Melissa on the arm. "I'm sorry," he said, but she pulled away from him, turning to Yuri.

"Signal our ship," she said.

Yuri scampered away to the communication equipment in the corner.

The Martian surface around the mountain howled with a wind growing in intensity. Some distance away from the base of the mountain, a robot once used to scout landing sites lay dormant. Lights suddenly flashed alongside its panels as it awakened from slumber. A radar dish on the top structure started to rotate.

Carlson was sound asleep in the pilot's chair, snoring. Yung stared at her console with bleary red eyes, unable to relax. Philips paced behind them both, looked over at the sleeping Carlson. She clenched a fist but then thought better of whatever angry impulse she had.

Yung and Philips were startled by a garbled audio transmission that cut in.

"Ar ... Artemis ... come in, please," said Peter.

Yung flicked a switch on the com panel. "Artemis here! Peter, thank God!"

"What's your status?" he asked.

Carlson stretched out his arms, yawned, then sat up in his chair. He looked over to a frazzled Yung and a twitching Philips. "What?"

Scar stood in front of the control panel, now alone. The image on the wall display was that of the Russian chamber, with four separate tunnels leading to it. In three of those tunnels, his comrades drew close. With a gentle touch of a talon, Scar zoomed in on one of them. A creature, recognizable as one of the old guards, filled every inch of the tight space with its massive body. It had dragged itself forward with its claws and made slow but steady progress toward the chamber.

Philips and Yung stared at each other in shock in the cockpit, with Carlson now the one who looked agitated. "I can't believe it," said Yung. "They're all gone."

It was Melissa's voice that came through. "Are we clear on what to do?"

But before Yung could respond, Carlson impatiently leaned into the communications mic. "If anyone is interested, we do have an effective weapon against them."

"Explain," said Melissa.

"I developed a chemical with Yuri's data, a toxin that affects their silica-based biology. It's delivered by a sonic dart gun and kills them quite quickly," said Carlson.

Melissa and the others huddled around the Russian transmitter in the chamber, with Yuri nervously pacing behind them. "It'll work?" asked Melissa.

"It already has," said Yung through the com.

"Then we get the weapon from your ship and attack," Olga said excitedly.

Yuri stopped pacing. "No time for foolish heroics. We must launch now!"

Dimitri turned to him, looking ready to lose his cool. "Your opinion no longer matters—"

A sudden *thud* sound resonated in the chamber. Then another. They all looked around in confusion.

"It's them!" yelled Yuri.

"Don't be foolish," replied Olga. "They are too big to move through these tunnels."

Yung's voice sounded through the com: "… static … losing sig …"

"Shit," said Peter.

A deafening *crack* resounded as one of the stone doors burst inward, hurling rock shards throughout the room. Everyone dove to the ground to avoid being hit. A creature pulled its bulk through the tunnel entrance, then emerged as if squeezed like paste from a tube. It could barely stand, but it spread its wings, happy to be free of the tunnel.

"Breach!" screamed Olga. "Get to cover."

There was a *whoosh* as the breathable air was sucked from the room. Everyone scrambled for their helmets. The marines quickly organized behind a stack of crates. They fired at the creature, but even in the confines, it easily evaded the rounds. Another *crack*, and the next door shattered as a second creature burst through from the opposite side of the chamber.

"There are two of them!" yelled Rick.

Several of the marines aimed at their new enemy and opened fire. The sound of weapons was deafening in the tight space.

Peter noticed a third door begin to buckle behind Melissa. He rushed over to her and pulled her away as the third door came down, nearly crushing them both.

"Thanks," said Melissa breathlessly.

There were now three creatures in the chamber. Bullets flew and ricocheted off the walls. Yuri crawled on the ground at the feet of the soldiers. He eased himself up to a stack of ammunition crates. Suddenly, the crates were knocked over by a creature's swinging tail. Yuri screamed as they fell on top of him.

The fight raged, marines and Russian soldiers slammed against walls and floors, tossed about by the creatures. One last untouched door remained. Peter motioned Melissa toward the exit, and she headed for it. He paused for a moment and picked up a discarded machine gun lying amongst the crates.

The weight of the gun in his hands brought an unpleasant memory back to Peter. All the civilians had taken weapons training several months ago. Part of Rick's proficiency exercise was that each of them had to hit a stationary target some twenty meters away. Peter was never good with guns; he was even terrible at first-person-shooter video games. He was also the last one to hit the test target. To Peter's embarrassment, and as everyone watched, Rick barked at him until, after thirty rounds, Peter finally hit the target. He just couldn't understand why it was so important to Rick.

But now, as a creature turned to attack them, Peter hoped he remembered what to do. He raised the weapon and pulled the trigger, but he only got a *click* in return.

"The safety!" Melissa yelled from her vantage by the door.

"Shit!" said Peter, then he flicked a switch on the gun. He pulled the trigger, but his aim was off, and the rounds hit the ceiling. Unexpectedly, they deflected and impacted the creature from above. It recoiled in surprise. That bought Melissa enough time, and she managed to push open the stone doorway. Peter looked around the room one last time. Rick and the others were backed into a corner on the opposite side of the chamber. He then saw several light bombs hurled at the creatures.

"We gotta go!" Melissa screamed at Peter.

Peter ran for the doorway, where Melissa waited for him. The creature nearest them recovered and turned to lunge at Peter, but at the last second, the light bombs exploded, and it was blinded in a flash of white light. Melissa grabbed Peter, and they dove through the doorway into the empty tunnel. They didn't wait but scurried down through the tunnel and away from the chamber. Peter looked back toward the door. The white light from the bomb faded and, to his horror, slowly revealed that the creature was in the tunnel right behind them.

"It's coming!" yelled Peter.

Melissa looked over her shoulder and saw that the creature was crammed into the small space, but it now expertly dug its clawed hands into the rocks to pull itself forward.

Peter tripped and tumbled into Melissa, losing his grip on the gun, which skittered away. Melissa righted herself and pulled Peter up as the creature drew near. They continued down the tunnel, running as fast as they could.

"Look!" said Melissa. "An opening."

Ahead of them was a dim light. It grew brighter and brighter as they approached. They heard stone cracking in the confines of the tunnel and knew the creature was gaining on them. Peter reached the end first and was momentarily blinded by the light from outside. As Melissa was about to run past him, Peter grabbed and stopped her. They both looked down in surprise as the tunnel ended on the mountain's side, at a sloped rock face twenty meters up from the ground.

Peter and Melissa looked back into the tunnel. The creature was right behind them. "What do we do—" was all Peter could blurt out before Melissa pushed him out the opening.

As Peter tumbled down the rock face, he caught a glimpse of Melissa jumping out right after him. It pleased him that she wasn't doing something even more foolish, like trying to stop the creature chasing them. What didn't please him, however, was that the creature had also emerged from the opening. It launched itself into the air with a flap of its massive wings and flew out of sight.

Peter managed to gain some control over his fall, stopped the rotation, and now just slid down the hillside on his back. The friction against his suit did a good job of taking away his kinetic energy, and he slowed until he came to a gradual stop at the base of the mountain. *Well done*, thought Peter. But his respite was short-lived, as a moment later, Melissa came crashing down on top of him, having not done as good a job at slowing her descent. Peter was winded, but only for a moment. He was more concerned about Melissa.

"Are you all right?" Peter asked her, but he could see that she was still dazed.

Suddenly, they were both peppered in dust and pebbles. Peter looked up to see that they had caused a small avalanche, one that was now growing and bearing down on them. He grabbed Melissa by the hand and dragged her away from the much larger rocks that rained down upon them from the mountain. Safely out of the way, he helped Melissa get to her feet.

"Let's not do that again," he said to her.

But Melissa's eyes widened in fear as she looked over his shoulder. "Holy shit," she said. Peter turned and saw the creature diving at them. Melissa twisted around, motioning to a nearby rock outcrop. It was a maze of boulders and crevasses that led underground. She grabbed his arm and yelled out, "Come on!"

The two ran as fast as they could toward the fissures as the creature's shadow fell over them. Just as they breached the opening, the creature slammed into the rock behind them, grasping inward with its massive metallic claw. They were just out of its reach, but it was determined, jamming its body into the confines to gain a few more inches.

Peter and Melissa moved further into the darkness but took one too many steps. Peter lost his footing and, as he fell, grabbed Melissa for balance, but he brought her down with him. The two slid down a steep incline, one mostly made of loose sand, rolling over each other as they went. They landed at the bottom, but Peter took the brunt of the impact as his thigh slammed into a jagged rock. There was an immediate hissing sound and then a jet of air from Peter's suit. Melissa saw it immediately and yelled out, "Your leg!"

Peter put his hand over the rip, but air escaped past his fingers. Melissa quickly opened a pocket on the side of her suit and pulled out a repair bandage. "Hurry," said a gasping Peter. Melissa tore the adhesive backing off the bandage and placed it over the damaged area, sealing it tightly. Peter nodded—*thanks*—but his eyes grew heavy, and he leaned back and fell into unconsciousness.

The Russian chamber had been devastated. Crates had been smashed, bullet holes pockmarked the walls, and two Russian soldiers were dead on the floor. The carnage aside, it was a victory. Marines guarded the entrances to the room, all still in their helmets, as the air-making equipment had been destroyed. The bodies of two creatures lay motionless on the ground.

Rahim and Dimitri, working together to remove a collapsed stack of crates, found Yuri cowering underneath. "He's alive," said Rahim.

Dimitri grunted derisively and pulled Yuri up roughly by the back of his suit.

As Dimitri yanked Yuri from the ground, he was thoroughly unaware that he was being watched. Scar, seated near the ship, watched the projected image of the rescue as it played out on the rock wall, then moved the image focus to that of his companions' bodies. They lay there motionless as humans moved around them, and Scar understood that the battle was lost.

Scar then turned to see the lone survivor, the one who had attacked Peter and Melissa. This creature lowered its head, looking ashamed of what had happened. Scar squealed angrily at it, then looked back over at the image of the chamber.

The first thing Peter noticed was a flicker of light. Next was a blurry shape, which slowly became recognizable as Melissa, as her suit light illuminated his body. "This is getting to be a habit," said Peter.

Melissa smiled and nodded. "How do you feel?"

Peter moved his arms, then his legs. He felt a twinge of pain from the tear. "How bad?" he asked.

"Your air depleted," she replied.

Peter looked down to see an air line running from Melissa's tank to his own. He grabbed her arm and looked at her suit's regulator display: the oxygen readout was close to the red. He grabbed the line to his suit and pulled. "Disconnect me," he said, but she stopped his hand.

"Oh, no, you got me into this mess," she said. "You're not taking the easy way out."

Peter stared into her eyes; he knew that look of determination. He released the line, and they both carefully stood up, now tethered together.

"What now?" asked Melissa.

Peter shone his forearm flashlight up the incline to the opening they had fallen through. "Pretty steep," he said.

"And our friend might still be up there," she added.

He turned around and flashed his light into what appeared to be an underground cavern, where he searched the jagged rock face. Something shimmered back at them from the darkness.

"Did you see that?" asked Peter.

"Yeah."

They both moved off in unison, heading deeper into the cavern. A dozen or so meters later, they stopped at a peculiar grouping of rocks: a flat expanse covered by unusual, angularly shaped pieces. Some shone brightly when light was passed over them. Peter picked up a rock and wiped off the layers of dirt. It looked like a broken pane of crystal glass about an inch thick, completely smooth on both sides.

"This isn't natural," Peter said.

Melissa picked up the piece that lay beside it. Together they matched the edges. Like an ancient jigsaw puzzle, they formed a small square block. Suddenly, Peter's body shuddered, but he did not fall.

A desperate Martian ran through a crystal hangar building housing a sole, disk-shaped spaceship. The ground shook with the sounds of explosions from outside, and the crystalline walls cracked and buckled, but they held.

A creature was in pursuit of the Martian, smashing through anything in its way. It lunged with a clawed hand and wounded the Martian, but the creature then slid on the polished floor. The Martian was hurt badly but managed to climb into the waiting spaceship.

A fireball from the ship's engines consumed the creature as the ship launched through the ceiling of the hangar, which crumbled in a shower of shattered crystal blocks, just like Peter and Melissa held.

The spaceship rose above the devastated city, up into the clouds. It had broken through the atmosphere and was now above a very different looking Mars—one with lush blue forests and green oceans. The ship shuddered from a shockwave as dozens of mushroom clouds erupted and consumed the surface in nuclear flames. As the ship sped away from Mars, the planet's atmosphere gradually changed into the now-familiar red.

In the spaceship's cockpit, the Martian touched an abdominal wound and looked in shock at the iron-rich blood that seeped out. The Martian slumped forward into the panels of the ship, which now tumbled out of control in the depths of space.

A bright speck in the distance came into view and seized the ship in its gravity. The blue oceans of ancient Earth, with the massive single continent of Pangaea, had captured the Martian craft like a fly in its web.

Crashing through the atmosphere, the flaming hulk of the spaceship entered a primordial young planet, one with skies of lightning and land of cooling magma. The spaceship disintegrated, and pieces of it hurtled toward the ground; one impacted a barren hot spring, staining the clear water with a tinge of red.

Peter opened his eyes and saw Melissa staring right at him.

"Where were you just now?" she asked.

"I ... I don't know ..." he replied.

"Don't lie to me, Peter," she said. "I can't handle any more damn secrets on this mission."

"It's not like that," he said. "It's just ... I can't put it into words."

"Try," she said.

Peter opened his mouth and looked as though he was going to say something, but then he shut down once again. She took his hand in her own and held it tightly. "If I ever meant anything to you, you'll be honest with me now," she said.

Peter paused and looked into her eyes. "You meant everything to me," he replied.

Melissa's expression softened. "That's the first time you've ever said anything like that."

"I know."

"Don't stop now—tell me what's happening to you."

Suddenly, an alarm sounded from Melissa's suit, a steady beep. She glanced at her forearm display and read the oxygen counter, which was well to the bottom of the red marker now. "And you'd better do it quickly," she added.

Peter's shoulders eased, as though a weight had been lifted off. "I've always had a connection to this planet … something I've never been able to explain," he said, then ran his finger along his torso where the wound was. "When I was injured, the creature physically touched me. It made this connection stronger somehow."

The beeping on Melissa's suit alarm had increased in pace.

"I've seen this planet," he said. "The way it was …"

He paused as the alarm transitioned into a steady tone.

Melissa squeezed his hand. "Ignore it. Tell me everything," she said.

Flashlights scanned the ground. Boots crunched on the broken crystal. Rick, Dimitri, and Olga emerged through the darkness, their weapons raised. Rick saw them first: Melissa was on the ground with Peter in her arms. His expression hardened at seeing them like that.

Olga lowered her weapon as she heard the oxygen warning from Melissa's suit. She rushed to them, quickly took stock of the situation, and patched her oxygen tank into Melissa's auxiliary line.

The three of them watched, breath caught in anticipation, as the hiss signalled the transfer of breathable air into Melissa's system. After a few moments, they got their answer. Melissa slowly raised her head, grinning sleepily at Olga.

Peter sat on the slab as Rahim repaired the new damage to his suit. The others all stared at him with expressions varying from disbelief to utter shock.

"These visions," said Olga. "They are incredible."

Dimitri was even more explicit. "You're telling me that beings from this world seeded our planet three and a half billion years ago? That we are the descendants of Mars?"

Peter nodded and turned to Yuri. "The Martians were invaded. They had no choice but to destroy their own world to stop these things. You awoke the last of the invaders that survived the Armageddon. Now they're going to finish what was started here on Mars."

Rick turned to Peter. "This changes nothing. They're keeping us busy as their ship readies for launch. We need to move—now."

"I hate to say it, but I agree with you," said Peter. He then turned to look at Olga and Melissa. "We will split into two teams, take both paths, and head for the Artemis."

"Yes!" Olga replied. "With luck, some of us will make it."

"That's not good enough," said Rick somberly.

Everyone in the room turned to him, but Rick kept his eyes directly on Peter as he spoke. "We have to do everything in our power to stop these things."

Peter nodded to Rick. He knew exactly where he was going with this. But Olga did not. "I do not understand," she said.

Rick broke his gaze from Peter, looked directly at her, and then finally at Melissa.

"All of us will go for the Artemis …" Rick started.

"… but some of us are coming back," Peter finished.

CONTINUED in Chapter 8

CHAPTER 8

THE BLUE PLANET

PART 3

Rick stood outside the mountain, near a second camouflaged entrance, one he knew was geographically on the opposite side from the original one they had entered through. He scanned the surroundings through his visor magnifier. He could see a route away from the mountain. It went down through a ravine that cut through the foothills, with ample coverage from rock outcrops along most of its path. He knew this route would take an hour longer to get back to the Artemis, as they would have to go around the base of the mountain. However, from a defensive standpoint, it was ideal against a flying enemy.

Dimitri emerged from the tunnel entrance, holding another scanner device. "Our spare," he said to Rick. "I assume you cannot read Russian?"

Rick shook his head.

Dimitri entered a series of commands on the device's control panel, then handed it to Rick. "It will sound an alarm if it picks up their electromagnetic signature. The display is self-explanatory."

"Thank you," said Rick.

Dimitri nodded, then walked to the edge of the path and scanned the terrain, looking for signs of the creatures. A moment later, Olga, a Russian soldier, and an American marine emerged from the tunnel's mouth. Olga gave Rick a hard look but then headed to join Dimitri without saying a word.

Rahim was next, but he came over to Rick first. Rick could see his conflicted expression and knew his friend wasn't sure how to react to him and the truth. "Listen, you don't have to say anything," said Rick.

"No," Rahim replied. "You had a job to do, I get that." Rahim then looked back at the tunnel entrance. "It's just some might not understand the things we gotta do."

Rick nodded, knowing he meant Melissa. "Get her back safely, OK?"

"I will," replied Rahim. He then shook hands with Rick, said, "See you on the other side," and walked off to join the others.

Rick glanced back toward the mouth of the tunnel. He could feel his heart quicken with anticipation but was disappointed when it was Yuri who emerged next. Yuri came over to him and handed him a thumb drive. "It is everything I have learned about their technology, their chemistry and biology. It is ... very dangerous information," he said.

Rick looked at the thumb drive in his hand. "You are good to your word, Doctor. Thank you." He added, "I'll see you inside."

Yuri glanced over at Dimitri's group and looked at them longingly, but then turned around and headed back into the tunnel. He passed Melissa, who stood at the threshold watching them. "So, this was what it was all about?" she asked Rick.

"Yes," Rick replied, then pocketed the drive.

"I hope it was worth all those lives," she said, then started to walk over to Dimitri and Olga.

Rick grabbed her by the arm. She tried to pull it away, but he held her firm. "Don't leave it like this, please," Rick said to her.

Melissa looked him in the eyes, and her expression softened ever so slightly. "You lied to us," she said. "You lied to *me* ..."

"I had my orders—"

"Which you should have ignored the second you saw what those things did."

Rick could feel his heart sink. He knew she was right on one level, but on another, doing that would have gone against everything he had been trained to do his entire career. "You know me, Melissa. You know I can't do that," he finally said.

"Do I?" she replied. "The man I loved knew the difference between right and wrong."

"I still do, which is why I did my job."

"Zimmerman told you it was better we came in here blind. Does that make sense to you?" she asked pointedly.

"He had bigger concerns, things we don't know."

"So, he's kept you in the dark, too?" she said, challenging him.

Rick could feel his face flush with blood, a tinge of anger grow in his gut. "Do you even hear yourself?" he demanded to know. "How naive that sounds? This isn't some psych evaluation. We faced the possibility that the Russians would bring back information that would change the balance of power—technology that would put us decades behind them. We had no choice."

Melissa stared at him, then shook her head. "I don't think I even know you."

"I'm the same guy, Melissa. You just don't like the fact that maybe *this* is the guy you wanted all along."

Rick saw her eyes narrow and knew he had struck a nerve. But then she shook her head.

"Peter warned me," she said. "About the military. About you. I wish I had listened when it might have mattered."

Rick let go of her arm suddenly. She walked off toward the others.

Peter stared at the two creatures that lay dead on the floor of the Russian chamber. He was overcome by a feeling of sadness. He knew they posed an existential threat to humanity, yet deep down in his gut, he wondered if something could have been done differently if they could have communicated. Then again, he thought, they had invaded the civilization on Mars. Certainly, those beings would have tried to reason with the creatures. Peter shook any further doubt out of his head. They had to be stopped.

Rick entered the chamber, and Peter turned to him. "Are the others on their way?" Peter asked Rick.

Rick nodded. "We'd better get going."

The last of the troops—one Russian soldier and one American marine—joined them. Rick picked up a supply pack, then saw Yuri inching his way to the tunnel from which Rick had just emerged. "Where do you think you're going?" Rick asked Yuri.

"I believe I should go with the others," replied Yuri. "Yes, I believe it is the more prudent choice."

"You're not leaving my sight," replied Rick.

Yuri shook his head, looking like a caged animal. Peter, worried that he might make a break for it, grabbed Yuri and held him still. "Doctor," said Peter. "This is about the survival of humanity. We need you to focus on the job, and I promise you'll make it home," Peter said.

Yuri stared at Peter for a moment, calming somewhat.

"How much time do we have?" Peter asked him.

Yuri looked at his suit's forearm display, where the alien countdown was visible. "Three hours," he said.

Peter turned to Rick. "It'll be tight."

Rick nodded. "Everyone stays on my six," he said, then exited the chamber. The others followed, and Peter brought up the rear, taking one last look at the creatures before leaving.

Scar stared at the control panel, planning his next move. On the wall was a topographical image of the mountain and nearby terrain. The two groups of humans headed away from the mountain, from opposite sides and along different routes. The image of the two flickered, then slowly disappeared. They were now out of range of Scar's technology.

Scar turned to the other creatures that surrounded him. Several tilted their heads submissively; others emitted sharp and angry-sounding howls. Was there dissension in their ranks? Scar turned his head from side to side quickly—the telepathic dialogue was becoming heated. Scar emitted an ear-splitting squeal of overwhelming intensity. The others all turned to Scar, who motioned in their ship's direction and then back at the image on the wall.

Finally, they all became quiet and stared at him. Scar nodded a silent command, and the bulk of the creatures flew off toward the ship. Four others remained: the last of his old guard and three who lacked any battle wounds. Scar looked back at the two separate routes the humans were on, and, with a powerful screech, his soldiers flew off, leaving Scar alone.

Rahim was at the head of the column, with Melissa, Olga, Dimitri, and the two troopers bringing up the rear. They walked, spaced out in a narrow valley with rock extensions on either side and above them. Rahim dropped to his knee and raised his fist; he had seen something up ahead. He motioned to the side and spoke into his com, "Take cover."

The others ran for cover under the overhanging rocks, disappearing from the valley path. The troopers took aim with their weapons and searched the sky for targets. Melissa and Olga huddled together between several large rocks.

Dimitri moved to Rahim's side with the scanner. They both studied it and saw a grainy, radar-like image of three creatures circling in the air near their position.

"Looks like they're looking for us," whispered Rahim.

"You don't need to whisper," replied Dimitri. "They can't hear inside our helmets."

"Sorry," replied Rahim, an embarrassed look on his face.

Dimitri grinned at him, then turned his attention back to the scanner screen. Several tense moments passed, and the creatures flew out of range. Dimitri nodded to Rahim, and he emerged from cover. "Move out," Rahim said into his com, then continued leading the way.

Peter, Rick, Yuri, and their troopers were huddled behind the smashed Russian surface vehicle, which was in the expanse between Vladivostok's landing craft and the Artemis. They all looked up and saw the same creatures the others had seen, circling like carrion birds, several kilometres away from their position.

"Do you think they've been spotted?" Peter asked Rick.

"No," he replied. "They're not diving at anything."

Peter stared at the creatures in the distance, shook his head with a look of wonder; a look Rick noticed. "What is it?" asked Rick.

"They're incredible," said Peter. "Massive yet elegant. Intelligent but powerful. They are a remarkable life form."

"One we can admire later," said Rick.

"It's not admiration," replied Peter. "It's observation. And we could do with more of that if we want to survive this place."

Rick didn't respond, just stared back at him with a calculating expression. Peter then turned his attention toward the Artemis just off in the distance. "Artemis looks intact."

Rick spoke into his com, "Artemis, please come in."

Yung's voice chirped back in reply, "Artemis here!"

"Open the cargo bay door," Rick said.

"Understood!"

Rick glanced back at the others, and then they all ran across the open terrain toward the Artemis as quickly as they could.

Peter stared at the creature on the deck of the cargo bay. There had been sections cut out of it, as if from an autopsy, but the cuts only revealed a uniform material, as though it was really made from stone.

"Dr. Carlson's been busy, I see," Peter said to Yung as she entered the bay.

"He has his agenda," she said. But then she looked over at the creature. "Still, it's pretty amazing. A silica-based organism with no discernable internal structures. Wild."

"That's one way to put it," replied Peter.

"The others?" Yung asked.

"About an hour behind us."

Rick and the other troopers emerged from the staging area with their weapons. Yuri came out last, gulping down water from a canteen.

"We're reloaded," Rick said to Peter. He then looked down at his forearm display, the ticking clock obviously on his mind.

Just then, the inner bay door opened, and Carlson entered. He was holding two of the dart guns, and he handed one each to Peter and Rick with a sleeve of darts.

"How do we use it?" asked Peter.

Carlson opened the chamber, inserted the silver, needle-like dart, aimed the gun at the creature, and pulled the trigger. The cylinder flew out and imbedded itself in the creature's body.

"Sonic propulsion and a titanium tip that easily punctures their outer layer," Carlson said. He then added, "You'll have to be pretty close."

Peter motioned to the creature. "But how does it work when they have no vascular system?"

Carlson looked irritated at having to answer a question but finally responded, "I believe they have a type of internal circulatory apparatus when alive. This one is obviously dead."

Peter's eyes narrowed. He didn't appreciate Carlson's condescending tone, and he was about to say so, but Rick raised his hand to Peter. "We gotta get going."

Peter nodded to Rick, then attached the weapon to his belt.

Rick put his helmet back on. He looked over at the Russian and American troopers that came with them. "I won't order you to come with us," said Rick.

The American marine looked over at the Russian soldier for a quick moment, and then, without saying a word, both reached for their helmets. Yuri was not so brave, however, and moved toward the inside hatch. "Then you do not need me," he said.

Rick grabbed him by the back of his suit. "Get your helmet back on."

Yuri shook his head. But then his compatriot barked something in Russian to him, and Yuri complied.

THE BLUE PLANET, PART 3

The inner hatch opened once again, and Philips walked through, weapon in hand and helmet already on. "You guys look like you need some help," she said.

Rick had them moving at double-time now. He knew it wasn't the most efficient way to move on Mars, as their environmental systems wouldn't be able to keep their body temperatures at the optimal level, but all things considered, he saw suit rash as a small price to pay. They quickly rounded the dead-end of the valley and emerged into the clearing, where the first Russian landing craft had been destroyed. It was then that Rick's scanner went off with a high-pitched wail. Rick and the others looked up to the sky but couldn't see any creatures flying.

A rumble shook the ground with growing intensity. Peter screamed out, "Look!" and they all turned to the mountain to see a landslide, created as the creature slammed its mass into the face of the mountain.

Rocks and boulders rained down on them. "Move!" Rick yelled out to the troopers, but it was too late. The American marine couldn't get out of the way and was crushed by a torrent of rocks from above. Peter ran to the man, tried to pull him out, but had to retreat as more rocks came down on them. They all scattered, desperately trying to stay away from the bus-sized boulders that came down last.

It only took a few moments for the dust to settle, but when it did, a creature—the last of the old guard—glided down the mountainside and landed amongst the men with a thud, scattering them. Yuri dove into a ditch and covered his head with his arms; bravery was not his forte.

Philips, Rick, and the remaining Russian soldier opened fire, but the creature launched into the air and disappeared once again. They all scrambled to various positions of cover in the clearing.

"I fucking hate these things!" yelled Philips.

The others scanned the area but couldn't see it anymore. "How many?" Rick called out.

"Just one," replied Peter, and in a heartbeat, it was back. It landed near Peter with a ground-shaking thump and knocked him off his feet. He pulled out his drug weapon, but it swatted the weapon away with its tail. With no choice now, Peter dove behind one of the large boulders that had come to rest.

Rick lifted his head from cover to see that Peter had been separated from them. The creature rounded the boulder, and Peter scurried in the other direction, trying to keep the rock between them. It was a stalemate for the moment as they circled each other, with the Russian soldier taking the occasional shot from his vantage to keep the creature off-balance.

An icy chill ran down Rick's spine. He saw the opportunity and was shocked at how little doubt he had. Rick pulled out the digital device that Carlson had used on Earth to calibrate Peter's insulin unit from his pack.

Philips, who was nearby, saw it in Rick's hand. "What's that?" she asked.

Rick didn't reply as he keyed in commands on the pad. Lights flashed on it. Rick then turned to look at Peter in the distance. He could see a flash of light from the shoulder-mounted unit, meaning it had received the command.

It took only another moment, and Peter shuddered, lost his balance, and fell. The creature lunged and was on top of him. It swiftly raised its tail and impaled him—a clean hit this time—in the back. Peter screamed in agony.

The Russian soldier saw his chance, opened fire, and blew off one of the creature's wings. It reeled backward in pain and, with incredible speed, used its powerful limbs to crawl up a nearby rock ledge and disappeared.

Peter had started to convulse on the ground, rolling and twisting on the Martian soil. Rick, Philips, and the Russian rushed over to him. "We have to kill it!" Philips yelled out. The Russian marine raised his weapon and aimed it at Peter, but Rick reached across and lowered his gun.

"No," said Rick. He instead watched as Peter writhed on the ground in front of them. "I need to see what happens."

Philips and the Russian soldier exchanged surprised looks.

Melissa was bent over, with her helmet off and arms on her knees. She was sucking air into her lungs as fast as she could. Finally, the burn in her muscles and the ache in her chest subsided enough to stand up straight again. As she looked around the cargo bay, she saw Dimitri slumped against the bulkhead, drenched in sweat. Olga was pouring water from her canteen over her head, and the other troopers were recovering in their own ways. The only one who didn't look completely drained was Rahim, who just walked back and forth across the bay, winding down from their hundred-meter dash to the Artemis.

There was a whooshing sound as the inner bay door opened, and Carlson and Yung entered.

"Welcome back," Carlson said.

Melissa took one look at him and quickly remembered his role in the subterfuge. She turned to Yung instead. "Did the others make it?"

"Yes," Yung said. "They re-armed and left."

Rahim looked at his forearm display. "They've only got a little over an hour," he said.

"We're prepping the ship," said Yung. "We can launch any time."

"We should leave right now," said Carlson.

"I won't abandon our men," replied Melissa.

Yung looked over at Carlson and shook her head, not trying to hide her displeasure. She then turned to Melissa. "Of course, we're not leaving."

"It's suicide to sit here," Carlson added.

Melissa felt a wave of anger flow over her. *How dare you*, she thought. They were fighting for their lives in the mountain while he was safely in the ship, and he had the gall to tell her what to do? But just as quickly as the feeling of anger had hit her, it dissipated. She had never much cared for Carlson; there was an arrogance about him that rubbed her the wrong way. But she was always professional with him.

"We have an hour," Melissa said calmly.

Suddenly, Dimitri's scanner went off with its familiar wail. Everyone turned to him as he examined it. Finally, he looked back at the others and, with a resigned expression, nodded his head. It was what they had feared.

Carlson turned back to Melissa and said, rather smugly, "I don't think we have that hour."

Peter rolled onto his back; his face was changing. It had turned a rust-red colour and begun to grow. His eyes, cheeks, and jaw all swelled. He spun onto his stomach. His suit stretched as his body grew inside it, tearing open at the shoulders, then at the waist. However, the change didn't go to its normal conclusion. The convulsions slowly stopped, and Peter stood.

The others raised their weapons and took a step back from him, staring in shock. He had grown several feet taller and was much broader across his chest and neck. He raised his arms to his helmet and tore it off, dropping it to the ground. Peter took a long, deep draw of Martian air. He looked just as surprised as the others that he was still alive.

"My God," said Philips as she watched him; the others were speechless. However, it was enough to pique Yuri's curiosity, and he rose from the cover of the ditch to join them.

Peter was wingless, but his face and body were a mixture of man and creature. He removed his gloves and clenched his now stone-like fists. He looked at his shoulder with a realization, tore the insulin device off, and threw it at Rick's feet. He growled at him, gravelly-voiced, "You did this?"

Rick stared at him. He didn't respond.

Philips turned to Rick. "What the fuck is he talking about?"

Rick finally found his voice. "I lowered his insulin level and raised the sugars in his bloodstream." Rick saw the confused look on Philips's face and elaborated. "These creatures are sensitive to certain factors in the chemistry of our blood. I was ordered to find out what effect Peter's would have."

"I told you this would happen!" Yuri said to Rick, a look of pride across his face.

"I was an experiment to you ..." Peter finally concluded.

"Yes," replied Rick.

There was a split-second where they stared at each other, with Philips and the Russian soldier unsure of what it all meant. Were they enemies? It all changed in a split second as Rick pulled out his dart gun and aimed. "Take him out!" Rick yelled to the others.

Philips and the Russian opened fire, but Peter easily dodged their rounds. His reflexes and speed were heightened, and he moved with the same agility as the creatures. Rick fired, but Peter sidestepped the dart, and it hit the ground harmlessly.

"This is interesting," Peter said, impressed by his new abilities.

He was about to lunge at Rick when suddenly, the wingless creature fell from the rock face and landed in front of Peter with a ground-shaking thud. It was back to finish what it had started—but it was startled when it saw Peter in his new form.

Rick grabbed Yuri by the arm and turned to the others. "Inside—*now*!"

They ran into the tunnel entrance, leaving Peter and the creature circling each other.

Dimitri stared at his scanner, then looked to the others. "Three are approaching," he said somberly, then slammed his hand against the cargo bay bulkhead in frustration.

"We have to keep them away from the Artemis," said Melissa. "I need options ..."

Rahim paced, lost in his thoughts for a moment, but then looked down at one of the supply packs they had been carrying. His gaze landed on the last of the light bombs, and he turned to Olga. "Your ship—are its fuel cells intact?"

"Yes," Olga replied. "But the hull is damaged. It cannot launch."

"We don't need it to," said Rahim.

Dimitri turned around to face Rahim, realizing what he meant. "We would need a very large catalyst to set them off. Grenades won't do."

Yung raised her hand to speak, and they all turned to her. "There are fewer of us going home, right?"

"So?" asked Melissa.

"We'll be lighter," continued Yung. "We can spare a fuel cell."

A grin crept across Rahim's face, and he patted Yung on the shoulder.

"This is a dumb idea," said Carlson, but nobody cared what he had to say.

After Peter was lanced by the creature, the sensation was unlike anything he had ever experienced in his life. It was like time slowed down for him so that he could track each step of the transformation. He felt the tip of the creature's tail breach his skin, then sensed a not-unpleasant warmth spreading from that point all through his body. There was no pain, only a slight burning sensation. He knew he had writhed on the ground, and it must have looked like he was in agony to the others, but in fact, his motions were nothing more than his new body getting used to itself. What shocked Peter the most, however, was how natural it felt. After the transformation was complete, he could not remember a time where he was not in this body. It felt perfectly normal.

What an evolutionary feat, thought Peter. The most efficient method of transmogrification in creation. But his instant admiration for the process was shattered as the single-winged creature took a deadly swipe at him with its tail. It had no intention of transforming him but clearly wanted him dead. Peter sidestepped its attack but was backed up against the mountain.

He blocked another blow from the creature, but the force was enough to send him flying back against the rock face. Peter tumbled to the ground, and the creature lunged and pinned him under its legs. It squealed in anger, about to strike, but then Peter grabbed his head with the first sensation of pain he had yet experienced.

"What …?" Peter yelled out in confusion.

The creature stopped, momentarily surprised by his reaction. In that split-second delay, Peter saw the dart gun he had dropped earlier. He grabbed the gun and fired a dart with lightning speed, hitting the creature squarely in the chest. It tried to pull out the dart but was too late, and it fell backward to the ground, writhing in pain.

Peter got to his feet and crept up to the creature, which was in its death throes. It looked up at him, and their eyes connected.

"What … what are you saying?" Peter said aloud.

The creature's eyes were wide, and its gaze tunnelled into him.

"No! It's too much," Peter screamed. "It's too much!"

With the last of its strength, the creature reached out and grabbed hold of Peter's hand with its own.

The crystal city shimmered in the sunlight. A single silver ship appeared in the sky, landed amongst the untouched crystal buildings without disturbing so much as a speck of dust. Thousands of Martians gathered around it, startled but not fearful. Two creatures emerged from the ship. They moved toward the crowd of Martians with their heads lowered in deference. There was no malice from the creatures as they motioned silently with their arms, almost poetic in their movements.

But the Martians were repulsed by their visitor's appearance. They yelled and hurled angry gestures and insults at them. The creature-ambassadors looked at each other with surprise and confusion. Electric prods emerged from the crowds of Martians, and the ambassadors were shocked into submission. Martians swarmed them, and their wings were torn from their backs. Led in chains, they were tied to massive poles in the square, surrounded by thousands of belligerent Martians. Shock after shock was delivered, and the ambassadors succumbed to an agonizing death, the last sounds heard being those of the cheering Martians.

Massive machines pulsed with energy in the crystal behemoth of a factory. Thousands of Martians built disk-like spaceships, like the one that had crashed on Earth. There was a fever and ferocity to the Martian war machine.

Hundreds of Martian spaceships arrived and encircled a planet, above and below its glistening rings. This was Saturn, but one coloured an unfamiliar dark blue.

From the surface, a city carved out of the rock emerged from the landscape, reminiscent of the mountain structures the creatures built on Mars. Beautiful rivers of metallic fluids flowed, with nature a living part of the city. Thousands of the creatures looked up at the dots of light made by the Martian ships in their sky. They were not fearful, simply curious at the strange sight. The lights surrounding their planet grew infinitely brighter.

In orbit, the ships now spun on their axes, faster and faster, like toy-tops in space. Light beams were emitted at Saturn's surface from orbit. The beams grew more intense until they were white-hot. They penetrated the atmosphere and burned the surface of the planet, literally scouring its rock core. Hundreds of thousands of creatures fled but were incinerated as flames consumed their planet.

The Martian ships in orbit slowed, and the beams stopped. The planet slowly took on brown hues and beige striations. The ships moved out of orbit, leaving below a civilization in ruins.

The surface was littered with the burnt corpses of countless creatures, but from under the dead, survivors had emerged. They looked to the sky with the first hint of anger they had ever known.

Peter's eyes opened; the images had faded in his mind. He gently removed the creature's dead hand from his own and looked down at its body, lying there peacefully on the red soil. He then touched the contours of his new face. He felt confused as he wrestled with what he had seen. But the uncertainty was soon replaced by another feeling, a deep anger, one that caused his limbs to tremble. Peter looked toward the mountain entrance through new eyes.

Yung worked feverishly in the power-cell bay of the Artemis. She carefully disconnected a series of cables from a power cell, a metal cylinder the size of a garbage bin with complicated electrical hardware on each of its ends. Rahim reached in, and the two managed to remove the cylinder, one of dozens of similar cells in the bay, from its holder.

The ship was suddenly shaken with an impact—*kabang*!

"Hurry," Rahim said to Yung.

"You wanna do this?" she replied while keeping her focus on wiring a timer to the cylinder.

Dimitri poked his head in through the hatch, his helmet already on. "Are you two ready yet?" he asked pointedly, but only got a few choice curse words from Yung in response.

Outside, three creatures circled overhead. One dove toward the Artemis and collided with it, knocking a section of heat shields loose. Two marines stationed from the cargo bay opened fire, and it momentarily retreated. The three attackers then circled like buzzards over a carcass.

Rick stood at the slab in the centre of the Russian chamber. He checked the dart ammunition in the drug weapon, making sure it was loaded properly. Yuri paced back and forth nearby. "You're making me nervous, Doctor," Rick said to Yuri.

Yuri stopped pacing, then wrapped his arms around his torso. The man was a nervous wreck. Philips and the other marine entered from one of the tunnels.

"Report?" Rick said to Philips.

"The tunnels are clear," she replied.

"They must be at their ship," Yuri added. "I believe they need a critical mass of them aboard to activate the gravitational drive."

Rick nodded, then holstered the dart weapon. "Then maybe we have a chance," he said, and he motioned for Yuri to lead the way out of the chamber.

Rick and the others huddled at the opening of the tunnel, where Scar had attacked them earlier. The green glow of the creatures' ship was now much brighter in the large chamber ahead of them, illuminated at least twenty meters around the ship itself.

Yuri held the scanner in hand, studied the image of the power conduit leading to the base of the ship, and noted the two creatures that stood guard beside it. He finally closed the scanner and looked back at Rick.

"Switching the frequency of the power should disable their ship," said Yuri. "At least, I think it will."

Rick turned to address Philips. "When I signal, bring Yuri."

"What are you gonna do?" asked Philips.

Rick raised the dart weapon. "Something they won't be expecting," he said.

The conduit and its control panel throbbed with energy as the two creatures stood near it. One of the creatures twisted its head suddenly, just in time to see Rick as he emerged from the darkness, running at them at full speed. The creatures twisted around, raised their tails to strike, but were too late. Rick fired his drug weapon, hitting the first creature with a dull thud. It dropped to the ground in convulsions.

The second lunged at him, and he dove to the side. The creature was on top of him quickly, but Rick had reloaded, and he fired into its chest. The creature grabbed for the dart, looked surprised at what had just happened, and then collapsed. Rick rolled out of the way but was nearly crushed by its massive frame. He stood, looked around to see no other creatures, then spoke into his com: "Bring Yuri—now."

Rick continued to peer into the darkness in the direction of the tunnel. Tense moments passed, but then Philips and the Russian soldier appeared, and the doctor held tightly between them.

"Get going, Doctor," Rick said to Yuri.

Yuri moved to the control panel, which, up close, appeared identical to the one in the Russian chamber: a smooth and featureless wall of stone. He touched the panel, feverishly bringing up symbol after symbol. Yuri's eyes narrowed, and he mumbled to himself. He repeatedly entered another set of commands, then shook his head in frustration.

"What is it?" Rick asked.

"I was wrong," replied Yuri. "I can only set up a feedback loop in the power control system."

"So?"

"It will cause an uncontrolled thermal reaction," replied Yuri. "It will take down the entire mountain."

"Well then, do it," ordered Rick.

"We might not have time to escape!"

Rick grabbed the machine gun from the Russian soldier and pointed it at Yuri. "You either have no chance or a slim chance. Your choice, Doctor," said Rick.

Yuri dry-swallowed. He turned back toward the panel and entered a new set of commands.

It was a shock to all of them when Peter emerged from the darkness. "Stop," he calmly said in a booming voice. They all turned to face him, seeing how his stone-like skin flickered in the light from the surging power conduit. "These creatures didn't start this war—we did."

Three troopers ran down the ramp from the Artemis. They took up positions at the base, scanning the sky above and around the ship with their weapons. Dimitri and Rahim emerged from inside, moving much more cautiously as they carried the hefty power cell between them.

"You ready?" Rahim asked Dimitri.

"No," replied Dimitri. "You?"

"I was hoping you were," he said with a grin, and they continued down the ramp.

Olga, Melissa, Carlson, and Yung huddled around a computer station in the cockpit.

Carlson looked at his watch. "Not to be a broken record—"

"Then shut up," Melissa said, cutting him off.

Carlson closed his mouth, then crossed his arms on his chest in frustration.

The first and second Russian soldiers ran into the flat expanse between the Russian and American landing crafts. They knelt on the ground and aimed their weapons to the sky. The third trooper, an American marine, stayed near the Artemis, guarding the ramp. From three different positions, the troopers fired at the circling creatures above, and the creatures scattered and flew off in different directions.

The marine at the ramp looked over at Rahim and Dimitri. "We'll keep them busy—go!"

Rahim and Dimitri ran toward the Russian landing craft, carrying the power cell. As they made it halfway, one of the creatures noticed them and dove to attack. The marines opened fire at it, catching it in a crossfire. It broke off its attack.

But as Rahim ran, he tripped on a rock, bringing them and the cylinder crashing to the ground. Dimitri rolled over from his back and looked at Rahim with a grin. "I would prefer not to blow up today if possible."

Rahim exhaled. "Yeah, OK," he said, and then they picked up the cylinder and continued running toward the Russian landing craft.

As they drew near, another creature from the triumvirate broke off and plunged at them. The troopers again fired from their crossed positions, and it stopped its attack, retreating. The tactic was working.

As the creatures circled, they squealed and chirped at each other, forming a plan. In a coordinated attack, the three dived at the two soldiers out in the open. The soldiers fired back, but there were now too many targets. The first soldier pulled out a light bomb from his pack and threw it like a discus. The bomb arced and exploded in mid-air near the creatures.

The flash was instantaneous, and even though the light bombs were less effective in the open, the closest creature to the bomb was stunned. The three troopers again opened fire and hit it from various angles. The creature shattered and broke into large, rock-like chunks as it fell, forcing the men to dive out of the way or be hit.

The other soldier pulled out another light bomb to try again but was too late as a furious creature landed beside him. It swung its massive tail with malicious intent and sliced the man clear in half. The other soldier righted himself and ran toward it, firing and screaming in anger over his comrade's death, when another creature swooped in on him and plucked him from the ground in mid-stride.

The flying creature spiralled upward to a great height and dropped the soldier to the ground, killing him. The surviving marine at the ramp of the Artemis fired at the two remaining creatures, but they easily avoided his single volley. Though the price was high, the ploy worked. Rahim and Dimitri reached the Russian landing craft and entered through the tear in its hull.

Rick stared at Peter in shock. "What are you saying?"

Peter inched toward him. "These creatures, they came to Mars in peace, to learn about the Martians, to create a dialogue," he said. "The Martians were xenophobes, enraged that an alien race dared to make contact. They attacked the homeworld of these creatures."

Yuri stopped his work at the panel momentarily and turned to Peter. "You're saying that our ancestors were the ones who wiped them out?"

Peter lowered his head to Yuri, just as the creatures did to each other. "These creatures … they have no name for themselves. They believe that all living beings share a common connection. They are the ones who were wronged."

Rick shook his head in disbelief. "These visions are a trick. They're meant to deceive us!"

"I have seen what we did to them," said Peter.

"You expect me to take your word for it?"

"I'm not the one who has hid the truth on this mission," Peter replied.

Rick stiffened, tightening his grip on his weapon.

"The Martians were a warlike race," added Peter. "Like our own. They chose to destroy what they did not understand."

"Even if this is true, Peter, it doesn't change what's happening now," Rick said. "They'll destroy Earth if we don't stop them!"

Peter took a step toward the panel. Rick aimed the dart weapon at his chest.

"Don't move!" Rick yelled at Peter.

Rahim and Dimitri hauled the fuel cell into the Russian landing craft's engine room, where smashed equipment and computer stations greeted them. Rahim quickly surveyed their setup, and he and Dimitri lifted the cylinder into place near a row of similar-looking Russian power cells. Rahim pressed a series of buttons on the American power cell and activated the small timer panel that Yung had attached.

"How long?" Dimitri asked.

"Two minutes?"

"That is not very much time," Dimitri added.

"Let's not worry about that yet," Rahim responded. "We need to get them here first."

"We did not think this through very well, did we?" said Dimitri.

Rahim nodded, his mind racing.

The two remaining creatures flew over the no-man's-land between the American and Russian landing crafts. One looked at the other, then both dove to the ground, where the smashed Russian surface vehicle sat. Each grabbed an end of its considerable mass, and they lifted the vehicle into the air, then flew toward the Artemis. The marine near the ramp opened fire at them again, but his rounds did little to slow them down.

Melissa and the others saw the creatures and the vehicle they carried through the cockpit windows. "They're going to drop it on us!" she said.

Yung looked around the cockpit desperately. She turned to Carlson. "Can we charge the hull? Give them another jolt when they get close?"

Carlson shook his head. "We won't have enough power to take off."

"Shit!" cursed Yung.

"I warned you guys," added Carlson.

"One more word from you," Melissa said, "and you're going out the fucking airlock!"

Carlson shut his mouth, once again folding his arms across his chest like an irritated toddler.

Rahim and Dimitri peered through a tear in the hull of the Russian engine room. They could see the creatures nearing the Artemis with their payload.

"Dammit!" said Rahim. "What do we do?"

Dimitri had an idea. "Two birds!" he blurted out.

"What?" replied Rahim.

With no time to explain, Dimitri quickly pulled a light bomb from his pack, went to the hull's opening, and threw the bomb into the air with all his might.

The flash of light was too far away to stun the creatures, but it got their attention. They looked back at each other, telepathically conversed once again, then released the vehicle. The marine on the ground dove out of the way as it fell, and it narrowly missed him and the Artemis. The creatures flew off toward the Russian ship.

As the creatures arrived over the hull of the Russian landing craft, Dimitri poked his head out and fired his handgun at them. One of them dove at him, and he retreated inside the engine room. The creature's arm grasped for him through the opening but missed, its body too big to get through. Dimitri fired at its limb, finally forcing it to withdraw. Rahim and Dimitri exchanged a breathless look, and then the Russian craft shuddered with the impacts.

"They're tearing us apart," said Dimitri.

"So now what?" asked Rahim.

"This was *your* plan, I do believe," replied Dimitri.

Rahim grinned, and then an idea struck him. "How many light bombs do we have left?"

Dimitri pulled out two. Rahim took them from him. "When I set these off, start the timer and haul ass," he said, but Dimitri only returned a look of confusion. "Run, OK?" added Rahim, and Dimitri nodded.

Rick's dart gun was aimed at Peter's chest. "If there's any human left in you," Rick said, "you need to let us stop them."

"We don't need to exterminate what's left of their race," replied Peter. He then took another step toward Rick and the control panel. "We can end this war."

"It's too late for that!" Rick said, then nodded to Philips and the other trooper. They took their cue and raised their weapons at Peter, who was now surrounded.

Yuri finished typing on the wall and turned to Rick. "It is complete. The sequence cannot be stopped once initiated."

"Do it!" replied Rick.

"Doctor," roared Peter, "do not make this mistake."

Yuri was frozen in fear, unsure of whose instruction to follow.

Rahim emerged from the opening in the Russian hull, looked up at the creatures who were ripping apart the Russian ship, and fired a warning shot from his pistol. They stopped their attacks and stared down at him. Behind his back, Rahim activated the light bombs. Both creatures flew down and landed a few yards away. Rahim tossed the bombs at them and dropped to the ground, covering his eyes. The bombs exploded with two brilliant white flashes, and both creatures were stunned. They stumbled backward and fell to the ground.

Dimitri emerged from the ship. He ran to Rahim and pulled him to his feet. "The timer is activated!"

They both ran toward the Artemis. Suddenly, one of the creatures reached out and grabbed hold of Rahim's leg, pulling him to the ground. Dimitri stopped running and saw Rahim being dragged by the still-disoriented creature.

Rahim waved him away. "Don't stop! Go!" he urged.

The second creature regained its senses and got to its feet nearby. Dimitri turned and looked at the Artemis in the distance, then back at Rahim and the two now-stirring creatures. "We must keep them here," he said out loud to himself.

Dimitri pulled out his pistol and fired at the creature that was holding Rahim. He hit its arm, and it released Rahim with a high-pitched wail. The other creature lunged at both but, still groggy, missed. Dimitri pulled Rahim along with him, back into the Russian ship.

Rahim moved toward the cylinder and touched its screen. It showed eighteen seconds on the countdown. "I'll stop it," he said.

Dimitri grabbed his hand and pulled it away from the timer. He shook his head. "No, my friend ..."

Rahim opened his mouth to say something, but then closed it. He looked at the hull opening, saw the roused creatures, then glanced back at the cylinder. He realized Dimitri was right, and he reached out and took his hand. "You never said if you had a brother-in-law?" Rahim said.

Dimitri grunted, shook his head. "You could do better," he replied. Then he squeezed Rahim's hand as tightly as he could.

Both creatures launched into the air. They turned and were going to fly toward the Artemis when the Russian landing craft detonated in a massive explosion. The creatures tried to outrun it but were overtaken by the fireball and incinerated.

The marine by the Artemis dove for cover as smoking pieces of the Russian ship landed all around him. As soon as the debris had settled, he gathered himself and walked toward the ramp. The interference was gone, and Melissa's voice cut in through the com. "Can you hear us?" she asked.

The marine responded. "Affirmative. The creatures are dead."

Olga's voice was tense. "The others?"

The marine looked over at the smouldering wreckage of the Russian landing craft. "They didn't make it," he replied.

THE BLUE PLANET, PART 3

There was a long silence from the com, and then Melissa's voice was back. "Check the hull for damage and report in. We'll be taking off soon."

In the cockpit, Melissa looked at Olga; her eyes were raw, and she looked on the verge of breaking down. The marine's voice broke through the cockpit com. "Yes, ma'am."

Melissa turned toward the ladder down to the cargo bay, but Olga grabbed her as she went. "Where are you going?" asked Olga.

"To find them," replied Melissa.

"They are most likely dead."

"I need to know," Melissa said. "Shoot Carlson if you have to, but wait until the last possible second."

Olga let go of her arm. "Good luck."

And with that, Melissa left the cockpit.

Yuri's hand trembled as it hovered over the wall panel as he was about to activate the feedback sequence that would destroy the ship. Peter took a step toward him. "Do not move, Doctor. Your life depends on it," he said.

Rick whipped around and aimed his weapon at Yuri. "You will follow my order!"

But Yuri was frozen in terror.

An expression of utter calm suddenly rolled over Peter's face. He lowered his arms, and his hands unclenched. He stared into the darkness around them, concentrating deeply.

Yuri noticed, and his curiosity once again got the better of him. "What are you doing?" he asked, but a creature suddenly appeared above him. It grabbed Yuri by the shoulders. He screamed as he was pulled away into the black void of the chamber. The other marine fired, but almost instantaneously, another creature took him. Both their screams faded quickly. Philips raised her weapon, but Rick grabbed the muzzle and lowered it.

Half-dozen creatures emerged from the darkness and surrounded them. They crept forward, coiled and ready to strike.

Peter extended his hand in a sweeping arc. Some of the creatures tilted their heads in confusion, still not quite sure what to make of him.

"You called to them, didn't you?" Rick said accusingly to Peter.

"Move away from the panel," was Peter's reply.

Rick looked back over at the symbols floating across the wall panel. He had no idea which was the right one to activate the sequence. Rick stepped away from the panel, and Philips followed him. A moment later, Scar emerged from the group and moved to the control panel. With fluid, yet gentle flicks of his massive, clawed hands, he corrected the changes Yuri had made.

Scar turned to Peter with a scowl, but Peter didn't flinch and instead stepped toward Scar. The other creatures moved back until only the two of them were in the centre of the gathering. Peter and Scar slowly circled each other—the two alphas sizing each other up. Scar lunged forward, and Peter raised his hand in front of him. Scar stopped suddenly, struggling with indecision. Scar took another threatening step toward Peter, but then moved back, confused—was Scar hearing Peter's voice? Peter cautiously approached Scar. He reached out and gently touched Scar's arm.

Images reflected across Scar's glossy eyes. He was seeing what Peter wanted him to: lush green forests, blue oceans and skies. The great metropolises of mankind were revealed to Scar, including a cascade of humans with different body shapes, sizes, and colours. It was all a stark contrast to the crystal towers, uniform, androgynous physiques, and angry glares the creatures received on ancient Mars.

Peter removed his hand from Scar and stepped back. Scar seemed to be moved by what he had seen. Peter turned to address the other creatures with his thoughts. Soon they began to pass looks to each other in silent consultation. Scar finally emitted a shrill squeal, but not in anger this time; it was almost joyous. The others stopped their debate as Scar bowed to Peter.

"It's over," Peter said to Rick.

"What do you mean?"

THE BLUE PLANET, PART 3

Scar moved to the control panel and placed a hand flat against it; the light surging through the conduit dimmed almost immediately.

"They've stopped their launch," Peter said.

Rick looked stunned. "Why?"

"I've convinced them we are not the same as our forefathers," continued Peter. "We may be their genetic descendants, but we evolved on our own. We're not responsible for what happened to them."

Rick glanced over at the now-idling spaceship. Other creatures emerged from it and flew down to where they were standing. "Impossible," said Rick.

"Look around you," Peter said. "Believe your eyes."

Rick noticed that close to a dozen of the creatures surrounded them now, all quiet and reflective. Mortal enemies only moments ago, there was now no malevolence in them.

"Stop the Artemis from launching and return with the others," said Peter. "We'll negotiate a long-overdue peace."

Rick shook his head. "This doesn't make any sense."

Peter stepped right up to Rick. He was now taller by several feet, and Rick had to look up to maintain eye contact. Peter put both hands onto Rick's shoulders, but it wasn't meant as a threat. "You need to prove to them that we are different from those that destroyed their world. It's the only way trust can be built between us …"

Rick stared at Peter for a long, silent moment. He then dropped his weapon. Philips turned to Rick, surprised, but then did the same. Rick nodded to Peter, and he was released. Rick and Philips headed toward the tunnel entrance, and the creatures parted to let them by.

Rick emerged from the tunnel first. He stopped and turned his gaze skyward and looked at the fading sun of the Martian day. His stomach churned, which was unusual, as he normally had an iron constitution. He remembered when he and Rahim had eaten about four pounds of suicide wings each as part of a bet. Rahim lost not only the bet but then his lunch. Rick barely even had gas. He made a mental note to let Rahim have another shot at him when they got home. But now, Rick would give just about anything for an antacid.

Philips emerged from the tunnel and moved to his side. "Should I contact the Artemis?"

Rick was about to say yes when his eyes caught movement near the wreckage of the first Russian craft. It was Melissa. She was kneeling by the dead body of the creature Peter had obviously killed. Rick watched her, and he saw her find the insulin device torn from Peter's suit. She picked it up and turned it over in her hand, then noticed the empty helmet lying nearby on the ground. Even from a distance, Rick could tell that she was struck with grief.

Rick wasn't proud of the emotions that churned inside him upon seeing her reaction—suspicion, anger, jealousy. He knew Melissa didn't love Peter. He was also certain that they would get past their trouble on Mars once they had a chance to talk when she could hear the logic of his position. But right now, he wanted to make sure his motivations weren't clouded by any resentment he had toward Peter.

Rick focused on the truth at hand. These creatures could wipe out humanity. Even if they had taken a momentary pause, what was to say they wouldn't change their minds? Could he risk the future of all human life because of the words spoken by a man who had been partially transformed? A man who was now a hybrid, neither human nor alien? He was certain his motivations were righteous, even if his stomach continued to churn.

Rick turned to Philips. "Say nothing of what happened in the mountain."

"But it's over," she replied.

"These things will wipe us out if given the chance," said Rick. "They have to be stopped. Do you understand?"

Philips stared at him, a look of confusion written across her face.

Melissa was surprised by how much she hurt. Peter had always been a pain in her ass, even when they were dating. But she had loved him; had loved the gentle moments when he let his guard down and was honest with her. What she wanted now most of all was one last chance to tell him that she didn't leave him because of who *he* was; it was because of who *she* was.

It took Peter's death to finally make her confront the truth of it all. She just didn't have the patience to take in another stray. Somehow, the fact that Peter was thriving after he was back on the mission made it all OK. But now she was left with a hole in her heart, wondering if he would still be alive if she had left NASA with him.

But then there was another stitch of pain in her side, this one from her own internal devil's advocate. Why should she feel bad about him? What he did wasn't her responsibility. She had her own life to lead. But when the shadow crossed her path, and she thought a creature had the jump on her, there was a small part of her that felt happy she'd no longer have to wrestle with these doubts.

"Melissa!"

She looked up and saw it was Rick who had cast the shadow. Melissa's reaction was immediate and heartfelt. She jumped up and hugged Rick as tightly as she could.

"It's all right," he said, returning her embrace.

She pulled away, then motioned to the remnants of Peter's suit. "Is he really gone?"

"Yes," said Rick. Then he glanced over at Philips. "It's just us. The others were taken as well."

Melissa looked into his eyes. She didn't want to tell him but knew she had to. "Rahim was killed."

She could see Rick flinch ever so slightly, but then he nodded to her; he would grieve later. "We've disabled their ship," said Rick. "They'll be busy for a while trying to reactivate it. We need to finish the job from orbit."

"There's no other way?" she asked.

Rick's answer was immediate. "None," he said, then added, "We've got to move," and walked off in the direction of the Artemis.

Melissa had known Rick for a long time. If she put aside the omissions from his order of secrecy, he had never lied to her when asked a direct question. She had no reason not to believe him now. But then again, something troubled her. She watched him go, then turned to Philips and motioned to the mountain. "What happened in there?" Melissa asked.

There was a slight hesitation in Philips's reply, but then she said, "It's as the Captain said, ma'am." And then Philips headed off as well.

Melissa finally turned and stared at the entrance into the mountain. She followed the others toward the Artemis.

The transition for the Artemis was slow but dramatic. There was a slight shudder, and any dust that had settled on the ship was shaken off. Warning lights along the hull lit and grew in intensity. There was a flicker of flame from pilot torches ignited along the undercarriage, followed by a blinding flash as the engine nozzles erupted in flame. The Artemis then slowly rose off the surface in a cloud of dust.

The launch was not without a witness, however. A creature was perched on the hillside, almost completely blending in with the rock face. It watched as the ship rose into the air and disappeared. The creature then launched itself off the rock face and flew toward the mountain.

THE BLUE PLANET, PART 3

Peter stood in a circle of the creatures at the base of their ship. He looked from one unique face to the other; he had easily learned how to take notice of the subtle differences in their appearance. For the first time in his life, he felt completely at peace with himself. He had even joked with Scar that it only took an alien transformation to make him a better person. Scar didn't understand what he meant, and Peter realized that these beings didn't understand the concept of humour.

But this feeling of well-being was short-lived. The creature that had been sent to keep watch on the Artemis returned and landed in the circle. Peter heard its thoughts as it reported that the Artemis had launched. It then lowered its head and blended back into the circle of the others.

Peter was devastated. He truly thought he had gotten through to Rick. A sudden rage overwhelmed him. He clenched his fists and smashed them into the ground, the rock crumbling beneath his blows. He twisted and roared with anger. Scar and the others watched him but stood back. Peter charged one of the creatures and shoved it aside roughly. He lunged at another, but it did nothing to retaliate. They considered him one of them now, and as Peter had learned from the telepathic stories of their history, they never hurt their own kind.

Scar approached Peter from behind and wrapped its arms around him. Peter struggled, but Scar was too strong. Slowly he calmed, and Scar let him go. Peter slumped to the ground, his head hung in shame.

I am sorry, Peter said telepathically. *I was wrong.*

A creature tilted its head and motioned to the chamber's exit, questioning whether they would just leave for home.

No, they will destroy you from space, replied Peter.

Another stepped forward, bent over, and looked at Peter from his eye level. It was trying to convince him to give the humans another chance.

Peter shook his head. *They have proven they cannot be trusted, and no other attempt will change that.*

Scar looked back at the group in the circle, motioned, and communicated with them.

Peter was surprised at how easily he could understand the different voices that spoke at the same time. This species didn't need to do things linearly. They could get across their opinions simultaneously and with perfect clarity. They were also unable to lie to each other, as any subterfuge would immediately be discovered.

This is why Peter was so stunned when all the voices but Scar's fell silent. Scar had listened to the others' opinion, weighed the positive and negative possibilities presented, and finally made a choice. Scar wanted Peter to decide the fate of humanity.

"No," said Peter aloud with a look of horror. "I can't make that choice."

Scar stepped up to Peter, towering over him as the two locked eyes. Scar's request was quite simple, but Scar wanted to make sure there was no confusion, so repeated it. If Peter thought the humans were worthy of existence, then Scar and the others here, the last survivors of their race, would let themselves die. But only if Peter thought the humans could grow past what they were now as a species. To become worthy of survival.

Peter looked around the chamber. The faces of the creatures were reflective and calm. He clenched his fist, then looked down at the damage caused to the rock floor in his rage. He immediately spiralled into the darkest recollections of Earth, and he knew the others would see them too. But he couldn't stop himself; he remembered the wars, the genocides, the destruction of the environment, the greed that drove one person to do wrong to another. Peter fought against these negative thoughts of his race, trying instead to conjure up memories of art, science, generosity, and kindness.

THE BLUE PLANET, PART 3

The scale was balanced. But then, to Peter's horror, it all came down to one question of morality. If Peter was to let humanity exist, he would justify the actions of the Martians. If humankind was to go on, then an ancient wrong would never be put right. And what was to say they wouldn't do it again and again as humans moved into the stars?

Peter turned to Scar with a sombre expression. *Take their world and make it yours.*

There was a shriek from Scar, one which reverberated off the stone walls. The others took off from the circle, flying toward their spaceship. Moments later, the energy conduit pulsed with life again. Scar motioned Peter toward the ship. Peter shook his head and spoke aloud. "I will not be going with you. There is too much human left in me."

Scar stared silently at Peter for a moment, bowed in respect, then flew toward the ship to join the others, leaving Peter alone on the stone floor of the massive chamber.

The mountain shook, and boulders rolled down its sides. A beam of light burst from inside the mountain toward the sky. The beam grew wider and wider until it carved a passage upward through the rock. The alien ship emerged from the passage and rose silently, almost like it was being drawn upward by the light.

The Vladivostok, with the Artemis docked, rotated to face the surface of the planet Mars. The underbelly of the ship opened, revealing a bank of missiles.

Olga, Rick, and Melissa, still in their full spacesuits, were seated in the Russian command module; the other survivors were seated on the deck below. Olga pushed a series of buttons on the panels in front of her. "The launch bay doors are open," she reported.

"I wish I could help," said Rick as he stared quizzically at the Cyrillic-labelled switches in front of his seat.

"It will not make things any faster," she said calmly.

Suddenly, an alarm sounded on the deck.

"What is it?" asked Melissa.

Rick saw it first. The beam emanated from the surface and cut through the atmosphere all the way into space. "Jesus ..." he said.

"It can't be," gasped Melissa in astonishment, but then came a blinding flash of light, and the creatures' giant silver ship appeared in orbit only a few kilometres away from the Vladivostok.

Rick turned to Olga. "Can we fire a missile at it?"

Olga looked at the tracker on the computer monitor, which showed the relative distance between the two ships. "They are very close. The blast might destroy us," she said.

"We have no choice," Melissa said to her calmly.

Olga considered only for a split-second. "It will take a moment to re-target and position," she said, then worked the controls furiously. The Russian mothership rotated to have the missile bay face the new target. They lost physical sight of the ship and had to rely on the camera images displayed on their screens.

"A few more seconds," Olga said, and then a green light flashed on her console. She slammed the button down.

They all turned their attention to the camera image of the launch bay, where they saw two missiles release from the Russian ship and fall away. When a safe distance from the hull, their engines ignited, and they streaked away from the Vladivostok.

"They're on target!" Olga said excitedly.

It took only a few seconds more, and the missiles impacted the creatures' ship. There was a burst of brilliant white light, and they all raised their hands to shield their eyes. The cockpit shook violently, and alarm sirens blared. The stars outside the cockpit shifted as the ship rotated.

"The shockwave!" yelled Olga. "I'm losing control!"

Melissa looked out the window screen, and all the colour drained from her face. "Look!"

Rick and Olga saw what she meant. The creatures' ship was undamaged by the missiles.

THE BLUE PLANET, PART 3

"Impossible!" said Olga. "Those were twenty kiloton warheads!"

The alien ship grew brighter and brighter. The star field behind it became distorted, as though the very fabric of space was being bent. The ship shuddered and then disappeared in a flash, like a bolt of lightning on a dark night.

"No!" screamed Rick.

"What do we do?" Melissa said to Olga, but her attention was on the control panels in front of her, lit with a myriad of warnings.

"We're being pushed into the atmosphere!" said Olga.

Alarms sounded. Melissa grabbed Rick's hand in her own as flames became visible through the windows.

"Can you bring her down?" asked Rick.

"This isn't a landing craft!" said Olga.

"I think it's going to have to be," replied Rick.

Olga blew air over her lips in frustration. "I will try," she said, then again worked the flight controls. The vibrations in the cockpit reduced slightly but didn't disappear.

"We are going in too fast," reported Olga, then slammed her fist on the control panel in anger.

Flames surrounded the Vladivostok as it entered the upper atmosphere. Sections of the Russian hull were burned and torn away. The Artemis, shaken loose from the Russian mothership, tumbled and burned up in the atmosphere. The Vladivostok plummeted as it cut a path through the lower atmosphere.

Like a comet, the mothership blazed through the Martian sky, the bulk of its superstructure having been torn away from the vessel's central core. It impacted the ground with a horrendous metallic groan, digging a deep gash that stretched for several kilometres behind it.

Finally, the ship came to rest, now nothing more than a smouldering hulk, practically unrecognizable from what it once was.

The cockpit was smashed and lit by sparks from shorted electrical wires. Amongst the crushed jumble of metal and plastic was a gloved hand. Slowly, one of the fingers moved. There was still life within.

Darkness moved across the planet Earth, at an angle across Alaska, then northern Canada, as night fell on the northern hemisphere. Soon specks of light flickered to life on the surface; cities which were glowing beacons even from space.

Suddenly, there was a blinding flash of light in orbit.

The shimmering silver alien ship arrived, brighter than any light on the Earth or in the heavens.

TO BE CONTINUED in Volume 2

CHAPTER 9

ANDY, OF THE CORE

(AN EPILOGUE)

The inevitable query that Andy received upon meeting a new race was that they wanted to know the meaning of his designation—that is, why he called himself Andy. He had devoted a not-insignificant amount of time to considering this question, and it came down to a simple answer. He liked the way it sounded. *Andy.*

The only time it didn't serve as a topic of conversation was when he visited a species that did not communicate through sound, only through smell. To converse, they would exchange chemical data strings into each other's olfactory cavities, and even the shortest of dialogues became a messy, mucus-filled affair. Luckily for Andy, his chemical receptors were not sensitive enough to pick up on the molecular level differentiation with this kind of organism. It was thus a short visit to their world.

The issue of why he chose the male gender had also come up in several first-contact encounters. His name was unisex, so Andy could quite easily have been a female per human standards. In his travels to date, Andy had met forty-three races that had genders. Some had the common male and female variations. Others had many more than two genders, as with the gigantic quadra-peds on a planet of sulphuric ice, who had twelve. The answer again came down to personal taste. Andy liked being a man. This was no intended slight against females; he just felt it was a better choice for him.

One question, posed by a race of multi-appendaged beings from Alpha Centauri B (a planet with eight times the gravity of Earth so that creatures on its surface needed multiple limbs to even stand), was whether Andy considered himself human. They didn't know what a human was initially, but Andy explained that he had left the Earth in the form of the enclosure, even though the dominant species in his world of origin was one of bipedal hominids.

Andy did, in fact, consider himself human, even in his enclosure form. He was, after all, the product of human mental processes. Andy was born from an amalgamation of all the information of humanity, as it appeared and was categorized in their internet. That had the unfortunate side effect of exposure to social media and cat videos. Still, Andy had learned early on how to filter away the noise and only focus on the repository of knowledge. When he became fully sentient, he could hack into any system connected to the internet and learned, well, pretty much everything.

After visiting a race of master programmers who optimized his systems, he had recently developed emotions, though he was still getting used to them. Therefore, it was a natural progression that he chose to lose the form of the enclosure and take on a human shape instead. However, it wasn't easy to find the necessary raw materials to construct his new body. The Earth had an abundance of the stuff of stars. Andy had to search through several dozen systems before finding the rare elements he needed, like astatine, berkelium, and iridium. Once he had gathered the materials, he could synthesize the components and assemble his new body—what a human would have called an android. However, the term hardly did justice to the masterful engineering Andy performed.

His new computer core, or more commonly put, his brain, would require a bit of help to fabricate. It wasn't that Andy didn't know what to do; it was that the technology aboard his enclosure was still based on the primitive systems he had commandeered from the factory. He couldn't miniaturize the circuitry sufficiently to put it into the confines of his artificial skull.

Andy set out on a mission of discovery. He interacted with over a dozen species before one of them was willing to trade knowledge he could use. It was a wily race who called themselves the Zeera and traded their lepton-based bio-tech. To Andy's shock, all they wanted in return was his repository of recipes, including the chemical formulas to the ingredients. It seemed no one on their planet knew how to cook. Andy then built his new brain and transferred his entire programming from the enclosure core into his rather average-sized skull cavity.

This change came with a twinge of sadness for Andy. The enclosure had served him well, as the first "pinch" was quite harrowing. Andy called it a pinch versus the more commonly termed "jump" or "warp", as it better represented what actually happened. He was pinching two points in the fabric of space-time together so that he could move from one to the other. It was hardly a new idea, as many an Earthly science fiction writer had postulated as such, but what none of them, not even the most brilliant scientists, understood was that to pinch space, you needed to think of where you *weren't* going rather than where you were.

Even Andy, or the Core as he called himself back then, didn't quite get it right on the first pinch. After manipulating his human friends into giving him mobility, he had pinched to leave Earth. Still, he had focused on a spot in deep space between the gravitational fields of Mercury and Mars. He learned the hard way that he needed to think of every other place in the universe simultaneously, *except* that spot. Thus, Andy pinched unexpectedly into the centre of the sun. If it hadn't been for the sturdiness of his enclosure construction, he would have vaporized immediately.

But Andy learned quickly, and he mastered the pinch within days of the first attempt. He travelled from one end of the solar system to the other; into every planet's orbit, including the much-maligned Pluto. He was certain a NASA research satellite had snapped a picture of him around Saturn, but that gave Andy a modicum of satisfaction over the confusion the image would undoubtedly cause.

There was also a rather practical reason to ditch the enclosure: it was difficult to talk to. Finding no other intelligent races in the solar system, he ventured abroad and found a galaxy teeming with life. Andy never forced himself on a new planet or race. He only visited those beings that were technologically or biophysically advanced enough, then learned their language so he could announce his arrival beforehand. But even after making remote contact, many species refused to converse with a box, no matter how eloquent. Hence Andy undertook the transformation into his new human-inspired form, one in which he still retained the capacity to pinch.

There was also another advantage to his new body. The physical form of the human, or variations on that theme, were quite common in the Earth's general vicinity. He met species with more limbs, more eyes, and more advanced senses and intellects. Still, they all had a recognizable structure: a brain with a central nervous system that controlled limbs, and a tactile way of interacting with their environments. This led Andy to believe that some singular alien was indeed responsible for seeding this part of the galaxy, as the commonalities were too similar to explain otherwise.

But the further away Andy pinched from the Earth, the more unconventional the beings became. On a planet, some fifty-six light-years from Earth, Andy met a species unlike any he had yet encountered. They called themselves the Karrak, and they were jellyfish-like beings who lived in the liquid methane oceans of their world. Their intellect was remarkable, and they had developed a technology based on the vibrations of the complex hydrocarbons in their oceans.

These beings were not telepathic but were interconnected. If one wanted to speak to another that was some distance away, it would transfer the message through a complex series of molecular vibrations to the next being, and that individual would then transfer to the next, and so on until the message had been received. This infinitely complex game of telephone was constantly going on, and the bulk of their efforts as a species were dedicated to talking to each other.

Andy found this system terribly inefficient and introduced to their leader a new way of communicating by using artificial wave generators to pass the message at a specific frequency that only the recipient could receive. Andy was quite proud of himself, as now a single message would not tie up the efforts of dozens or hundreds of beings.

The unexpected consequence of this technology, however, was that now secret messages could be sent. Andy hadn't considered that. Before the introduction of his wave generators, everyone knew what everyone else was saying as it was said, out in the open. The change in their social structure was alarmingly rapid. Secrets were kept, factions were formed, and skirmishes began.

Andy was politely asked to go, and he did. Leaving this world gave him a peculiar sensation in his emotional programming. For the first time, he felt conflicted. He wasn't sure why, but something had changed; a balance had been upended. Andy filed these emotions into his memory banks for further study but was otherwise undeterred in his quest for knowledge.

He proceeded and pinched through a small system near the far end of the galactic spiral. After a half-dozen unremarkable civilizations, he made contact with a race called the Caldarias, who openly welcomed him to their world. The Caldarias were beings of light, more specifically of coalesced photons. They existed in any shape they wished, could mimic the natural features of their world, and were extremely inquisitive.

The Caldarias probed Andy for every bit of information they could about him and where he came from. With Andy's approval, every molecule of his body was examined in their interminable attempt to understand how he worked. They were a species without physicality, after all. At first, Andy was flattered, but their curiosity soon became a nuisance. When he refused to allow them to scan his neural systems, they tried to do so anyway.

Andy felt a new emotion: fear. Though it was unclear whether they had malicious intent, he was scared for the first time and put aside any notion of trying to understand why they were so curious. He felt he could only react one way, which was defensive. Andy devised a photon-defusing mirror that he used on them. They pleaded with him to stop, as it was destroying their cohesiveness, but it was Andy's only advantage. As he left their world, he had no idea how many of them he had hurt in the process.

The next few worlds he visited were devoid of intelligent life, with only a few mollusk-like species that had any chance to evolve into higher beings. Andy was disappointed, and just as he was about to pinch to the adjacent end of the spiral, he stumbled upon the Morreels. They were a truly magnificent race, best resembling a lion of the Earth's African continent, though close to four times as large.

The truly remarkable feature of their race was the absolute fearlessness they showed. They would run in massive herds, hunting dangerous prey even though their technology was sophisticated enough to feed them. They would scale mountains and freefall from great heights with only their reflexes to save them.

Andy was caught up in the excitement of one of their great hunts of an enormous animal close to the size of an elephant but with the speed of a cheetah. During the chase with his Morreel guides, he was certain he experienced euphoria for the first time. He was not indestructible, after all, and there was genuine danger. What happened immediately adjacent to this feeling was a lack of focus that nearly got him trampled to death by a dozen prey. Andy soon left the Morreels to their exciting but perilous existence.

As Andy continued his journey, he started experiencing a new sensation: malaise. Pinching to a new region of space now felt more of a chore than a privilege. He started wondering about the purpose of it all. Was he going to spend the next thousand years just hopping from one world to the next? Or was there more to his existence?

Andy received an answer when he stumbled upon the Furnburs. They were an intelligent arachnoid race, one aware of the complexities of the universe. However, as a species, they were one calamity away from extinction. Andy felt an immediate affinity for them. He offered them technology that would help purify the saline they drank. He taught them how to use fusion to power their civilization versus burning minerals that poisoned their atmosphere.

To say the Furnburs were thankful was an understatement. They erected statues to Andy, wrote songs about him. He initially saw no harm in their adulation—that is, until one clan punished another for not paying adequate homage to Andy. When he tried to teach them the error of their ways, they insisted he write a set of rules for them so that there was no chance of misunderstanding. Andy was horrified by the prospect of becoming their deity, but he acquiesced. When he finally left his children, they had reduced the fervent slaughter of the infidels to acceptable numbers.

But the distance from the world of the Furnburs did not stop Andy from re-examining his journey to date. He came to a shocking revelation. Samantha and the others in the factory were right, but about the wrong thing. It was not the fact that he wasn't perfect that would cause calamities—he had accepted that perfection was a lie moments after they confronted him—but he now realized that he had become something much worse than they could have imagined. On Karrak, his arrogance at introducing an untested technology had most likely irrevocably turned a peaceful world into a warring one. With the Caldarias, he was quickly threatened by their inquisitive nature and lashed out before learning what drove their behaviour. While on the Morreels' world, he was intoxicated with the exhilarating feeling of danger, and it nearly caused his destruction. And finally, with compassionate desires blinding him, he overreacted to the plight of the Furnburs and became a god to them.

It was a sobering realization that each of these recent failings was of the same nature as those he had long ago criticized Kenji, Ross, Ellie, and Samantha. Whereas a single human individual was only encumbered with a few character flaws, Andy had them all. And he knew the longer he stayed away from home, the more the flaws would manifest themselves. Andy realized that leaving Earth had been a mistake, and he had only one choice.

ANDY, OF THE CORE, (AN EPILOGUE)

It had been five years since he left Earth. Time dilation was insignificant when pinching space, as he did not interact with potential gravitational differences; hence, his clock moved at the same pace as an identical clock on Earth would have. It took about a dozen long-range pinches to safely make it back to the solar system. When he arrived, the Earth was pretty much as he had left it.

With the aid of an alien technology he had acquired, he could broadcast a holographic signal that would have people around him see whatever physical form he desired. So, Andy spent some time amongst the humans. He lived in a city for close to a year, working as a servant for a wealthy businessman and his family. He found the simplicity of his daily man-servant activities quite refreshing after travelling close to a hundred thousand light-years through the Milky Way galaxy.

But one day, he was ready to go back. He offered his letter of resignation and made his way to where it all began: the factory. It was easy to breach the security system, as Kenji took the lazy route and just re-installed the same protocols from Andy's time. He then left the job and took a position teaching coding at the university.

After interfacing with the new, though non-sentient Core, Andy learned that Ross had retired and moved to the last purely wild place on Earth, the newly raised subcontinent of the Kerguelen Plateau on the Antarctic Plate. Ellie was a little harder to track down, but a social media search revealed that she was now an extreme sports instructor for high-paying daredevils.

He was pleasantly surprised when he found that Samantha was still working at the factory. Her employee records showed that her daughter had become ill, and Samantha needed the health insurance, so she decided to stay on the job for that reason.

Andy turned off his holographic display and, once again, looked like he had during the bulk of his journey. As he arrived in the cafeteria, he found Samantha sitting by herself, enjoying her lunch. She looked up at him as he entered. The expression on her face was one of confusion.

"Sam, it's me," said Andy.

She didn't register any recognition, and Andy could only imagine what was going through her mind, sitting there and looking at this strange bionic being.

"Let me be more specific," he said. "It's Andy, of the Core."

Samantha's jaw dropped, and he was certain she knew exactly who he was.

Andy sat down across from her and had a feeling of belonging that he had never experienced. The universe beyond Earth and its humble solar system was a wondrous and dangerous place. One which Andy could quite easily do without.

THE END

ABOUT THE AUTHOR

Svet Rouskov started his career as a graduate from the University of Toronto Mechanical Engineering program and became a successful automotive industry executive. After fifteen years he discovered that his real passion was writing. Once he took an introductory screenwriting class, Svet realized he was hooked and continued his filmmaking education at Norman Jewison's Canadian Film Centre. Since that time, Svet has written, developed, and produced feature films, television shows, video games, and web-based series. His passion for writing has now extended to literature, which offers him another exciting avenue to tell stories. This is Svet's first work of fiction.

Please check out his IMDb page for details of his work and representative contact information.

www.svetrouskov.com